The Light Team

Jeff McNair

To Monica
You were a great encouragement to me. Thank-you!,
with love –
Jeff McNair
1 John 1:5-7

The Light Team
by Jeff McNair

ISBN 1-58169-005-3

For Worldwide Distribution
Printed in the U.S.A.

THIRD STORY WINDOW
An Imprint of Genesis Communications, Inc.
P.O. Box 91011 • Mobile, AL 36691
(888) 670-7463
Email: GenesisCom@aol.com

DEDICATION

This book is dedicated to Kathi, Josh and Amy.

ACKNOWLEDGMENTS

Special thanks to my friend, Mark Bernhart,
and the rest of the the "linklings,"
Rick Langer and Jon Lewis.

TYL

TABLE OF CONTENTS

PREFACE

You might read J.R.R. Tolkien's *The Hobbit* for enjoyment; however, should you try to find your way to Middle Earth using the maps included with the story, you will have great difficulty, as there is no such place. On the contrary, the biblical story leads real people to the real God through the accomplishments of a real Savior, Jesus.

The difference between fantasy and the realities spoken of in the Bible is tremendous. Yet, for the reader, the impact of combining the two is nothing short of extraordinary. *The Light Team* is offered to you as a creative account of the Gospel story of the Bible, imaginatively depicted through the medium of fiction. Yet it is the author's hope that *The Light Team* will lead others to the factual story in the Bible. Through *The Light Team,* some will perhaps discover the Bible, and through the Bible, find their way to the real God.

Obviously there are dangers and benefits to such an approach. A significant danger is that some might read *The Light Team* as if it were the Bible. This is a gross error. Although it is the author's intention to prompt interest in the Bible, license has been taken in the creation of this fictional account. For example, a sub-plot explores the idea of humankind's "free will" through the interactions between the characters of LiarLight—a satanic figure—and thgiL—the leader of the wraiths. The story relates that LiarLight created thgiL and the wraiths. This notion is not supported by the biblical account. Should the reader take this aspect of the story as the "Gospel truth," it will lead him or her astray. These and other ideas added to the story, although hopefully entertaining and instructive, must be examined in the light of the actual biblical account.

Potential benefits to this fictional approach to the Gospel story are present as well, "offering food for thought" while reading the actual account. For example, events happening behind the scenes—including interactions in the spiritual world and among the people of that time—may be presented. The novel provides the opportunity to directly treat topics of interest to the reader which might have been more indirectly addressed in the Bible. Also, readers who might not pick up a Bible right away and read it, could become engrossed in a good novel, which could stimulate their interest in reading the actual Bible.

So, please enjoy *The Light Team!* It is my hope that, if you have not yet met "Iaman" and the "Light" of *The Light Team,* this story will help to guide you to a meeting with them. Should you already be a follower of the Light, perhaps you will gain insights into Him whom you have trusted.

Chapter One
THE DANCE

The lone figure moves lithely through his dance. His balance and precision are unsurpassed. With each graceful leap, the dancer floats above the ground. Sinking to the horizon, the two staggered suns, Burn the White and Heart Red, flood the sky with a red hue pierced with shafts of white. Surrounding the dancer is what appears to be a countryside carpeted by deep purple flowers with colored centers. Although the petals are all of one color, the centers—the faces of the blossoms—are many pale shades. The spectral colors range from a dark, almost brown color, to a pale white. They stand silent and still as if in awe of the dancer. He represents all they ever desired or wanted to be. He is free, unrestrained by roots. Accompanying the stunning choreography is only the soft padding sound of his feet on the ground.

As Burn sets, Heart remains a while longer, producing a flaming horizon which highlights the silhouette of the perfectly proportioned dancer. This scene represents the height of beauty and grace. The performer appears to fly through the amber clouds, reflecting their changing moods. He performs each dramatic movement effortlessly, with fluid perfection.

The sky reluctantly surrenders its color as the red sun sets further. The figure now begins to give off a glow coming from a previously unnoticed inner source. The fresh winsomeness of the light only adds to the wonder. The presence is like that of a light being—a creation of light. In reality, the dancer is the greatest of all those created by the Light: the epitome of gracefulness.

The stage around which the flowers stand is set off by a scalloped pattern of gray jutting stones. They seem to have unusual markings on them. Some of the stone border is rounded at the top; other parts are perfectly square. Could the markings be words, perhaps names? Yes, it is true. The stage is surrounded by headstones. The dance occurs in a cemetery—the graveyard of all men.

The faces of the flowers surrounding the scene now come into focus. They are not flowers at all. The field of purple and pale is a sea of thousands of hooded figures. Each figure is perfectly still, head slightly bowed, motionless. The faces appear depressed. Tremendous mental suffering is evident; they look straight ahead as if remembering a great pain. These are the faces of the rejecters of the Light. The brief respite the dance gives them from sensory pain imparts little permanent hope. Had they physical bodies, they would be crying uncontrollably.

1

As the dance continues, motifs are repeated, movements reiterated; its themes of derision and mocking become evident.

This dance is a celebration of the death of those entombed; it is dark and empty, despicable and evil. Headstones are trophies, the graveyard a triumphant battlefield. The light emanating from the performer is self-promoting. He produces the glow to glorify himself. Like yellowing photographs, the decaying bodies remind him of his victory over them. They are gracefully defamed beneath his gliding footfalls.

Every time he performs the dance, he commemorates his victorious conquest of his prisoners solely with the weapon of fear. Every robed prisoner once again faces pain anew; they re-experience every moment as if for the first time. Each fresh pain is raw in its horror. Jeering laughter now accompanies obscene movements. Vulgarity and insolence are whipped into a frenzy of bravado.

He seemingly demonstrates his power over the Light himself. In the contest for followers, the dancer wins again, and again, and again. He taunts the Light with the assembly of his captives. He worships himself before the greatest audience ever assembled. The audience grows daily for each new dance. His followers clamor to be let in, and once in, are trapped. The assembly's worship of the dancer, forced though it may be, is a direct affront to the Light.

The dances also have a personal meaning: the dancer communicates his own rebellion from the Light. In the Light's presence, he regularly reenacts his original act of defiance.

Surrounded by his victories on every side, LiarLight loves the graveyard. His greatest achievement is death, and through death, he ultimately has a victory over every man. The crowd that surrounds him is comprised of his conquests. The graveyard is the platform of transition from mortal life to the spirit world; for many, therefore, it is a transition to total servitude to him.

Others, however, are not among the throng of despair. It is true that LiarLight still saw them die, some with great personal suffering. Those absent from the throng are followers of the Light. They fought LiarLight during their mortal lives. Although he enjoyed a victory over their physical bodies, they escaped his spiritual domain. Through death they live forever in a different spiritual existence—the presence of the Light. LiarLight has no influence whatsoever there.

A hooded figure approaches, watching the graveyard performance. He stops respectfully at the inner fringe of the circled audience. He fears the dancer, as LiarLight truly is to be feared. LiarLight owns his followers, holding their loyalty through a combination of fear, lies, and hopelessness.

The lone figure waits solemnly for the completion of the dance. His submissive demeanor is that of one attending a religious ceremony. He is respectful and silent. With head bowed worshipfully, he strikes a subservient pose and remains motionless until the dance concludes.

Finally the dancer completes his dance. As his final movement, LiarLight stands with his hands outstretched to the sky. In this position, he receives the worship he has given to himself, as well as the worship and fear of those who look on. His slow moving hands reach at the air greedily as if to take something that wasn't meant to be given to him or taken by him. Gradually his arms return to his sides. After an extended pause, he nods for the hooded figure to approach. The figure is DisLight, one of LiarLight's generals, who, with his head still bowed and eyes cast down, whispers to LiarLight.

LiarLight surveys the assembly. A visible shudder goes through the dark army, like a wind blowing through a field of withered and dead flowers. But this too is a part of the ceremony. Each hooded figure then stretches forth two gray and bony arms. Each hand trembles, like the dried bud of a dead flower when it is disturbed. The buds were the potential for beauty that never blossomed; the dead buds remain closed tight, each palm turned toward the earth, focusing the attention of the pale faces downward. As each head lowers, the countryside slowly fades to black. The enveloping darkness expresses the plight of the damned: like a flower abandoned in a desert without water, here there is no hope of refreshment from above.

LiarLight glowers over the field of darkness. Then he smirks and nods to DisLight. Together they leave the scene.

Chapter Two
LONE WARRIOR AND
THE LAMPLIGHTERS

The grizzled man made his way to the top of a small hill. His ascetic lifestyle in the dense thicket of scrubby wire trees caused him to look much older than he actually was. He is tall with straight, shoulder-length black hair and blue eyes. His wrinkled amber skin looks like sun-dried fruit. Being a Sopa, he also has the characteristic facial features of pale yellow skin, broad nose, and thick lips. He is known as the Lone Warrior, because he lives out there alone out of dedication to the Light.

The Lone Warrior was born in Rialto. All his life his parents told him that he was unique. "You have been selected by the Light! The Light has revealed to us that you are the one who will prepare for the coming of the greatest of all Light Teams! You will prepare the way for LiarLight's Bane—he who will defeat LiarLight!" The Lone Warrior's purpose became his defining attribute. He spent his life studying the Old Stories, looking for connections with the coming conquerors. Hour upon hour he spent researching the Light's interactions with people throughout human history. After years dedicated to this preparation, he received the impression that he was ready. So he set out to prepare the people for the coming of the One. In his mind he dreamed of people following the coming leader, of people flocking to the One partly because of his preparation of them. To concentrate on his task, he removed himself from the city. His life revolved around communing with the Light, studying the Old Stories, and coming down from the hills to prepare the people.

He laid his pack down in the usual place—an L-shaped rock under a twisted wire tree. He leaned backward to stretch his muscles, stiff from carrying the pack and from the many nights of sleeping on the ground. His five closest followers, who had been waiting there since dawn, greeted him respectfully.

"I never tire of the beauty of this place," he said, smiling and looking out from the top of the hill.

The vista from the peak spans the city of Bernardino, the surrounding countryside, as well as the imposing mountains. The fields—deep green squares of textured bumps from this view— are surrounded by saw trees with their spiky branches. Geometric patterns mottle the low hills and the expansive valley: they are the famous red orchards, a form of citrus from which the Redlands gets its name. The highest mountain, Gorgonio, is snowcapped most of the year while the others have snow in the cold winters only. During exceptionally cold winters, the lower mountains sometimes also receive a dusting of white.

The Lone Warrior's hill lies on the southwest end of Redlands. South, east, and west of the hill are areas covered with low growing dwarf cone trees, dotted with wild tobacco trees and sugar bushes. The wilderness is traversed by a dirt road which heads west from Redlands about five miles before it forks toward Riverside and Camden. The closest civilized area to Redlands is Bernardino to the north.

Lone Warrior stood in the clearing of the parched hillside. The true Light is in him as much as it can be found in any man. "Did you hear the baolas howling last night?" he asked them. "They sounded like a bunch of old women at a baby showing." The others chuckled. "They were close, too—close enough to reach out and pet!" The Lone Warrior is friendly in spite of his eccentricities. He is friendly, but painfully direct. Both of these qualities grew out of his intense love for people. People feel so accepted by him that they seem to have no need to put on a hypocritical front.

"People are so confused," he often says to his followers. "They are so confused they don't even know they are wandering with no direction and no purpose to their life and will deny it if they're asked."

He believes that evil is to be confronted, not overlooked or ignored. His followers sometimes cringe at his confrontations with people even though the Lone Warrior's confrontations are always loving. The ones he confronts have to reckon with his words because of the combination of their power and the love with which they are delivered.

Several days a week, he makes his way to this little hill to talk with groups of people, attempting to recruit followers of the Light. Some think he is a member of the Light Team. Many, including the LampLighters, think he is crazy.

Centuries ago, the Light chose to work with and through the Sopa Lamp-Lighters. He worked directly with the LampLighters, through miracles He performed on their behalf. The Old Stories tell of how He defeated their enemies and sent them great leaders. The LampLighters spoke to the people on behalf of the Light, teaching them the Light's standards for human interactions. But the people became rebellious and quick to turn from the Light and His teachings. At times, the Light would intervene again and raise up other LampLighters to speak for Him. When these Light followers were in leadership, there came periods of rededication to the Light when the people rejected LiarLight and returned to the true Light. These times also resulted in great prosperity for the Sopa nation. Unfortunately, LiarLight found the Sopas easily corruptible. In nearly every case, the leader either self-destructed or was killed by the people.

In recent times, the LampLighters became oppressively legalistic. The Old Stories contain specific regulations for human behavior designed to help people live well, but the guidelines were not intended to be the total focus of life. In spite of this, the LampLighters had elevated observance of the regulations above love for people and their needs. Following the Light was now oppressive under them as they substituted obedience for joy and legalism for love. The leadership had transformed a bright creation of the Light into a dim and disfigured reflection. Light service was equated with strict law observance. There were few LampLighters who still strove to function in accordance with the Light's original intent.

LiarLight often used the LampLighters to accomplish his work among the Sopas, but they were oblivious to the fact. If confronted with such an accusation, they would deny it; but the fact remains that it was true.

Today was not unlike most days. The narrow valley, just a stone's throw wide, separates the Lone Warrior's hill from Redlands proper. Between the hill and the east side of Redlands are red groves. When in bloom, the whole valley takes on the musky fragrance of its blossoms.

The valley has already filled with people from all over. Many have come on foot; although those who can afford them came on their ayugas—furry, four-legged means of transportation. The ayugas are tied to the placilla trees in a small grove that had been planted as a kind of a park many years before. The wind blowing through the two-toned placilla leaves produces a green and silver sparkle.

Every other day the people gather to hear the Warrior's powerful message firsthand. He had already developed a significant following, speaking to nearly 100 people on most days. Today a crowd of 75 to 80 awaited his teaching.

He began the day by going down into the small valley and greeting the people he knew. Many of them introduced friends whom he acknowledged with love and enthusiasm. While waiting for him, they sat in the shade, talking quietly amongst themselves.

After he had finished his greetings, Lone Warrior made his way back up the side of the hill. The crowd rumbled to a semblance of quiet in anticipation of his words.

"I try to describe the Light to you and help you understand who He is," he began. "I do know for sure that the Light is your only hope against the power of LiarLight. If you cling to the Light, you will have the power to ignore LiarLight's promises. You will see his lies for what they are, so that in the end, he will flee from you. Yet, this is not what most of you do. Instead, you talk with LiarLight; you dabble in his perversions. You pride yourself on having the power to 'resist' him; you listen to his lies. You inch as close to the edge of immorality as you can. Should you step too far, you say, 'I can handle it,' while simultaneously falling into line with his army of dupes. Hear me! His only desire is to destroy you. Renounce him!"

He paused, as a man rose to his feet. "Teacher, how does one determine what is of the Light and what is of LiarLight?"

Lone Warrior smiled back at the man. "I appreciate your question! At times it is difficult to determine what the Light's guidance is on an issue. However, if you consistently take to heart the obvious areas of guidance given you by the Light, and follow them, then the more difficult areas will become clearer." He smiles again at the man, "Do you understand what I mean?"

"Not really," the man replied.

"My friend, the Light tells us to speak to Him often during the day, almost without ceasing. He also instructs us to study the Old Stories. Do you do these things?"

The man hesitated.

"Well, I see by your lack of a response that you are not following the Light's general guidance. This guidance has already been given to you and applies to all. If you will not follow the guidance already given to you, why should the Light give you more guidance? Why should he give you any more specific guidance? You ask for more direction while ignoring the directions already given." The Lone Warrior shook his head. "Do you take the Light for a fool? My friend, I see your confusion about the Light comes from *your* inactivity, not the Light's."

Lone Warrior then looked out at the crowd. "I detect squirming among the rest of you. I appreciate this man's question and his unstated honesty. The same exhortation applies to each of you who are not actively engaging in following the general guidance handed down to you in the Old Stories."

The man who had asked the question heaved a sigh of relief. The Lone Warrior had not confronted him as directly as with some in the past.

So the teaching went. Brief statements with short explanations, followed by questions and answers. The people enjoyed the manner in which the Lone Warrior could make the Old Stories clear to them; in truth, they also enjoyed the confrontations. Each knew that sooner or later his turn would come, but this was "part of the game" for them. The risk involved in questioning him only added interest to the overall proceedings.

At the end of the day, the Lone Warrior made some concluding comments as he stared at the horizon. "The day will come when the Light's man will visit us and free us from LiarLight's tyranny. He will be our champion! As the Great Loser said in the Old Stories, he will be our 'advocate.' He will satisfy the Light's need for justice. The presence of the Light will be strong in him; there will be no mistaking it." Today was like many other days; he often alluded to the coming of the future leader of the Light Team.

He then looked piercingly into the crowd. "Some of you think that I am a Light Team member. I haven't the stamina, nor is it my role in life. I am a mere man, imbued with no special power, called to no such place. However, the one who is coming will lead a new Light Team. It will be his team that will strike the death blow to LiarLight and his followers. I am here to prepare you for his arising, as told in the Old Stories. Be aware! I feel the time of his coming is close."

He finished his teaching and gave a few directions to his followers. Another day of instruction was concluded, the time was late, and he was weary. He collected his few things and set out for home—if you could call his hovel in the wilderness a home. The air grew chilly as the suns set one at a time behind the foothills. How much longer would he be able to continue? Was he really who he thought he was? He paused for a moment on the road to gather his strength. He took a deep breath, heaved a sigh, and was about to walk on again when he felt an arm around his shoulder. The presence of the Light surrounded him. It was a presence that brought reassurance to his beliefs, a presence that covered his inadequacies with peace and victory. He suddenly knew he was being embraced by the one who would lead the next Light Team.

As the Lone Warrior gathered his courage to look at him, the man asked, "Give me your teaching; I want to hear the message."

The Lone Warrior looked upon the younger man. He wore loose jeans, boots, and a billowy, tan shirt. He was tall with shoulder-length black hair. A beard covered much of his face. Heavy eyebrows, which nearly met in the middle of his forehead, added to the intensity of his gray-green eyes. His complexion was a ruddy amber. His posture indicated that he was a strong man. He stood straight, and his rolled-up sleeves revealed the forearm of a workman: veins bulging against stiff muscles.

"You want to hear the message from me?" the Lone Warrior replied. "It is I who should hear the message from you; it is your teaching that I have anticipated!"

The man replied lovingly, "Let it be this way for now. You have fought well, winning the ground of your own mind. Others also do battle because of the truth you have shared. The Light has restrained LiarLight in part by causing him to underestimate the power of your words." The Lone Warrior was moved by this commendation, but he could never have expected what was to follow.

"I would honor you by hearing your teaching," said the man, as he sat at Warrior's feet.

In grateful disbelief, the Lone Warrior shared his teaching. At first the honor was so great that the message was accompanied by weeping. As his

8

composure returned, he felt tides of joy well up in him. He had seen the fulfillment of his teaching. His life had meaning; his message was good and true; he feared nothing.

When he finished teaching, the younger man rose. "Well done, good and faithful servant. Your words are true. Because you have been faithful with this message, your name will be mentioned among the greatest of Light Team." The man then looked the Lone Warrior directly in the eyes. "I desire that you finish your days in peace. However, LiarLight will see to your demise. Prepare yourself for what lies ahead. I leave you now as I must prepare for battle. But before I depart, I perceive that you have a request of me."

"Please, what is your name, that I might tell of it to my followers?"

The man smiled affirmingly. "I am Iaman. Leader of the Light Team."

Chapter Three
LIARLIGHT'S AWAKENING

As they walked from the graveyard, DisLight informed LiarLight that his generals were assembled. He had been instructed to summon them for a meeting immediately following the dance. LiarLight felt it was time to finally address something that had been bothering him in recent days.

LiarLight had expected the coming of his challenger for many years, but had gotten complacent. The "Times of Anticipation," as they were known, lasted much longer and were far more productive than he had dreamed. Several had arisen to oppose him, but in each case he met the challenge and defeated the challenger; that is, each died. There were occasional rumblings that LiarLight would address through one of his generals, but in the end, none were worthy of concern.

Several years back, however, he noted a change. He wasn't quite certain, but he felt that he detected the movement of some of the original members of the Light Team. LiarLight knows each of the members of the original Light Team. As depicted in the Old Stories, the original Light Team was one of the greatest creations of the Light. They were designed to be His servants, to carry out His good purposes. The greatest, the most beautiful, and the most powerful of them was LiarLight. The record in the Old Stories is not entirely clear, but it alludes to the fact that LiarLight made the decision to reject the Light. He reasoned that someone as great as he could never be a servant—he should be served, not serve. These thoughts were the seed of his dissension which ultimately led to his rebellion against the Light.

Since his break with the original Light Team, the hatred grew between him and his past partners. Some lesser team members, like DisLight, followed LiarLight. They saw his break as an opportunity for themselves to increase in stature on a new team. Although deep down they knew that it was the power of the Light that gave them and all the members of the Light Team their special abilities, LiarLight seemed to produce his own Light. He persuaded them to believe that it was he who generated the Light that gave them their power. Scores left to follow him.

At times, the defectors discussed among themselves where the true Light came from, and at times they doubted LiarLight's claims. Only his highest ranking generals ever dared speak such thoughts. However, if one of them garnered the courage to discuss the question with LiarLight directly, it seemed impossible to put down his claims. It was as if LiarLight knew his thoughts before he did, and could always put down any argument. All who tried to engage him in a debate were doomed to fail, since the only way to defeat him was to flee and hold to the power of the true Light. LiarLight allowed a slight glimmer of dissension only among the elite of his followers. In this way he was able to keep them thinking that following him was a logical decision they had made. It was LiarLight's belief that this slight amount of flexibility increased the loyalty of the elite of his followers. Questions of any kind from lesser followers, however, were dealt with deftly and painfully.

Over time, LiarLight's army, living and dead, became great. To LiarLight's credit, in the life of every one of his followers there came a moment when each one chose him over the Light. Once someone made that decision, rarely did he return to the Light; he was most often lost forever. Most of them did not know the truth that no one is ever lost to the Light; the Light always knows and cares for him.

Through the ages, LiarLight's mind became increasingly warped, ready to bring destruction on anyone he chose. This was partly the result of his rejection of the Light and partly due to the use of his powers of deception upon himself. It is a known fact that people who reject the Light experience hardship, both during their lives and in death. However, this is not to say that bad things do not happen to good people; hardship doesn't necessarily mean that the person experiencing it has rejected the Light. LiarLight many times uses it to try and wear down the followers of the Light. But without the Light in a person, there is nothing to stop LiarLight from having his way. He acts in such lives with reckless abandon—his preferred mode of operation.

If LiarLight were a human, he would be the undetected serial killer, the handsome and friendly rapist whom no one suspects, the child molester loved by his victims. In some ways LiarLight lost his mind; in other ways, his sanity is evident in his self-control. Control coupled with insanity is nothing less than evil, and that is what LiarLight is—pure evil.

People often misunderstand LiarLight's motivations. They think on the things that tempt them and assume that those are what also excite a presence such as he. Little do they know that the acts themselves are inconsequential to someone like LiarLight. His pleasure comes from the attitude of disobedience that he engenders, and the power he wields over individuals in persuading them to abandon the truth. He challenges the Light in the presence of the disobedient parties. Like a ringmaster at a circus, LiarLight calls the Light's attention to the "center stage" where people—the Light's own creation—act out their disdain for the Light under the glare of spotlights. The lost crowds cheer as the Light looks on, unwavering. The disobedient acts provide the ultimate satisfaction—power—for LiarLight. But he does not rejoice merely in his power over the actors, although there is some joy in that; he delights in his apparent power over the Light himself.

11

Still, LiarLight could not explain the ominous feelings he had been having recently. It seemed the original Light Team was on the move. He remembered first feeling anxious some 30 years prior. Less than a year later, there was a major disturbance. It included a tremendous spiritual disruption involving a multitude of Light Team members, followed by ominous quiet. In response to rumors that a new human Light Team leader was to be born from among the Sopas, he directed Lightbender and CounterLight, two of his generals, to seek out the child and destroy him. They instigated dramatic measures through the Summas, another ethnic group, resulting in a period of widespread misery and death that marked the beginning of the race wars. It was the Summas who were in power; they carried out the mass-killing. Thousands of Sopas and even many Saties, the third major ethnic group, were also killed in an effort to destroy the predicted leader.

Over the last 30 years, the power of the presence grew greater than any LiarLight felt in past millennia. Interestingly, the new presence was nearly identical to the Light itself; LiarLight could not distinguish between the two. Although he detected the presence, he became confused between the new presence and the ever present power of the true Light. It seemed that the arrival of the new Light Team was imminent.

LiarLight readied himself for the meeting with his generals. He changed from a dancer to a dark presence. LiarLight used many forms, depending on the deception he was projecting. The form he chose now was shadowy and ill-defined—like someone approaching in a dark alley. He moved in a manner where he appeared to be anywhere at any instant. He made sure his appearance would give no indication of his concern.

Before meeting with the generals, he reviewed his impressions. He thought over his feeling of increasing oppression and wondered what was happening to cause the feelings. Remembering back to the events of 30 years ago, he recalled that his agents had indeed instigated much suffering. Unfortunately, they had not created any significant change to diminish the disturbance he originally felt. Suddenly a realization hit him. *Why did I relent, if the presence still remained?* He cursed himself and his minions. *How could I have been so stupid?* he berated himself, wrenching his mind for answers.

He knew of the Old Stories fabricated by past human Light Team members that predicted his ultimate downfall. To date, those predictions had not come to pass. True, many men had come claiming to be the fulfillment of the past predictions. Each insisted he was the one predicted, the one who would ultimately destroy LiarLight, but they were actually agents of LiarLight himself. How clever had he been to use the old legends about his own defeat as a means to divert even more followers from the Light! One has to know the enemy in order to defeat him.

Could this force that I detected 30 years ago have developed sufficient strength to challenge me? I have dealt with the Light for centuries. It is amazing how perfectly the presence mimics the Light Himself. The presence is so much like the Light, it cannot be counterfeit.

Perhaps a Light Team member has defected: another like me is attempting to establish himself as a rival to the Light. He comforted himself with this explanation. He thought about past Light Team members who could possibly rebel: An-Avel rebelled once, but ultimately found his way back. Ghozman rebelled several times. He even tried to escape the Light, but he never thought to set himself up as a direct rival to the Light. Paso-Lomon won great battles for the Light, but ultimately his rebellion led to perdition. He eventually returned to the Light, but only as a shadow of what he once was. Besides, they were all men. *No, I myself am the only past Light Team member of any significance to have successfully challenged the Light,* he concluded.

He smiled to himself for a moment of self-satisfaction, but then anxiety abruptly overtook him. *Could I be seeing the arising of my challenger as predicted in the Old Stories?* The thought horrified him. He, more than any other created being, understood the power of the Light (which was why the Light felt immensely grieved at LiarLight's absenting himself from his presence, though LiarLight could know nothing of the pain of this betrayal). During lucid moments, he wondered why the Light permitted him to engage in the wickedness he had come to love. Increasingly, however, he fell prey to his own deception, persuading himself that his own light was preferable, providing the atmosphere for the type of deeds he reveled in. However, like the incessant liar who begins to believe his own lies, the line between truth and lies regarding his own power had lost its clarity. Perhaps the power of blackness had swallowed up all the whiteness within him so that the light was extinguished in him, himself taking on deeper and deeper shades of darkness.

Suddenly anxiety hit him again, as a realization came over him: *The Light tricked me!* He reeled at the thought. *I've ignored the presence because the Light fooled me! What other explanation could there be? Did I not recognize the presence 30 years ago? Did I not address the issue? But had not the presence also continued while I ignored it?* Fuming, he cursed the Light repeatedly. Then he stopped. *Why am I so aware of this presence now? If the Light has hidden this thing from me, why am I suddenly aware of it again at this time?* He smiled as if having solved an intricate riddle. *This Light presence is now prepared to engage me.* He paused. *The Light has never approached a confrontation with me in such a manner before; I wonder what He is planning.*

LiarLight's mind moved again to the meeting with his generals. They must not find out about his manipulation at the hands of the Light, as the notion would destroy their confidence in him. He would put the blame on the generals whom he assigned to address the presence. What did it matter that the Light's finger was obviously the cause of the oversight? This monumental error must be addressed, swiftly and discreetly.

Before meeting with the entire group, LiarLight called Lightbender and CounterLight to himself. With angry and maniacal fury, he dispensed his wrath upon them. Dazed, Lightbender returned alone to the group of waiting generals.

LiarLight collected himself, and using the full extent of his super powers, once again assured himself that he was winning the war with the Light. His demeanor changed. The leaf shaking in the wind became the steadfast trunk. It was time he demonstrated the extent of his power. *I will find this presence and destroy it!* he vowed amid countless, frightening curses.

Chapter Four
THE JUSTICE LAWS

"All rise! The Court of the City of Camden is now in session, Magistrate M. Schall presiding." Camden was the capital city of Calvada in the Redlands.

There was the shuffling of boots over the red dust as all in the courtroom rose to their feet.

"Please be seated," he said as he took his own chair. The old, basket-woven chairs squeaked as the people sat. "Will the jury chairman please rise."

A rather large man in his best bib overalls stood to his feet. His shoulder-length black hair framed his dark, tannish yellow face and bright blue eyes. He blew his broad nose at this perfectly inappropriate time and took a moment to wipe off all of the remaining residue. He was of the Sopa race and was accompanied by a small, thin Sopa woman. The laws required that two members of each race should sit on the jury to decide all matters of ethnic violence. With him were two women of the Satie race. One was short with dark brown, almost black skin. Her nose was thin as were her lips. Her hair was a light brown color and tightly curled so that it clung closely to her head. The other was taller, with a reddish tint to her hair. Two other members of the jury were men with light pink to peach-colored skin and black hair. The lids of their eyes appeared tightly closed and slightly oblique. These distinctive features, along with their added height, were common to the Summa race.

"How does the jury find in the case of the LampLighters versus the Government of Calvada?"

"We find the defendant, the Government of Calvada, not guilty."

Immediate celebration and depression—depending on which side of the aisle you sat—arose in the room. In a recent confrontation between seven LampLighters (the religious leaders of the Sopas) and government police, the LampLighters were killed. Although no one was really sure how the case would be decided, many suspected that the government would not be found guilty of ethnic violence. The tripartite government, comprised equally of members of each race, always seemed to be unassailable on ethnic grounds. Additionally, should they be found guilty, who would be punished to fulfill the requirements of the Justice laws?

The magistrate silenced them with a raised hand. "With a verdict of not guilty, the Justice laws are not applied. Case dismissed."

The Justice laws were developed some nine years prior, at the end of the 21-year race war. The war had begun when the Summas, who were in power at that time, became threatened by LampLighter claims that a new leader had been born among the Sopas. The Sopas did little to calm the Summas' fears. This leader, supposedly the greatest in history, would become the equivalent of the king of the country. Although no one specifically had been named, the LampLighter holy books, known as the Old Stories, claimed that the new leader would arise from a small, out-of-the-way town known as Barstow. The Sopas' political rallies centered on the government soon to come. They planned to remedy past wrongs. The tyrannical Summa leaders felt threatened and overreacted. Using government troops largely comprised of Summas, they systematically killed all male Sopas from the age of birth to three. Many pregnant women, and even many Saties, were also killed. In the end, a war broke out among the three races. Each ethnic group considered both of the other groups its enemies. The nation was in total upheaval. Saties killed Summas and Summas killed Sopas. It was a free-for-all. The national infrastructure of commerce and the rule of law was destroyed. In addition, nearly a third of the population was killed. Cooler heads finally prevailed, and all sides in the conflict ultimately agreed to a cease fire for reasons of self-preservation. If the war had not stopped when it did, there would have been little left to fight over.

A group comprised of representatives of each of the three races was founded and named the Interracial Council. It convened to try to resolve the differences among them. Although there was a long history of problems, the atrocities of the recent war only led to further separation. Something had to be done to bring the three groups together so the Interracial Council took on the task and miraculously built a fragile peace.

The Interracial Council proposed a two-pronged solution. First was the formation of the tripartite government. The governmental hierarchy was basically the same as it was under the Summas; however, now there was equal representation for each of the three groups within the government with leadership positions set aside exclusively for members of each race. The 15 regional governors or magistrates were also equally divided among the races. Thus if a Satie magistrate resigned or died, he/she could only be replaced by a Satie. There was, therefore, a semblance of stability. Of course, not all members of a particular race agreed politically. Some were more ethnocentric than others, and some were were more conciliatory than others. However, these ideas were inconsequential as far as the make-up of the government was concerned. Each race was responsible for selecting its own representative, and election funds could only come from within a candidate's own ethnic voter base. Therefore, other races could not be blamed for election results. This notion carried over into the lower echelons of government as well.

The second part of the solution became known as the Justice laws. The Justice laws were developed by the Interracial Council in an attempt to prevent future racial war through extreme yet equitable measures. In cases of ethnic violence, the Justice laws allowed for a victimized group to bring those who caused the violence to trial. Should the defendant group be found guilty, and particularly if guilty of murder, a leader from the convicted group would be put to death. Additionally, the leader to be executed was selected by the accusing group. Most often, the closest local magistrate was responsible for facilitating the selection and carrying out the sentence. The executions were public and brutal. These laws generally had the combined effect of causing leaders to become more circumspect in their actions, while concurrently satisfying a victimized group's need for justice.

As barbarous as it seems, this system produced the desired result. The public executions reminded the people of the horror of death, and the comparatively more acceptable outcome of one individual dying, rather than continuing ethnic warfare. Every ethnic group had been convicted at least once, and a leader executed. Many thought this was a good thing since the most extreme of the leaders were the ones who were chosen to die and they would no longer have the opportunity to pick at the scab of racial healing. The wounds of the community would finally be given the opportunity to mend.

As the people began to disperse from the courtroom, the attorney for the LampLighters, a Sopa, walked across the aisle to the Satie, a government attorney. "You prepared a good case, counselor, but we both know the government was guilty."

"Are you saying that our system of law doesn't work? Do you mean to imply that murderers can get off free?" the defense attorney shot back.

"We both know it's hard to convict a triracial government of racially motivated murder against one of the groups it's supposed to represent, particularly when the Justice laws are involved." He waited briefly for a response, then continued, "Today's finding in favor of the state could lead to more violence. If I were you, I would counsel the government to quickly make a gesture of conciliation toward the Sopas."

"Is that some sort of threat?" the defense attorney retorted.

"Threat? Not really, but I know the LampLighters. There are fringe groups within them who will see this ruling as motivation to strike back." He paused. "How quickly we forget the race wars! What's that saying. . .about history repeating itself?"

The prosecuting attorney just stood there fiddling with his papers.

"Look, this is no threat; it's only an observation. I just think the government can forestall retaliation if they were to do something to appease the LampLighters in some way. You have their ear; so, please pass on the message."

"Listen, I'll see what I can do," he said as he walked away. "This was a somewhat unique case," he said over his shoulder.

"Thanks!" The prosecuting attorney wanted to say more, to try to convince his counterpart to make a greater effort, but his attempts would come across as little more than envious parting words. He could only hope for the best, as the LampLighters were indeed a force to be reckoned with.

Although the LampLighter religion had lost its power and appeal to many since it had become a system of ceremony and law, a remnant of the group honestly sought the Light. Some were the product of families who worked to keep the spirit of Light-following alive. Although they participated in the LampLighter activities, they did so with limited satisfaction. Often they were misunderstood or ostracized for their persistent claim that there was so much more to following the Light. They cited examples from the Old Stories of how the Light had raised up great men and women to accomplish His purposes. Men like Paso-Lomon and Tears, and women like Rotechord and Mutiold made a difference for the Light.

Some even spoke of the Light Team. The Light Team would be assembled once again by the Light and bring freedom. No longer would people be forced to live under LiarLight's tyranny. The Light would usher in a new day. Ultimately, there would be peace.

Yet the leaders of the LampLighters were unsure. Their study of the Old Stories convinced them that those predictions were for a different time. They felt that the people should look to them, the Light-appointed guides. They claimed that it was only through their leadership that the people would find direction and vision; the LampLighter leaders were the future and the Light would work through them alone.

If the appeals of the leadership would not subdue those who were unconvinced, the LampLighters used the political power they wielded to threaten fellow Sopas. This combination of religious and political muscle kept most of them in line.

It must be remembered that most Sopa citizens were simple people: they were farmers, orchardmen, or ayuga breeders who hadn't the education to take on the LampLighters. In the end, some braved the wrath of the LampLighters and followed after charlatans who came along claiming to be the leader of a new Light Team. The LampLighters made examples of these folks upon their disillusioned return.

Still, there were those both inside and outside of the LampLighter organization who truly sought the Light. The did their best as well to lead others to a more complete understanding of the real power of the religion of the Sopas.

Chapter Five
THE MEETING

Lightbender bristled from the cursing he and CounterLight had received over their failure to destroy the presence when it was first detected. After all, why would LiarLight suddenly act so crazy over something that occurred some 30 years prior? He also wondered what happened to CounterLight. Pondering these disturbing questions, he addressed the assembled generals as they waited for LiarLight.

"Something has caught our leader's attention," Lightbender began. "It relates to events of 30 years ago, when CounterLight and I dealt with the Sopas. If you recall, we were instructed to destroy a presence of which the Leader was aware. It was CounterLight's and my impression that the issue had been taken care of. It seems, however, that the presence persists." He corrected himself, ". . . due to CounterLight's error, the presence persists." Lightbender paused, "In the future, the Leader will not tolerate such incompetence on the part of his generals. As you notice, CounterLight is no longer among us."

The generals stared back confused. Where had he gone? Could he have tried to go back to the Light Himself? Those who knew Counterlight and the evil he had perpetrated felt there was little chance of that. Maybe he was banished to some kind of nowhere land; they had heard of such a punishment in the past. Even Lightbender didn't know where CounterLight was, although he gave no indication of this fact. Wherever he was, they all knew that they didn't want to be there. Knowing that LiarLight had sent him away reinforced their fear of him. What really happened to CounterLight, no one but LiarLight and the Light knew. Most likely, he suffered in a lost existence somewhere between the Country of the Light and LiarLight's realm.

Lightbender wondered what happened to set off LiarLight. Lightbender claimed to have come up with the idea to orchestrate the killing of all the infant male Sopas by the Summas. At the time, this act pleased LiarLight. Perhaps that's what saved him from a fate similar to CounterLight's; Lightbender himself didn't know.

There were six generals in all, including the now absent CounterLight. Besides Lightbender and DisLight, there was also NulLight, FauxLight, AnihiLight and thgiL. All but thgiL were recognized as a kind of elite class, as they had been high-ranking members of the original Light Team. All the original team members were male in appearance. They were strikingly handsome;

19

however, there was something about them which was different from those who never left the Light's service. Those who served LiarLight looked older: the difference was like that of a 25-year-old in comparison to a 40-year-old. LiarLight's generals appeared to have a weathered look and an "edge" to them. Looking at them, cruelty and anger were etched in their faces. These elite generals (LiarLight included) had been closer to the Light than any other created beings. Yet they had chosen not only to reject Him, but to actively fight against Him.

Original Light Team members—whether in LiarLight's service or not—distinguished themselves by using the word "Light" in their names. No other dared to do so. The final general was thgiL. thgiL didn't like the fact that she could never be at the same level as the other generals, in spite of her unimpaired obedience.

thgiL was the chief of LiarLight's wraiths. LiarLight considered thgiL his greatest creation. However, LiarLight recognized a critical flaw in himself as a created being: he was created with a free choice. But LiarLight would not make the same mistake with his creations: they would have no choice but to follow him. thgiL and the shadow-wraiths were created to corrupt the Light's creation of humanity.

Initially, LiarLight and his generals were themselves involved in the corruption of humanity. As the human population grew, and their task became more encompassing, it seemed appropriate for LiarLight to assign multiple agents to harass individual persons by observing their weaknesses and throwing them into confusion and inaction. This had the result of deflecting them from seeking the Light and preventing them from influencing others to do the same. The ongoing dribble of Light Team defectors helped somewhat, but a greater army was necessary. In response, LiarLight commissioned thgiL, and being pleased with her performance, sent others like her who were less powerful, but able to complete the task of sabotaging people's attempts to reach for the Light. The generals then moved to positions of directing thgiL, the wraiths, and the lesser status defectors from the Light Team.

It is difficult to describe thgiL's appearance. She is a spirit-presence, having no real physical character. The quality of being seen is a physical characteristic common to humans, but of little value in interactions in the spirit world. Yet, if it served LiarLight's purpose for the wraiths to be seen, they appeared as delicate, ethereal women. Seeing thgiL and the other wraiths, however, it is obvious they are all made of the same stuff.

When thgiL was created is unknown to her. She remembers events in human history which give some indication of an age, but time had always been a strictly physical commodity, bearing little impact on the spiritual.

All the creations of the Light are designed to follow him. However, the

Light desires followers who choose to follow him. He desires a relationship with his followers, be they people or his original spirit creations. The Light recognized that the only way to have a relationship of any value is to relate with those who choose the relationship. The Light also recognized that there is risk in creating such beings: from the creator's perspective, they may choose not to relate to him and may reject the creator as LiarLight did. However, the creation of free choice tells volumes about a creator. The gift of free choice reveals the desire for relationship; and with that intention, the Light created His creations with free choice.

LiarLight cared little about such relationships. Does one relate to the hammer in one's hand? His underlings were merely tools, to be wielded at his whim. Creations deprived of free will reflect only their master's consuming desire for power; there is no need to initiate contact with them except to tell them what to do.

The generals who conspired with LiarLight were a different story: LiarLight interacted with the generals who left the Light with him, only because their power increased his power. Although he had to relate to them, he found it tedious.

thgiL was an enigma, and so defied classification. Created without free will, she had served LiarLight for as long as she could remember, and knew nothing other than that existence. However, LiarLight had to keep thgiL's mind continually in check. Sometime after her creation, he recognized a flaw in her. There was never a danger that thgiL would do anything other than LiarLight's will; rather, the problem came when she was confused or distracted by questions about her existence. She was not designed for self-examination; for without choice, why self-examination? At times, however, LiarLight would become preoccupied, forgetting his need to shore up her mental defenses. During these times, he observed she would become less effective as a servant. If she could discern LiarLight's will, she would do it, but at times she would become confused. On these occasions, LiarLight would discover her confusion, and his rage would result in thgiL's punishment. Although her errant behavior was no fault of her own, LiarLight refused to admit he had neglected to take care of this flaw in her. Besides, thgiL's punishment delighted the other generals. In the past, he had thought of destroying her and starting over, but somehow he was prohibited, as if the time for new creation had passed.

The wraiths were also flawed. LiarLight had instilled in them his instinct for self-preservation; he thought this would result in stronger, scrappier fighters. What he got instead were fighters who were quick to run in the face of danger in order to save themselves.

In some ways, thgiL and the other wraiths, or "thgiLers" as they were sometimes called, embodied perfect followers. They sought LiarLight's will so they could do it. They claimed obedience as their sole purpose for existence, and they acted out that claim. They were totally dedicated to his service; they delighted in bringing about his objectives.

What thgiL lacked due to her flaws, she made up for in violence. Working under Lightbender, she inspired the killing of the Sopa children. She had actually come up with the idea, suggesting it to Lightbender. She cared little about who received credit, however, but was concerned only that her master's plans were achieved.

Ultimately, thgiL had become one of the generals. thgiL was the only general worthy of LiarLight's complete trust. The others disdained her because of the closeness she appeared to enjoy with LiarLight. In reality, there was no closeness at all between the two: thgiL was a tool, and LiarLight wielded her. When there is need of a hammer, the hand seeks it out. With no nail to hit, the hammer is forgotten. Without free will, thgiL also cared little for relationship. thgiL would let nothing come between her and LiarLight. Her master's words were the law, and she was completely dedicated to him.

Today LiarLight's generals waited for him at the typical place of meeting. He spent a significant amount of his time at a particular spiritual location. His followers knew how to find him at this address, but it was not a linear or even a two-dimensional address. One didn't go to such and such a place and make a left looking for a particular landmark. In the spirit world, beings move directly to locations; directions are unnecessary. LiarLight's meeting place was one of those locations.

Suddenly, LiarLight's shadowy figure appeared before the generals. thgiL immediately fell on her face before him; this was her typical greeting. The others separated from thgiL and simply bowed their heads in respect. thgiL reverently arose, but would not look toward LiarLight's face.

LiarLight addressed the assembled generals.

"My Generals," he began, "I have detected a growing presence on the earth; I want you to seek it out, and report back to me—directly to me."

"How will we know we have found the presence you seek?" thgiL asked respectfully.

LiarLight turned to thgiL. "Seek the one true Light. Anyone who seeks the Light will be ultimately drawn to the presence of which I speak," answered LiarLight. He then turned toward the others. "However, beware of the Light," he warned. "Do not be influenced by what you will find; the true Light has the ability to corrupt you from the path you have chosen." LiarLight sneered as he thought back. "He will try to woo you to himself with remembrances of past days—days which I remember. I am disgusted when I think of groveling before him. Never again!" LiarLight sneered at the generals. "Seek him out, but beware: the jealousy of the Light rages against those who have renounced Him. Remember, you have chosen to follow my light."

thgiL was saddened by this affront. "I desire only to do your will!" she responded pleadingly.

LiarLight snapped at her, "What do you know of desire? You are an object!"

The generals smiled disdainfully at thgiL. LiarLight turned back toward them and seared them with his stare. "The Light exists for the opportunity to destroy you. There is no turning back; you are unforgivable." The generals stood unmoving. "Yet, should you attempt to turn to him, you will feel the power of my wrath." LiarLight scowled at the generals. Gradually he smiled, reflecting the smiles they had flashed at thgiL. "CounterLight now knows my capabilities."

Those words caused a simultaneous chill to come over all but thgiL; they had been the agents of LiarLight's wrath themselves in the past. They acted out the depths of his depravity. In spite of this, their fear was not entirely of LiarLight, but of the true Light Himself. LiarLight was particularly conscientious in his efforts to train the minds of his followers regarding the Light; he vehemently focused his super powers to this end. Yes, they feared him. However, the intensive, ongoing efforts of LiarLight did in part achieve the opposite of what he had intended: in order to maintain their allegiance, he inadvertently pointed out the formidable power of the Light. Instead of lessening their fear so as to enable them to carry out his subversive purposes, their dread increased all the more and threatened to decrease their effectiveness. Because their leader admitted the almost irresistible attraction of the Light, their fear of the Light was all consuming. Nevertheless, they proceeded to search out the Light as they were instructed, but not without strong misgivings.

Chapter Six
DIALOGUE IN THE DESERT

Two days passed. DisLight appeared and approached LiarLight. thgiL knelt at LiarLight's side. DisLight was both exhilarated and baffled at the same time. *I found the presence! But how would LiarLight receive the news?*

Upon DisLight's arrival, LiarLight was distracted with his own thoughts. Finally he acknowledged DisLight's presence. He looked upon him incredulously.

"I have found him!" reported DisLight. "The image of the Light. He's in the desert. But, he's—he's . . ."

"He's a man," LiarLight finished.

"He's sent . . . ff-for you. I mean, he's ss-sent me to . . . gg-get you," stuttered DisLight, himself in disbelief.

LiarLight became enraged. "A mere man has sent for me? I will destroy him!"

"He has the presence," replied DisLight sheepishly.

thgiL became incensed. "Let me destroy this fool, my mentor! How dare he command you!" With that, thgiL rose as if to leave.

LiarLight was taken aback. "Wait!" He motioned to thgiL, who fell to her knees before him. "The presence I have been feeling is housed in a man?" He ran through the Old Stories in his mind. *Did not they tell of a man being his ultimate downfall? Of course they did!* He cursed as he once again reflected on his suspicion that the Light was manipulating him. *Of course, the Old Stories predicted a man would bring him down. The Light's power surely must have clouded my understanding of the events of 30 years prior.* His mind began to clear like the dissipation of a cloud in a stiff breeze. *Of course it was true,* he thought. *My challenger was to be a descendent of Paso-Lomon. Yes, my challenger was to be a human. Why did the idea initially surprise me? Had I always assumed my challenger would be a super-being like myself or one of the other members of the original Light Team? Or was it only recently that I had been confused on the issue? Why is the Light doing these things to me? There were human members of past Light Teams. The Light hadn't expended the same effort with his human agents in the past; they were easily accessible and eminently corruptible. There must be something different about this human challenger.*

24

His expression softened. "So he sent for me, did he? Well, I suppose I should not keep him waiting," he chuckled to himself.

LiarLight turned back to DisLight. "From your thoughts, I see that he is in the desert . . . and he what? He sent for me . . . to help him prepare for battle?" LiarLight was astonished. "This man is a fool!" he said, shaking his head. "So filled with the presence, and yet such a fool." He thought to himself, *I must reacquaint myself with the Old Stories; if this is a part of the plan described there, I must proceed carefully. The Light is a clever foe: he will often act in ways that would appear simple yet below the surface are complex. Brilliance in simplicity—that's the Light.*

LiarLight surveyed the scene. Before him was an expansive desert. The bottlebrush bushes with their wiry stalks, which sucked up the nightly dew, grappled with the desert for life. Wind-worn rock bit through the orange sand in unusual, grotesque shapes, as though a titan had been amusing himself there and left his artistic creation intact for all to admire. The twin suns reflected off each rock, creating interesting color changes if one looked quickly from left to right. In the midst of the sculpted terrain sat a solitary man. He looked pathetic: he was sweat and grime, skin and bones. There was nothing about him to merit a second glance. He was just a man, dying of heat, thirst, and hunger. His lips were swollen; his skin parched and sunburnt.

It was Iaman. After leaving the Lone Warrior, he went out to the desert east of Cabazon to prepare himself for what lay ahead. His preparation took place during the preceding five weeks in the desert. Here he was tested and hardened in his dedication to the Light. Mentally he was still sharp, but physically he was drained.

His hands, though trembling, beckoned LiarLight to come. This recognition surprised LiarLight, as he had not yet made himself visible to mortal eyes. The shock also jolted him into an awareness of the incredible presence of the Light evident in the man. This presence was indeed the one he had felt for the past three decades. He knew that this man was filled with the presence of the Light. Could he be the Light? The presence he manifested was so formidable, he decided to approach him as if he were in fact the Light.

"How interesting to find you in this form," began LiarLight. "A bit inhibiting, wouldn't you say?"

The man didn't respond. Gradually, he looked up at LiarLight with love. "You were once great among the members of the Light Team. You were given power and beauty greater than any other. Yet here you stand, disinherited and cursed, before me today."

It was unnerving to hear such words come from the mouth of a man. Now LiarLight was really confused. The answer gave him no indication of who was speaking. LiarLight steadied himself. *This is a mere man. Independent of the presence within him, this is a mere man!* He thought back on his successes in the past. *How many men have challenged me in the past? How many survived the challenge? They too were filled with the presence of the Light. True, this man had a greater evidence than those in the past; he would simply be a more significant challenge.*

LiarLight began again. "You have had a hard existence out here in the desert. Your skin is taut against your bones. You have not even the strength to stand. Yet, the Presence is so evident in you. Call on the Light to renew your strength. Surely, he would not have you die in such a manner. I perceive that you and I are to be considerable foes. I love a good fight and am not the type to relish defeating someone in your condition. Call on the Light to refresh you, and we will have a battle that shall be sung of for generations!"

The man was unmoved. After several moments in which he gathered his strength, he replied. "LiarLight, there is more to the existence of a man than his physical body. I am sustained only by clinging to the Light." The statement exhausted him; at its making, he looked like he was at the end of his strength.

Undaunted, LiarLight changed his approach. "You are certainly very weak. In addition, you are alone." He glowered at him. "Is the Light to which you cling concerned about you at all? Would such a caretaker allow you to fall into this condition?" He challenged him, "Would such a protector give me access to you in your current state?" At that moment, LiarLight transported the two of them to the height of one of the ancient rocks. He supported the weakened body at the edge of the precipice. "Something is wrong! You have been abandoned! Throw yourself down and the strong arms of the Light Team will come to your aid. Such a sight would be an undeniable proof of the Light's power."

The man limply shook his head from side to side. "I have no need to test the Light; nor will I use my body to force His hand." He looked up at LiarLight. The purity in his eyes caused LiarLight to look away.

LiarLight was clearly ruffled; his super powers had no effect. The man's will seemed impenetrable. LiarLight had never explored such a disciplined mind. He attacked the man's psyche with all his power. In an instant, he showed his conquests; legions of followers were paraded before the man. Looking down from the rock, they saw all the riches and kingdoms of the past, present, and future.

He turned to the man. "All these will I give to you." As he spoke, the splendor of kingdoms as never seen before or since was assembled beneath Iaman's feet as they dangled over the edge of the rock. "Only flee the Light and cling to me!"

At this, the man gingerly rose to his feet. His exhaustion caused him to pause as he gathered his strength. The strain could be heard in his raspy voice.

26

"For centuries, our battlefield has consisted of the minds of men. Your lies have persuaded many. However, the battle has now intensified: I have become a man." He paused and caught his breath. "The battlefield will now be my mind, a fully human mind. My only power will be the power of the Light. Be warned, though, a new Light Team is arising, led by me, Iaman."

The anger welled up in LiarLight. Every part of him screamed to attack this man who openly defied him. He longed to tear his flesh, to beat him, to cause him agony. He ached to torture the man, to cause him to cry out in pain for mercy. He wanted to humiliate him in every possible way. *Oh, to malign you with ridicule, to drown you in the spit of deriders!* LiarLight's depraved mind surged with hate.

But somehow, he couldn't act. LiarLight stood limp; he couldn't even move, a fact which only intensified his maniacal state. He couldn't even look away. He tried to at least refuse attention with his mind, but he found himself listening.

Iaman then glanced toward the visions of riches that amassed below. "As for your temptations, I am not impressed by your trinkets . . ." his eyes looked with compassion upon those who were under LiarLight's control, ". . . although I lament those who have bought your lies. It is only the Light who offers any hope; I will cling to Him alone." He then paused for a final gasp of strength. Slowly, he turned toward LiarLight. "As for you, depart from me."

In an instant, LiarLight found himself far from him.

Chapter Seven
THE ROAD TO BARSTOW

After being restored by original Light Team members, Iaman headed for
Barstow, where he grew up. The journey gave him the opportunity to recall
his boyhood days. The familiar words of a song went through his mind. He
hummed it to himself, voicing, " . . . as I think of my home, I think of the man
I've become." The place for him to go at this time in his life was back to
Barstow. There were to be many changes on the horizon.

He made his way through Bernardino and Devore. He walked up over the
hill just above Devore. He turned and saw the entire valley behind him. The
suns rose to his left. In a patch of sunlight, a tall bulber with its tiny front legs
and long back ones stood motionless except for the occasional twitching of
its furry, black and white tail. Its too-long ears stood erect. The dense shrub-
bery was overgrown and rugged, and the suns scorched it all. The vista of silhouetted mountains, foothills, orchards, and bottlebrushes in the distance
caused him to hesitate. As he surveyed the scene, he smiled, taking it all in.

Standing there, he saw an approaching cart. At first it was little more than
a dot with a trail of dust. In a few minutes, he began to make out two powerful looking white ayugas in front and a tall driver. The cart moved at a good
pace, although not hurried. The cart itself was filled high with boxes that rose
above the head of the man who controlled the reins. The paneled sides rose
about four feet with boxes randomly sticking above the sides as if peering at
the scenery. Behind the driver's seat were three stacks of large white seed
sacks. Iaman flagged down the driver, who brought the cart to a stop.

"What do you need?" asked the driver. The ayugas sputtered and stamped,
anxious to be back in their stalls.

"Greetings to you!" Iaman responded cheerfully. "Are you heading for
Barstow?"

The man smiled. "Yeah, you want to come?"

"Yes, can I get a ride?"

"I guess so. Come on up."

The driver watched as Iaman climbed up onto the seat next to him. His
sleeves were rolled over each of his biceps, where the knot of a muscle looked
like a bulbous growth on his arm, which otherwise seemed a little thin. His
head was covered with a dusty gray hat with a broad brim, its darker band

blending with the sweat stains. He looked weary yet determined to get to his destination.

Upon settling into a relatively comfortable seat, Iaman took a long breath and exhaled with an expression of deep relief.

The driver appeared lean and wiry. He exuded a tough confidence like that of a streetwise brawler. He took off his wide-brimmed hat and wiped his brow on his sleeve. His hair was black and combed straight back. Two strips of gold skin appeared to be working their way up to a meeting at the top of his sparsely covered head. His bright blue eyes with golden flecks were like the underside of a blue-bellied salaver with its scales interspersed with tufts of yellow hair. He adjusted his hat so that it leaned back off his forehead, gave a few clicks of his tongue, and the ayugas trotted on.

Iaman extended his hand, "I'm Iaman."

"Albert." They knocked hands in typical Sopa fashion. "If you don't mind me saying, Iaman, you look like you could use something to eat. I got some biscuits and water right behind the seat. Help yourself."

Iaman reached back and opened the bag. The white flour dust mingled with the dust of the road. He grabbed three biscuits and turned around, offering one to Albert. "Thanks," he said as he took one.

"'Iaman'—that's a bit of an unusual name. How did you come by it?"

"It's from the Old Stories. My mother gave it to me."

Albert cringed. When he heard "Old Stories," he thought "LampLighters." Had he inadvertently picked up a LampLighter? He wondered what he should say now. Albert softened as he watched his passenger casually eat his biscuits and look around at the sawbrush blossoms that shot up like white torches. Albert had always been curious about the Old Stories, although he never took the time to get any formal training in them. Most of his life he had tried to hide his lack of knowledge. He was like the non-reader who tried to bluff his way through a world of readers. A lack of knowledge about the Old Stories in that culture was tantamount to illiteracy. To compensate, he developed a short temper and a strong punch. Few people questioned him about anything unless they were sure they wouldn't ruffle him. Albert decided to take a chance and ask the man about the Old Stories even though it was hard for him to admit an inadequacy to anyone, particularly a stranger.

"From the Old Stories, huh? Do you know much about the Old Stories?" Albert did his best to be nonchalant, not wanting to let on that he himself knew very little about the Old Stories.

Iaman smiled. "Yeah, I do know quite a bit about the Old Stories," Iaman replied. Iaman picked up immediately that he was not talking to a learned man. However, he detected Albert's vulnerability beneath his hard exterior.

Albert became excited. At last he would have the opportunity to remedy a deficit he had possessed all of his life. The trip to Barstow would likely take ten hours. He would suck the marrow out of the ten hours of instruction. Chances are that he'd never see this man again either, so he decided to be totally honest about his lack of knowledge.

"You know, Iaman, I never was much for book learning. When I was young my family was pretty poor, so I went to work as a boy. It's not easy for me to say, but I really don't know much of anything about the Old Stories." Albert couldn't believe he had just confessed his shortcoming to a complete stranger, but he felt better for doing so. His passenger seemed like a nice enough guy. At the same time, he decided that if the man laughed at him, he would boot him off the moving cart.

Iaman smiled again. "You are a wise man, Albert. The first step to learning is recognizing what you don't know."

No one had ever spoken positively to him about his lack of learning—particularly not a stranger. The surprising affirmation made Albert's eyes misty. He looked away as if checking the side of the cart. After a moment he turned back, once again composed.

Iaman began to share, "The Old Stories have been handed down over several thousand years. They tell the story of how the Light has worked in human history to accomplish His purposes. You see, the Light wants an ongoing relationship with all the people he made. But some of them chose to deliberately disobey Him. Being pure and just, the Light cannot interact with them; yet the Light still desires to have a relationship with them. The Old Stories describe the process by which the Light is reestablishing a relationship with people."

Albert listened intently over the clopping of the ayugas' hoofs. "I had always heard that the Old Stories were about LiarLight getting beat," Albert interjected.

"You're right! LiarLight's defeat plays an important part in the Old Stories. You see it's all tied up in reestablishing a relationship with the Light. LiarLight desires nothing more than to separate people from the Light. To him, each act of disobedience against the Light is a victory. So he works to fool people into renouncing the Light." Albert nodded his head. Iaman continued, "Much of the Old Stories detail accounts of battles between people— human members of past Light Teams—and LiarLight and his gang of fallen Light Team members and wraiths. In some cases, these people have won great battles for the Light; in other cases, LiarLight has tripped them up with wealth, or sex, or power. Also in the end, each of these noble warriors has died. So in one sense, LiarLight has defeated them since they no longer have direct access to the world of men."

30

"Am I right in thinking that LiarLight will eventually be beaten? Or will people always die?"

Iaman shook his head and smiled in appreciation of the astuteness of Albert's question. "Your questions in no way betray a lack of training about the Old Stories. Yes, you are right; ultimately the fatal blow to LiarLight will come through the defeat of his greatest weapon—death. The Old Stories predict it. No, LiarLight will not always rule over the earth. Even now his days are numbered. In fact, the next Light Team to arise will be the one that will defeat him."

A chill ran through Albert's body as if he had been let in on some secret known only to the spirit world. As the words sunk in, his eyes squinted with a question. "How do you know these things?"

Starting at the beginning, Iaman spent the rest of the trip talking about the Old Stories with Albert. As he recounted each event, Iaman described its relation to the coming Light Team and its leader. As he listened, Albert recognized that although the team would be important, the leader of the next team was the one predicted. It is as if the entire focus of the Old Stories pointed to the coming of this leader. Filled with the Light, he will teach people the truth, but he will not be accepted. As Iaman said, "He will be a 'man of sorrows' and 'acquainted with grief.'" This was unfathomable to Albert. Why would one who had the power to defeat LiarLight submit to sorrow and grief? He understood that it had something to do with satisfying the Light's justice, but he simply couldn't get his mind around the idea.

The instruction continued for the rest of the day and on into the evening. Finally they arrived in Barstow. Iaman experienced mixed emotions about once more being in the city of his birth.

Chapter Eight
PREDICTIONS FULFILLED

The city of Barstow was a small city compared to Bernardino. It was located at the crossroads of two major commerce routes. Over time, people settled there seeing the opportunity to make a living from the travelers and commerce which made its way through there. Few people went to Barstow to see Barstow. It was more of a stopover on the way to Bernardino or Camden.

The commercial district was little more than six stone's throw square with merchants' stalls running along the main street. The streets, which moved away from the village square, had homes randomly spaced along them.

As the cart moved through the streets, Iaman reminisced about his boyhood days in Barstow. He remembered the hours in his father's blacksmith shop and his mother's cooking, and the time he got his first ayuga. It didn't matter how many times he returned home; his mind always filled with such memories.

His father was now deceased, and his mother lived alone. He had several kinsmen who lived in the area, so he didn't worry about his mother. He had not written to tell her that he was coming, so she would not be expecting him. He still hadn't decided whether to visit her first, or complete his business. Deciding on the latter, he indicated to Albert to stop ahead in front of the village lodge.

"Where are you planning on staying tonight?" Albert asked.

"I was going to see if the lodge management would allow me to sleep in their barn."

"I've got a little shed on the other side of the town. At this hour, I'm not gonna do any deliveries. Why don't you come with me? The shed is small, but I've got a couple of fresh hay bales we can break up to sleep on. In the morning, we'll go our separate ways."

"It's much appreciated, Albert," said Iaman.

They slowly drove the cart across the village. Half an hour later, each man had a makeshift bed of fresh hay, and was nodding off to sleep. In the morning, Iaman awoke to the sound of rustling hay as Albert prepared for his labors of the day by engaging in his usual rhythmic exercises.

"Thanks, Albert, for the place to stay."

"Glad to help out." Albert finished one last set of situps and turned to

Iaman. "Well sir, I appreciated the chance to talk with you. I hope we run into each other again sometime." He then stuck out his fist.

"I'm sure we will," said Iaman as he warmly knocked Albert's hand with his own. With that, Albert climbed on his cart and was off.

Iaman moved outside and stretched. He looked around to get his bearings; it had been pitch dark when they had ridden in. On the ground was the sack of biscuits Albert had shared with him the previous day.

A short distance away, above the clapboard buildings of the small village, he spotted the bluff where the LampLighter meeting hall was located. Grabbing the half-empty bag of biscuits, which Albert apparently left for him, Iaman headed for the LampLighter's early morning meeting.

In spite of their problems, there were many among the LampLighters who honestly sought the Light. They endeavored to help people in the same manner as the Lone Warrior. Unfortunately, however, the leadership was dominated by a very different type: these leaders saw the LampLighters as a means to obtain power over the masses. After all, the political leaders were the only ones more powerful than they.

The LampLighter meeting hall was a simple, stucco covered, adobe structure. The morning suns hovered above the horizon, warming the clay bricks. By noon, they would have soaked in a good portion of the day's heat. For now, they still held the cool of the evening. The interior of the building was Spartan. Gray-brown walls met a dusty planked floor on which sat a series of tightly woven benches. About 80 people could be seated for a meeting, with perhaps another 30 standing. A raised platform took up the southwest corner of the room, and the benches were oriented so that the audience could view the proceedings that would occur in the corner. Immediately to the left, in the southeast corner, a door led to a small separate room where the leaders would meet. Typically, once the people were seated, the leaders would enter from there. They then took positions in the first row of benches where the seats of honor were reserved for them.

The weekly meetings of the LampLighters drew a variously motivated crowd. There were those who were honestly seeking the Light and were looking for direction; those who attended out of fear of what would happen to them for not attending; political zealots who saw the LampLighters as the only hope for independence from the ruling political structures; and others who came for a variety of personal reasons. Into this assembly walked Iaman.

It was customary to start LampLighter meetings with readings from the Old Stories. Occasionally they would have a stranger read the section for the day. If someone were willing to stand before the group and read, chances were he was a LampLighter who was traveling, or at the least, was unashamed to be identified with the group. Those who refused to read made themselves highly suspect. They might be asked to leave the meeting or even the village. In every case, strangers were always monitored.

Iaman entered the room and moved to the front. He took the reader's position on the far right seat of the front row. None of the LampLighters recognized him, but each assumed one of the other leaders had selected him as the reader. The meeting began with some singing and announcements. At the appropriate time, the master of ceremonies nodded to Iaman to come forward to perform his reading. As he arose, the men in the room removed their broad-brimmed hats. The order of the service was fairly common wherever you went. Iaman stepped forward and took the book. He opened up to a familiar section, and began to read:

> The Light has filled me.
> This is the hour to tell the truth to those who,
> > for want of knowledge, own lies.
> On behalf of the Light, I offer freedom to
> > those who are in bondage.
> On behalf of the Light, I offer the ability to
> > once again see things as they really are.
> On behalf of the Light, I offer the removal of
> > accusations.
> On behalf of the Light, I announce the hour
> > predicted of old: the Light Team arises.

Those who listened were amazed. They had never heard the predications of the arising of a future Light Team read with such authority. They marveled, as the words seemed to be his own, rather than those of an ancient writer.

The feeling that swept the room was broken off by Iaman. As he raised his hands, the room became suddenly silent. Iaman's voice electrified them. His delivery was slow and deliberate. "This prediction has come true today," he paused, " . . . in your hearing!"

But the people were distracted. Someone recognized Iaman. He leaned to his neighbor in the audience and asked, "Isn't that the old blacksmith's son? What was his name? Uh, William—yeah. Isn't that William's son?" Others overheard the comment, and many began to nod in agreement or talk to their neighbor indicating that they too recognized him.

Iaman's assertion didn't register. The people twittered among themselves about how wonderful William's son had turned out. What a pity William wasn't alive to see him! In a moment, some remembered him as a boy playing in the streets. Others recalled his dexterity in maneuvering his ayuga on Race Day.

34

Recognizing their distraction, Iaman cut them to the quick. In a voice that rose above the din, he rebuked them. "The day will come when you will accuse me of hypocrisy. You will say, 'Not only could he not defeat LiarLight, but he is defeated by common thugs. So, you were going to save us from LiarLight? You couldn't even save yourself.' Believe me, your knowledge of me clouds your eyes as to who I really am." He paused. "You await the arising of Light Team? I repeat: this prediction has come true today," he paused, "... in ... your ... hearing!"

At this, there was pandemonium. The leadership felt as if they were blindsided. Screaming, "Blasphemy!" the LampLighters grabbed Iaman and spirited him off. No one had ever dared to desecrate the Old Stories in such a manner. The example of his death would be a warning to self-proclaimed Light speakers of the future. Their goal was to hurl him off the cliff on which their meeting hall stood. The crowd swarmed to the edge of the cliff, surging forward and fanning out across the ledge. Iaman was not among them.

Later it was said he had disappeared, or had become a ghost. In reality, his power was such that, unbeknownst to them, he had simply walked away. He did not see his mother on this visit.

Chapter Nine
CHANGING OF ALLEGIANCES

The Lone Warrior awoke and shook the cobwebs of sleep from his brain. He stretched and then stopped, remembering the events of the previous evening. He smiled and said to himself, "Last night, I met Iaman!" The thought filled him with joy. "So, Iaman is the name of the one I have been waiting for." He stood up and stretched some more. "Iaman." He now hurried to ready himself. His "home" was little more than a cluster of sugar bushes and bottlebrush trees about a mile up a path from his hill on a small butte. The trees provided shade, and the bushes gave him some degree of privacy. He could leave a few things there without fear of them being stolen.

Quickly he picked up his things and made his way from the butte, travelling over a narrow path, which sloped severely on one side and had a sheer drop into a canyon on the other. As he wound around to the left past the canyon, there was a broad field thick with tall, yellow grass. Then there was a gentle, 20 stone's throw rise; once on top, the entire valley opened up before him. According to his custom, he laid down his pack and paused. As he stood looking out on the valley, he spoke to the Light, "O Light, I ask for guidance in talking with the people I will meet today. Help me to loose them from LiarLight's chains. Thank you for bringing the one, Iaman, who will free your people. Thank you for giving me the courage to carry on all these years. Thank you that my message is true." He paused for a second as the realization came over him. *What am I going to do now?* he thought to himself. He was not worried; it simply occurred to him that he no longer had to talk about the one who was to come. *He is here.* The thought grabbed him again. He shouted, "HE is here! He IS here!" He smiled. "He is HERE!" He thrust his fist high into the air and laughed out loud. He continued to chuckle joyfully as he picked up his pack and went on.

With a spring in his step, he arrived a bit earlier than usual at his teaching hill. His loyal followers looked at him with curiosity, wondering what was up, but he only smiled at them. He decided not to tell his followers about Iaman before the other people arrived. In a few minutes he wanted to change his mind, but decided to stay with his plan. As the larger following began to arrive, it was all he could do to keep quiet about the important news.

The people shuffled onto the hillside accompanied by the din of movement and conversation. The Lone Warrior arose and held his hands up to quiet them down. Slowly the hillside became quiet. A smile came over his face; he beamed. The suns reflected the tears as they welled up in his eyes. "I met him who will free us from LiarLight."

His closest followers looked up suddenly in disbelief. "What?" several of them whispered.

He looked at them and nodded his head. "It's true!" He turned back to the large group, "His name is Iaman, and he will lead the new Light Team, the one predicted in the Old Stories. He walks among us!"

With the announcement, his five closest followers jumped up and began shouting and screaming for joy! "Thanks be to the Light!" one shouted. "The Light has fulfilled His promise!" said another.

They hugged and shook the Lone Warrior's hand. Some of the staunchest of the following also rejoiced at the hopeful news. Though the rest of people marveled, the LampLighters were confident that the Lone Warrior had finally lost his mind.

"Where is he?" one of the LampLighters at the back of the crowd shouted. At first he couldn't be heard. "Where is he? Where is he?" he shouted again. The celebration slowly subsided as the people who heard him looked questioningly at the Warrior.

On the third try the Lone Warrior finally heard him and tried to reassure him, "I don't know at the moment, but he will return."

"Oh, so he's not here—but you saw him?" one taunted.

Another LampLighter at the front turned to the crowd and said loudly, "Hey, if he is the leader of the Light Team, maybe he has super powers?"

He turned and challenged the Lone Warrior, "Well, does he have super powers? Maybe he'll fly over us at any moment!" They laughed among themselves, enjoying their sport.

The Lone Warrior was undaunted. "The coming of the Country of the Light is at hand! Why should Iaman's coming be any different than the days of Krauz the Lightseer? Remember, the Old Stories tell of ridiculers in his day as well. Because of their lack of trust in the Light, they were destroyed."

"So you are now like Krauz?" the LampLighters shouted back. "Your claim about the Country of Light only increases our concerns. Why don't you tell these people the truth!" That was about as close as the LampLighters would come to calling Lone Warrior a liar or a fool since they feared the people.

The next day, the valley was covered with hundreds of curious followers. The word had gotten out that the new Light Team leader had arrived. The credible testimony of the Lone Warrior brought the people. For the first week after his announcement, the crowds kept growing.

The Lone Warrior staunchly returned to presenting his message. He began by saying, "I have met our champion! I have met him who will defeat LiarLight!" From there on, his message was much the same as in the past.

The LampLighters, however, intensified their taunting. The mocking went on for five weeks, then six weeks, and now seven weeks. The people were becoming impatient. It was one thing to talk about something fantastic, but to claim to have seen the fantastic with no corroboration is quite another.

"Where is the one you speak of?" the people asked skeptically.

"The timing isn't right," the Lone Warrior responded. "In the Light's time, he will return to us."

This explanation was insufficient for many. His following dwindled under the incessant taunting. Eight weeks, then nine weeks passed. On an average day, less than 50 now came to listen to the Lone Warrior. Then, in the midst of his teaching, surprising them all, the Lone Warrior cried out, "There!" A single figure appeared walking toward them on the road from Bernardino.

"There he is! He is Iaman, leader of the new Light Team!"

Mayhem broke out. The people rose, grabbed their things and chased after him. One yelled, "Are you the Light Team Leader?" Another shouted, "Where did you come from?" Still another bellowed, "Are you going to kill LiarLight?"

Iaman just continued walking resolutely. He appeared friendly and smiled, but would not respond to their questions. He approached the Lone Warrior and they embraced. Then they parted, and Iaman walked away, heading toward Redlands. The people followed. Iaman knocked their hands warmly and stooped to pat the heads of all the children he passed.

The sudden confusion surprised the LampLighters. Grabbing a passerby, one of them asked, "What's going on?"

The passerby retorted, "Haven't you been paying attention? The Lone Warrior says Iaman has returned!"

"Iaman? Who is Iaman?"

"The one who will save us! The one predicated! The leader of the new Light Team!" With that, he hurried off.

As the people bolted, the Lone Warrior remained on his small hilltop, surrounded by his most loyal students; a satisfied smile covered his face. His followers hungered to follow after Iaman as well, but their loyalty to the Lone Warrior was too strong. They devotedly remained with him.

At last the Lone Warrior spoke to them, "My friends, why do you stay here with me? Your future lies with Iaman."

"What do you want us to do?" one of them asked.

"That is for you to decide," he replied. "However, if it were me, I would follow him." He paused. "You see, he must increase, and I must and will decrease. My future will not permit me to follow." With that he grabbed his pack and left them, walking back toward his home in the hills. For a moment of indecision, they stared fondly after him. Then they looked at each other, joy and sorrow mingled. Finally, one stood and left in the direction that Iaman had taken. One by one, each began taking the path toward Redlands.

Chapter Ten
STAR QUALITY

As the group crowded behind Iaman, two followers—Clarence and Scott—wrestled with the throng to get alongside of Iaman. Scott craned his neck as they jostled along, trying to see where Iaman was in the midst of them all. Scott was tall and handsome. He had black hair, soft brown eyes and a winning smile. Being fastidious about his clothes, he always looked sharp and well-groomed. He was no dandy—just a rugged yet crisp looking man. "I don't see him!" he shouted back to Clarence.

Clarence struggled to stay with Scott. Six foot in height, he was leaner and wiry. His broad brimmed hat was tipped back and covered his neck. An unruly strip of black hair stuck out from under his hat, intruding on his forehead. Several days of stubble showed on his cheeks, chin, and neck. Looking on his face, one was drawn to his pale blue, almost eerie looking eyes. His short temper was evident by the manner in which he would shove back those who got between him and Scott.

Scott moved up on Iaman's right side as Clarence suddenly burst through the crowd in front of them both. They struggled with what to say to Iaman. They had heard what the Lone Warrior said and had seen Iaman ignore the questions shouted at him. Clarence smiled at Iaman, then nervously looked away while putting his hands in his pockets and fell in alongside Scott.

For some reason they became anxious, as if they were approaching a dignitary. Their hearts burned; more than anything, they desired to talk with him. In his own way, each thought to himself, What could I have in common with the future leader of the Light Team that he would want to converse with me? They continued to follow, looking for the opportunity to engage him. Clarence gestured to Scott with his hands and mouthed, "Say something to him."

Why would he want to talk to me? Scott thought to himself. *He ignores everyone else—well, not ignores—but he isn't answering their questions.*

Finally, unable to wait any longer, Clarence leaned around Scott and blurted out a question, "So, where do you live?" Immediately, he felt sheepish. *What a stupid thing to ask.* Scott looked at Clarence, rolled his eyes and shook his head. At that moment, they knew that they had blown any opportunity of impressing him. They looked for a way to get lost in the crowd once again.

Surprisingly, Iaman stopped. Recognizing their embarrassment, he turned and smiled at them. With a wink he said, "Come and see."

They did indeed go and see, and spent the entire day with him. The day flew by. They felt like hurried children wanting to stop and look at everything. Time was their enemy, and they had no weapon to stop it.

They learned that Iaman was born in Barstow. During the time when the Summas persecuted the LampLighters, killing all the firstborn children, his parents escaped with him to the outback of Maxima. Later he came back to Calvada, settling in Barstow. His father was a blacksmith. Iaman had learned the trade as well, and he delighted in telling them the ins and outs of the business. Apparently he was also an expert ayuga rider, thanks to his father's tutelage preparing him for Race Day.

The highlight of their visit was listening to Iaman's discussion of the Old Stories. He could quote long sections with great authority and then go on to explain the meaning to his listeners. They marveled at his knowledge and understanding. He could illustrate any idea with a story. These stories came from his experiences growing up in that region. He connected with the people by talking about reds, placilla trees, or the desert—things familiar to them. The questions they hurled at him he now fully answered. By evening, only a few people remained, the others having gone their separate ways with stories to tell of the intriguing man they had met.

As they walked home from East Redlands to Bernardino that evening, Clarence and Scott agreed that they noted something different about him.

"You know, it's as if there's a presence, some kinda presence or something in him," said Clarence.

Scott agreed, "But it wasn't immediately evident; it wasn't until we'd spent most of the day with him that I began to see it."

It was surprising to them that they both saw the same quality in the man. They struggled with how to describe it. They paused for awhile and rested by the side of the road. As they pondered their day, they stared up at the stars.

Suddenly Scott jumped up, "That's what he's like! He's like the stars!" Clarence thought about it, and then with a puzzled expression said, "Sorry, but I don't know; I don't get what you mean." He paused. "Well . . . I guess he does have a kind of a—you know—a glow."

Scott grabbed his arm. "Yeah, that's right—a kind of a glow, but not like a light or a glowing ember." He looked up. "He's more like the stars. We've been sitting here and looking up, right?" Clarence nodded. "Little by little, our eyes have become more used to the darkness out here," he explained. "And as we've stared, more and more stars have gradually come into view. Now we can even begin to see great clusters of stars. If we were to just glance up at the sky we wouldn't see them, but the longer we stare, the more stars come into view."

"I get your meaning now: Iaman looks just like anybody else, like any other man; but another look shows that he is a smart man." His eyes looked up as he reflected on the teaching he had received that day. "I have never heard the Old Stories explained so clearly."

"That's true," replied Scott. "A second look would show how great a teacher he is."

Clarence interrupted, "You know, I bet he's a great leader, too. I think I could follow him just about anywhere."

"True, but that's not it either. There is a quality about him—I guess you could call it 'star quality.'" He thought for a second. "Yeah, star quality! It's like . . . looking up at the stars: you see more of them the longer you stare." His face lit up as he made another realization. "But that's not the only thing! I could stare straight ahead into that field, and not see anything more than I would see at a glance. You need two things: the concentrated stare and the right thing to look at."

With that, the discussion ceased, as they tried to recall the vistas that opened as Iaman had opened himself up to them. As they sat there, both came to the same conclusion. "I want what he has," said Scott.

"You heard what the LampLighters have been saying, over and over—I've gotten sick of it—about the Lone Warrior. Do you think what the Lone Warrior said is true?" Clarence asked. "He's always been reliable in the past, at least as far as I know."

"You mean, about Iaman being the next leader of the Light Team?" Scott looked away thoughtfully. Then he stared for a moment at the expanse above him. "You know, I think I do believe it."

Chapter 11
BROTHER TO BROTHER

Once they reached Bernardino, Clarence and Scott separated, each going to his own place. Both of them spent a restless night thinking over what had happened that day. In the morning, they woke with a vigor to go share with others what they had heard from Iaman.

Clarence and Scott each had a brother. The four of them together, Scott and his brother Steve, Clarence and his brother Albert, were in the dry goods business—that is, they transported bottled goods, flour, seed, and other household products to outlying areas. Their years of hauling large packages had made their bodies limber and strong.

Scott didn't really resemble his brother Steve. Although shorter than Scott by two hands width, Steve was more solidly built—he was an athlete. The difference in height, coupled with Steve's lack of hair, caused people to question if they were really siblings. However, what hair Steve lacked on his head, he made up for on his face. Steve's beard grew well down onto his chest, and was as thick as steel wool. The main similarity between Steve and Scott was their almost identical voices. People never realized their sibling relationship until they would begin to speak; then the connection became obvious.

Clarence and Albert were much more similar in appearance, both being tall and lean with an angry, hungry look. Clarence had a unique way of speaking, which was at times annoying to the others.

People marveled at the relationship between the two sets of brothers as each pair had such different personalities. Steve and Scott were the "no nonsense" kind of guys who were at the same time fun-loving. Steve, in particular, could gather men together and quickly gain their trust. His involvement with several groups of men at different times in his life resulted in lifelong friendships. Although not necessarily the leader of these groups, he was obviously an influential member, well-respected and enjoyed. Scott was also a leader, but in a different way: he seemed to instinctively understand people's motivation.

The business, originally started by Steve and Albert, significantly jumped forward when Scott came on board. He had a knack for knowing not only what people wanted, but also how to package a product in a way that appealed to them. His ability, however, was more than simply good business sense: he connected with people, understood where they were coming from, and could relate to them. Steve just shook his head at Scott's ability with people. He would say, "I was sitting there with you and had no idea what was going on." That refrain was so often repeated that it became a joke amongst the four.

Albert and Clarence were quite different from Scott and Steve. On the exterior, they were seemingly calm and friendly, but there was a short distance for them between friendliness and anger. Another joke amongst the brothers related to how hotheaded the two could be, particularly Albert. Albert would say, "I don't understand why you guys say such things—I'm always such an even-tempered guy!" Steve would shake his head and with a smirk, reply, "Whatever you say, Lilly." "Lilly" was a nickname given by a co-worker to Albert; when used at inopportune times, it started his fuse sizzling.

Clarence, although not as hotheaded as Albert, could be very judgmental, unforgiving, and impulsive. People claimed the brothers' volatility was due to their upbringing. In fact, behind his back, their father was known among the townspeople as "Thunderhead," due to his ranting tirades. Albert and Clarence often relate to anyone who'll listen that their most memorable incident was when as kids they spoiled the neighbor's swimming hole with dead lizards and various animal droppings. The neighbors never did find out the identity of the culprits; but Thunderhead found out, and the household storm that day was the stuff of family legend.

The S&A Dry Goods business of the four men was highly visible in the Redlands-Bernardino area. One could hardly pass a day without seeing a cart with the characteristic S&A logo. The trademark white ayugas that were used to pull the carts was Scott's idea, which made their carts even more noticeable.

The importance of their business to the local area had resulted in their good reputation being well-established. They were honest, reliable men who lived quiet lives and worked hard.

This unlikely group was in business together, and over time became increasingly close, in spite of their differences. They trusted one another and literally lived for each other. It was into this scene that a somewhat changed Scott and Clarence appeared in the morning.

In the morning Scott lay in bed and rehearsed how he would approach Steve. He wanted to tell his brother about his experience with Iaman the day before. He wanted Steve to catch the feeling that he himself had experienced. Upon hearing Steve rustling around making breakfast, Scott threw on some clothes and went into the kitchen.

"Hey brother, look at this!" Steve pointed to the news captions from the local transcriber: "'Five Summas and Two Saties Killed in Ethnic Violence.' They say the attack was in retaliation for a decision awhile back, where they let the government off for the killing of seven LampLighters. Let's see, the attack was in Rialto—hey, that's not too far from here. It says they caught one of the guys, and I guess their leader is a political rabble-rouser named Elie. 'A national effort is underway to find and capture him.'"

"So how did you enjoy your day off?" Steve asked, changing the subject. "You hadn't gotten in by the time I went to bed. Albert and I had a drink together and then turned in."

Standing there, filling the doorway, Scott prepared his words. To his dismay, they rushed forth from his lips: "I met the most amazing man yesterday. We saw him when we were out by the Lone Warrior's hill. The Lone Warrior said he is the next leader of Light Team; I really believe that he has star quality." Scott waited for a response.

Steve paused with his plate of biscuits and gravy in one hand, and a cup of coffee in the other, gave him a puzzled look and smiled. "So you met the leader of the Light Team on your day off?" he reiterated sarcastically. "How nice." Steve shook his head and sat down at the table. "I was delivering yesterday, over by the LampLighters place, and we got to talking. You know, some of the LampLighters have been saying that they think 'old LW' has finally lost it with his talk about how he met the new Light Team leader—but get this—no one else has seen him. I respect LW, don't get me wrong; but look at him. Living out there in a bush on some hillside, eating Light knows what, can really get to a man after a while. And besides, the LampLighters don't believe him." Steve looked up at Scott from the table.

Scott was insistent, "Well, the leader that LW has been talking about for the last couple of months did show up yesterday. His name is Iaman, and Clarence and I spent the day with him—what an incredible guy!" Scott looked back at Steve appealingly.

Suddenly caught by the seriousness in Scott's eyes, Steve stared back. Although often good for a joke, he knew Scott was not joking.

Clarence and Albert had been loading dry goods when Albert said, "Hey, let's take a break!" Clarence had been quiet all morning; Albert hadn't said anything, but did give him several questioning looks. He knew Clarence would get around to talking about what was on his mind when he was ready. Clarence leaned against a cart while Albert sat on the ground with his back against a couple of sacks of seeds. He took off his hat and wiped his brow with his sleeve.

"What do you think about old LW?" Clarence asked. "You know the LampLighters really think he's crazy. Do you think he's crazy, or is there something there?"

Albert continued wiping his brow as he thought for a second. "Well, I'm no fanatic, if that's what you mean."

Clarence continued to stare.

Albert looked exasperated. His voiced raised a bit: "What are you after? Sure, I've heard his teaching once or twice, and I suppose what he says makes sense about fleeing from LiarLight and all that. I guess I just think some of it is just so much talk!" He calmed down. "How are you supposed to flee LiarLight when he's got all the power? No, there isn't much hope until the Light kills off death by getting rid of LiarLight—that's what the Old Stories say."

"Well, what about the Light Team?" Clarence asked.

"Yea, what about it? It seems that it ought to be arriving sometime." He looked back at his brother. "All I can say is, don't hold your breath." Deep in his heart, he wanted to believe, but the predictions felt like fairy tales. He thought about his time on the road to Barstow a couple of weeks back with that stranger. The stranger did clear up a few questions for him.

Clarence would not let up: "Well, do you think LW is reliable?"

Albert was getting agitated. "I don't think he's a liar, if that's your meaning." Albert leaned back and sighed, "He's been out in that desert a long time. I'm sure he wouldn't deliberately mislead people; he'd have no reason to."

Clarence gathered up his courage and prepared for his brother's onslaught. "Yesterday, Scott and I went to hear LW. He gave the same old teaching about fleeing LiarLight, and you know, the coming of the Light Team; but this time he said that he had met the one who would be the leader of the team predicted in the Old Stories. If that wasn't enough, he pointed out a man in the crowd. He said his name was Iaman; I met him and asked him where he lived, and if he was the leader of Light Team."

Albert sat erect and held up his hand. "Wait a minute: you said his name was 'Iaman?'" he asked intently.

"Yeah." Clarence shook his head affirmingly and then went on. "Anyway, Scott and I followed him, and he invited us to come to his house. The whole day. . . we ended up spending the whole day with him." Clarence looked up as if remembering his words from the previous day. "I've never met another man like him before; he explained the Old Stories, made them so clear . . ."

Clarence continued, but Albert was not paying attention. Albert thought to himself, *Could he be the guy who rode with me to Barstow?*

" . . . not like the LampLighters, not at all . . ." Clarence went on.

Albert thought, *He talked about the Light Team, but he never said anything about he himself being the leader of the Light Team.*

" . . . the guy really—you know—we felt as if we could follow him . . ."

Albert interrupted pointedly, "And Scott felt the same way?"

"Yeah." He paused looking at Albert quizzically. Albert stared with the revelation. "He said the guy, Iaman, had something he called 'star quality.'"

Clarence went on to describe what star quality was, as well as many of the details of the day. To his surprise, Albert didn't react negatively. He listened with rapt attention, occasionally staring off in thought.

"You know, I know where he lives," said Clarence.

Chapter 12
LIARLIGHT'S DECEPTION

LiarLight smarted from his confrontation with Iaman in the desert. He had underestimated this man with the presence.

He still hadn't resolved his initial question about whether Iaman was the Light. The idea seemed ridiculous. *What possible reason would the Light have for taking the form of a man? A man is so vulnerable, so basic, so simple. Why not become a higher form of creation? Why not become one of the original members of creation? Something like me.* He puzzled over what could be on the Light's mind. Then again, he might not be the Light at all. He could just be a man that the Light has tutored over the past 30 years. A kind of "Super Light Man." He pondered some more. *What did it say, "a man, a descendent of Paso-Lomon, will be my downfall?"*

He continued in thought, but could not resolve the pivotal question of who Iaman was. One thing was for certain: since his humiliation in the desert, he vowed that he would no longer be misled by the Light. The defeat crystallized in his mind his suspicion that the Light was manipulating him. The events which unfolded around Iaman fascinated him; like brain teasers or pieces of an intricate puzzle, he pondered them trying to arrive at the elusive answer. His defeat had sobered him to a heightened state of carefulness.

Then there was the Lone Warrior. LiarLight was angered as he thought about him. DisLight was to incite the LampLighters to action, but his prompting did nothing. LiarLight had underestimated the Lone Warrior and overestimated the power of the LampLighters. He also hadn't figured on the Light's direct involvement. It seemed the Light's fingerprints were everywhere. He set his mind to have revenge on the Lone Warrior. He would control the damage caused by him. What is more important—he would destroy him.

It was obvious to LiarLight that Iaman was in the process of finding Light Team members. Hundreds of people were already following him, listening to his teaching; it sounded similar to that of the Lone Warrior, but with more authority. Additionally, LW always spoke about the future—the coming of the Light Team. Iaman, however, spoke about the present: events that were currently unfolding. An inner circle seemed to be gradually developing around Iaman. It would simply be a matter of time before the Light Team was assembled and the members given their powers. At that point, the team would begin its assault on LiarLight's kingdom.

LiarLight sought a better way to monitor the situation as it developed. *If sent, one of my generals would be easily detected. Hadn't Iaman seen me in the desert before he revealed himself?* Then the obvious broke into his mind. *Why not use a member of the Light Team? The idea percolated for a moment. No human has ever fully given himself over to following the Light. There is always an area of their mind accessible to me.* He smiled at the thought. *Perhaps Iaman will not be able to distinguish the evil thoughts in his loyal team members from those I will plant in the one I control.* His mind raced again. He would study the ones selected by Iaman for the team to understand their strengths and weaknesses. *My agent must initially be like any other loyal member. Later, I will corrupt the selection for my own purposes.*

LiarLight resolved to carry out the plan. He would monitor Iaman's movements, occasionally mounting a token attack. He would use the LampLighters to trip Iaman up with their incessant questions and arguments. A few examples of Iaman looking foolish would certainly cause many to fall away. He knew during this phase of the strategy he would take his lumps. However, he would endure these minor, early defeats to lull Iaman into complacency about him. LiarLight figured, *If I were in the same situation, I might even become overconfident; and I am superior to Iaman.*

He recognized, however, that his final victory would come through the corrupting of one of Iaman's followers. A team member would eventually betray Iaman; a team member would be his downfall. How fitting!

The plan was perfect; his confidence returned. He would see Iaman dead, and the great Light Team scattered.

His plan would take time: time for the selection and training of the team members, and time for LiarLight to make his selection and to ultimately gain control of his agent. As he thought about it, he realized again that he would have to face defeat, at least in the short term. However, his early defeats would sharpen his followers, including the LampLighters that were under his control. His allies would have the opportunity to see Iaman's strategy. Could I even dupe the Light into revealing his hand? He smiled at the possibility. My early defeats will also lead to overconfidence among the new members of Light Team. I can use such overconfidence. It is a short jump from overconfidence to pride.

LiarLight considered which of his generals would be best able to carry out this plan. It is somewhat risky to place a past member of a Light Team so close to an individual who seemed to be the Light. There was only one safe choice: thgiL. Was she not his greatest achievement? Had he not created thgiL to corrupt the minds of men? Additionally, there was the benefit of thgiL's lack of free will. It would be impossible to corrupt her; she would be immune to temptation. She would be able to get close to Iaman and not only remain

47

pure, but even be disgusted by the teaching she would hear. Only she was totally devoted to serving LiarLight.

He would put his plan in motion, and the waiting period would begin. For now, there would be little for him to do, so he turned his attention to the Lone Warrior.

LiarLight was brilliant; his plan was perfect. The leader of the Light Team would die at the hands of his own team.

Chapter 13
THE TEAM

It was indeed Iaman's desire to establish a new Light Team. He recognized that the efforts of past Light Teams had not significantly affected the plight of people in their battle against LiarLight. His strategy, however, would be quite different: he would fulfill the predictions articulated in the Old Stories. The battle he would engage in would result in the downfall of LiarLight.

The plan itself was clearly laid out in the Old Stories, although depicted with metaphor and imagery. The Old Stories were so skillfully laid down that most readers could not see the connections between past and present events. These readers included the LampLighters who denied the pivotal message of the Old Stories. They aggressively denied the notion of a new Light Team. Their defensiveness was partially due to the fact that they saw the serious implications: a new order would dislodge them from the positions of power they had come to enjoy. They fixedly set their jaws against such a possibility.

On the day Iaman was with Clarence and Scott, he also spoke with a large group of people. While some went back to their homes, others stayed and spent several days with him. Evidently the Lone Warrior's assertions regarding Iaman had been heard by many. As a result, much of the crowd that had been following LW began to follow Iaman.

Early one day, Iaman left his home in East Redlands and travelled with a few people to Bernardino. As he entered the city, he headed for the S&A Dry Goods Company. In the midst of a number of slat faced buildings stood a large structure covering what seemed a complete city block. The S&A logo was painted above the large double doors of the warehouse, which was an immense, plain wood barn, about twice the width of typical ones.

Iaman paused and looked at the workers moving in and out like red ants on an anthill. Four carts with two white ayugas each were out front. The carts were backed into the dug-out driveway that formed a loading dock. While sitting in the driveway, the cart beds were level with the floor of the building itself, and had a group of eight men busily loading them. Unnoticed by the laborers, Iaman walked past them, up the steps, and through the front doors.

Inside, the expansive room was filled with boxes and large sacks of various shapes and colors. Along one wall were eight ayuga stalls. Dusty rectangular prisms of light streamed in through the doors leading to the outside from each of the stalls. The aroma of ayuga feed and manure filled the air.

Iaman smiled at this familiar scent which brought back so many good memories of working with his father. In the back of the expansive warehouse was a room built in each corner. Iaman saw two men sitting at a table covered with papers. The light, which seeped in through the closed back doors, outlined their silhouetted forms like a dark painting in a gilded frame.

The men at the table looked up at the stranger approaching them, himself silhouetted for them by the bright light of the large entry doors. Clarence and Scott immediately recognized him. Scott ran to get Steve to introduce him to Iaman. At that moment, Albert walked over from one of the ayuga stalls wiping his brow with his sleeve.

"Hello, Albert," said Iaman.

Albert recognized him immediately. "Hello!" he replied in wonder.

"You guys know each other?" Clarence asked.

"Yeah," said Albert, "We met on my Barstow run. I gave . . . Iaman . . ."
he continued after Iaman nodded, "I gave Iaman a ride to Barstow."

At that moment Scott came charging in with Steve in tow. "Steve, this is Iaman, the man I was telling you about: the leader of the new Light Team."

Iaman looked at Steve. His eyes glowed with pride and love, and he smiled as if greeting a lifetime friend. He breathed deeply and then spoke, "Steve, it is true: I am the leader of the Light Team. Join me and join my team."

Iaman then looked upon the others. "Together, we will venture into LiarLight's domain and win victory for the Light. Join me!"

They decided right then and there to leave everything—home, business, comfort—and followed him.

As they left, Scott grabbed one of the workers who had been loading a cart. As the others looked on from a distance, they saw the confused look on the man's face. Scott gestured with both hands as if to say, "It's all yours now," and walked back toward the group. The man just stood there with his hat in his hand scratching his head. The others loading the cart looked on as if they knew something was up but weren't quite sure what, as the two sets of brothers left with the stranger. Years later, the brothers thought back on how quickly they left to follow Iaman. They couldn't explain it, but they knew it had been the right thing to do.

They walked together up the street when the wind suddenly whipped up and swirled around the men. Albert chased his hat as it was blown from his head. As quickly as it came, the wind died down again. Several bottlebrush branches rolled aimlessly. They passed the gunsmith's shop and the lodge, which were north of S&A Dry Goods. Iaman then crossed the street and headed straight for Cy's Place, the local fermented drink establishment. As these places go, it was a sleazy one. The LampLighters had been trying to get it closed down for several years, but it remained open all the same. A competing one had eventually opened south of the warehouse where the more respectable people went to socialize. As they stepped onto the sidewalk in front of the place, the four brothers were already puzzled: the leader of the Light Team . . . going into an establishment like Cy's Place?

Clarence spoke up, "Iaman, you know I don't think we oughta be going in here. There is another place—a better one if you know what I mean—back down a ways, if you want a red stinger." Iaman paid no attention, pushing open the swinging doors and going in; the brothers hesitated, then followed.

Cyrus had been watching Iaman pass by the window. One of his girls, Kelly, a beautiful woman with long, black hair, had gone to hear Iaman teach on one of her days off and had been impressed by him. When she mentioned how she had spent her day off, she received a great deal of razzing from her co-workers. She had felt extremely uncomfortable with her work at Cy's since then, but looked upon herself as being so morally polluted that she was unsalvageable. She therefore tried to put Iaman out of her mind . . . But here he was, approaching! She had been seductively sitting outside with several other "silk-and-lace" clad "ladies," and ran inside to tell Cyrus of Iaman's approach.

Being a man who kept abreast of current events and local happenings, Cyrus knew who Iaman was, and what LW had said about him. He was also vaguely familiar with the Old Stories that predicted the arising of a new Light Team. He was shocked to see Iaman coming toward his office. *Perhaps I will be the first that Iaman will vanquish,* he thought to himself. He had been accused of being a vulgar, immoral, licentious man and knew the accusations were true. He was embarrassed to have Iaman walk past his harem of lewd females. Cyrus hoped they would be silent, but he didn't have anything to worry about—Iaman's striking presence silenced them all.

Iaman walked straightaway into Cyrus' office. Kelly huddled in the corner, wanting to be as inconspicuous as possible. Cyrus tried to remain calm, but he fidgeted nervously with papers on his desk and prepared for the worst.

"Join me!" Iaman invited.

Cyrus was taken aback; he couldn't believe it. Kelly's jaw dropped. She was so shocked, she fell against the wall where she was standing. Finally, the words, "Join me," registered in their minds. Surprising them all, Cyrus followed Iaman outside.

Scott and Clarence looked at each other. Clarence leaned over to Scott: "It seems being on the Light Team is not the great honor I thought," he whispered behind his hand. Their dreams were dashed as they left with Cyrus. Albert and Steve gave each other a "What's going on?" look. Clarence and Scott tried their best to put on a brave face for their brothers, but they too were bewildered.

They walked out of Cy's Place and went up a couple of blocks to the park. Iaman led them to the center of the park where they sat on the steps of a marble statue honoring T. Willits, the first Bernardino magistrate. There they sat for the remainder of the morning. Iaman taught them, but no one would broach the topic of Cyrus. The man himself, however, was distracted.

His head bobbed from side to side avoiding the glances of passersby like one of the purple-feathered birds that frequented the park.

* * * * * * * *

Around lunch time, Seth came up to Scott and Steve. He was friendly and gregarious; whenever he was alone, it wasn't for long. He was of medium height for a Sopa, with dark hair and eyes. A dramatic actor on the side, he was good for a joke. He could take the most bland story and embellish it with his antics to the point that everyone would be rolling with laughter.

Energetically, he said, "Hey you guys, why aren't you . . ." then his eyes caught Cyrus' and his sentence trailed off curiously, ". . . down at the shop?"

The two only gave a look in Iaman's direction.

"Seth! I'm glad to see you! I've been looking for you!" said Iaman. "Join us: be a member of Light Team!"

Without hesitation, Seth shrugged and joined the rest. All afternoon they walked around Bernardino talking all the time, getting to know one another. Seth knew the brothers pretty well, but none of them knew Cyrus. They tried to be cordial, but they just didn't trust him—his reputation preceded him.

Later that day, they broke up for the evening meal. Clarence and Scott went back to the warehouse to take care of any problems that may have arisen during the day after their sudden departure. Seth took the opportunity and went looking for Josh only to find him sitting under a tree. When he saw his friend, Seth started running toward him. Josh was quite tall and athletic, but carried himself modestly. His suspenders pulled his billowy shirt against toned muscles, and his rolled-up shirt sleeve barely fit over his forearm.

"Josh! Josh! I found the one predicted in the Old Stories!" He paused, trying to catch his breath after almost tripping. "The leader . . . of the new Light Team . . . His name is Iaman . . . and he's from Barstow!"

"Barstow?" Josh recoiled with squinting black eyes. "Can anything good come out of Barstow?"

Seth shrugged, responding, "Come and see!"

Reluctantly, Josh joined Seth to find Iaman. He continued to munch on a bulber leg as he and Seth approached Iaman. Looking up at Josh Iaman said, "Now here is a man's man: a man with a sharp mind; honest, forthright, and yet compassionate."

"How . . . Where do you know me from?" asked Josh taken aback.

"I have seen you on several occasions in the village," replied Iaman.

Josh was amazed. "You are the leader of Light Team!"

"You make that affirmation because I said I saw you in town?" Iaman chuckled. "You'll have greater proof than that!"

52

* * * * * * * *

The following day, they were off again walking around Bernardino—Iaman teaching, the team listening. They returned to the park they had visited the day before. A bit of a commotion was in progress. A man named Lupe was standing on a wooden box and lecturing the crowd. Apparently, his topic was politics. He was small in stature but well-built, and the fire of his convictions was convincingly conveyed to all. As Lupe spoke to the people, they occasionally responded with hearty shouts and loud cheers.

"I say we've been under the thumb of government for too long. How long will we shoulder the yoke of our oppressors? Seven of our brothers are dead, and how have the Justice Laws helped us?"

The people cheered enthusiastically.

A slightly older, well-dressed, dark-skinned man of medium build spoke up from the crowd as he gradually made his way forward. "Lupe, Lupe, Lupe, there you go again! Who has filled your mind with these ideas? You excite the people with your rhetoric, and they go out and are silenced by the government. Change won't come from stirring up the people to hatred and violence. But change will come through the sharing of ideas. One informed life will result in more positive gains than the sticks and clubs of a hundred incited by you!"

Lupe recognized the voice of his antagonist and friend. "Michael, Michael, Michael, there you go again. It's now noon: have you been to work yet today?" The people chuckled. "The life of a professor is easy at the university. You don't face the same challenges as those among us who do real work."

Michael smiled and shook his head. "You should update your arguments; the people tire of your trite repartee. You must have forgotten that I no longer work for the university . . ." he said sarcastically, ". . . although it is not as easy as you imagine. I have a 'real job,' as you would say, in the business world. Will all of your political arguments be as easy to dispel as your forgetfulness about my work?" The people smiled. "Oh, by the way, do you have a 'real job' these days?" That retort caused many in the crowd to snicker behind their hands.

One of Lupe's compatriots shouted out, "We work to free the people!" Lupe silenced him with a hand and turned to the people.

"Michael misses the intellectual debate of the university," Lupe replied. "He enjoys the stimulation of argument and counter-argument." Michael raised his eyebrows and nodded his head as if to say, "It's true." Lupe held out his hand to Michael, "But he would be with us, if it came to it."

Michael took his hand. "My friend, you know me too well," Michael smiled. "But that is my point: I don't want us to come 'to it.' If we were to

53

come to blows with the government, the streets would fill with blood—our blood—and my blood would most certainly mingle with yours. Yet, should we return to the days of the wars? I'd rather my sweat mingled with yours in productive work that makes our corner of the world a better place. I'd rather my thoughts mingle with yours as we seek a way to live well, a way to live with those different from ourselves that also honors the Light. These do I prefer over . . . over bloodstained streets."

Michael then turned to the people. "Lupe makes your hearts burn over the political injustice all of you face; my heart burns as well. But freedom from oppression will not come from government; it cannot come from government. The Light is the source of true freedom." Lupe couldn't argue with that statement, so he stepped down. Together they walked through the crowd.

Lupe leaned over to Michael. "Did you see who is on the fringe of the crowd?" he whispered.

Michael stuck his head up and looked around. "No, who?"

Lupe pointed, "Over there to the left, standing with the dry goods guys."

Michael saw the man Lupe referred to. "Is that Iaman—the one the people have been talking about?" Michael asked.

"It's got to be—I heard that the dry goods guys have left everything to follow him."

"The dry goods brothers are following him?" inquired Michael, surprised. "Aren't they pretty stable guys?"

"Yes, but so is LW."

"True enough, but religion is his business. Now the dry goods guys are just solid, regular men." Michael paused. "Huh? So they left their business to follow him? I find that pretty amazing. I don't know them very well, but they always seemed to have a . . . reliable common sense about them. He must be a very charismatic man, this Iaman. Let's go introduce ourselves," said Michael. Lupe nodded, and they moved in Iaman's direction. The people separated before them as they walked over to Iaman.

Iaman saw them approaching and reached the palm of his hand out to Lupe. "Hello. I am Iaman," he said.

"I am Lupe, and this is Michael," Lupe replied.

"A pleasure," said Michael as he met Iaman's hand with his.

"That was an interesting exchange. You both spoke of freedom. Would you honestly like to free people from their greatest oppressor?" Iaman questioned. He saw the fire in Lupe, who loved his people very much and was consumed by his political idealism.

Lupe's eyes riveted Iaman, "I would do anything to shatter this yoke of oppression!"

Michael looked at Iaman with a sidelong glance. Was this man toying with him, or was he real? He hesitated for a moment as he thought. *I would be free of my oppressor? But do we mean the same oppressor?*

Iaman turned to Lupe. "Join me, and we will defeat the Great Oppressor—LiarLight himself. Together we will venture into his kingdom and carry off his greatest prize!" Iaman replied.

"I'm with you!" Lupe responded unhesitatingly.

Lupe looked into Iaman's eyes; they caught Lupe up and filled him with awe and fascination. The gleam in Iaman's eyes electrified him, but at the same time he wondered if he didn't also detect a tinge of sadness.

"I will follow you as well," replied Michael.

* * * * * * * *

As people observed the team, they had mixed reactions. Lupe was familiar to them. He had very definite political opinions and was happy to share them. He was also quick to tell you that you were wrong if you didn't agree with him. He felt the country was going "downhill fast," as he would say. He was very open about the fact that he saw participation in the Light Team as a fantastic career opportunity—to be a part of the only potentially viable alternative to the reigning political establishment. He mostly kept this opinion to himself around Iaman, but everyone, including Iaman, knew Lupe's motivation.

Iaman handpicked three other men to be members of the team: Bertrand, Wendell, and Edward. Bertrand was a quiet man, but it was evident to Iaman that he had a lot going on beneath the surface. He appeared cerebral, calculating, and sensible. He kept his distance when anyone tried to approach him. He was clean-shaven with short-cropped hair. There was nothing particularly unusual about his appearance: he was of average height and build, with dark hair and dark eyes. But his background was somewhat mysterious—people wondered where he came from. Neighbors of his said he was very friendly, although he generally kept to himself.

Wendell was just the opposite. He was about 55 and balding with gray on the sides. Always friendly, energetic and joyful, he was a delight to be around. Wendell was the kind of guy who at one moment would be discussing a fine point of following the Light and the next moment would be putting a stuffed skin of a poisonous ahshaker in someone's saddlebag, waiting for their reaction. All who knew him liked him. More than once he raised Albert's ire, but he also brought many a smile to Iaman's lips.

Different from both Bertrand and Wendell was Edward. He was paranoid; he was the type that would worry even if he had nothing to worry about. None of the team actually knew how he came to be a member. He seemed to just show up one day and was introduced by Iaman as the final member of their team. Edward was intensely concerned about everything. One minute he was fretting about the size of the crowd that followed them; the next moment he lamented speaking gruffly to a stranger. He agonized about his mother and was uneasy with so many people around. He tried to hide his apprehension, but it was written all over his face. Even when he was silent, you could tell he was fretting over something. He became known to them all as Edward the Worrier.

Iaman knew the consensus among his team was that Edward was a bad choice. He overheard whispers, "Him . . . a Light Team member?" Michael was dubbed a likely choice, and Wendell was understandable, but Edward? Some tried to look at his selection another way, thinking that if Edward could be a Light Team member, anyone could. In other respects, he seemed like the others, except for his considerable weight—another of his worries. Edward continually bothered the other team members with his worries and concerns, and they openly showed their impatience with him. Iaman, however, always treated him with kindness.

* * * * * * * *

In all, Iaman chose 12 men for the Light Team—Steve and Scott; Albert and Clarence, the sons of Thunderhead; Josh, Seth, Lupe the patriot, and Cyrus; Edward the worrier, Bertrand, Michael, and Wendell.

Chapter 14
THE TEAM GATHERS

This group of 12 rather ordinary men formed the team. Gradually, they were beginning to get to know each other. Seth was already pretty well acquainted with the dry goods brothers; Josh knew them as well, but only from greetings on the street. And Lupe and Michael knew each other from their political exchanges in the park.

Cyrus was the most distrusted at first; however, the men began to see a genuine change in him. None of them had personally known him in the past, although all of them knew *about* him prior to joining the team. Their experience with him was quite the opposite of what they had expected; in the few weeks they had been following Iaman, it was obvious Cyrus was becoming a different man.

Prior to joining Iaman, Cyrus was always surrounded by many "friends". These men were opportunists at best: they hoped that through their friendship they would get sexual favors from Cyrus' girls without having to pay, and sometimes they did. Occasionally one still would approach him with a jovial sexual innuendo that caused the team great consternation. Cyrus would do his best to turn it away with explanations that he'd changed, and that he was no longer in that type of work. The bewildered looks he received from his former associates expressed in no uncertain terms they thought he had lost his mind. To combine the ideas of "Cyrus" and "follower of the Light" in the same breath was ludicrous. The typical comment was, "Cyrus has found religion?" The typical response was, "Well, I guess there's hope for anybody!" or, "There *is* a Light!" Yet, to his credit, Cyrus stood his ground. At this point in his life, he didn't mind if people saw him in a different light.

His break with Cy's Place was remarkable; it was as swift as it was complete. In spite of the public opinion against him, he had an established clientele, and if anything at the time of his joining the team, his business was on the upswing. His leaving to follow Iaman was a shock to most of his prostitutes. Yet, several of his "girls" were encouraged by his move and took the opportunity to leave as well. Kelly was right on Cyrus' heels as he left to follow Iaman. She figured Cyrus was no better than she, and the great Light Team leader called him to follow, so why not her? She could follow as well. She was encouraged when a couple of the other women came with her. They remained on the fringe of the group, but they followed nonetheless.

By this time, the men had had the opportunity to follow Iaman for a whole month. He arose early, spending time by himself. As soon as they awoke, he would begin teaching them and the crowd that soon gathered. Meals were eaten at the regular times. Although they were meager, no one hungered.

Even though they were selected and set apart for some reason as members of the Light Team, the 12 saw little difference in their daily interactions with Iaman as compared with those of the general following. At times, they were disappointed, wondering whether this was all there was for them. But it was still too early for them to form serious doubts about their mission. The confusion that clouded their minds, however, was soon to become a basic characteristic of their journey with Iaman, and a major stumbling block when it counted most and important decisions had to be made. One can bet LiarLight wanted to keep them in the dark for as long as possible, and that he sent his best agents to maintain their obtuseness.

Many of the people remained skeptical about Iaman and his team. They remembered others who had come at various times in the past claiming to be the next leader of Light Team. Some who followed were later embarrassed by their gullibility when the charlatan was finally unmasked. Others weren't so lucky. In the people's remembrance, there were at least two occasions when followers of a self-proclaimed Light Team leader ultimately took their own lives. As a result, one couldn't help but be skeptical.

The men who followed this Light Team leader, however, were very different—they were solid, hard-working men with good reputations. Most were known for their common sense. When men like Steve followed Iaman, you couldn't help taking a second look. This fact calmed the fears of many of Cyrus' friends. *There must be something there,* they thought.

The LampLighters had a particularly low regard for sex peddlers like Cyrus. The very presence of Cy's Place in the community mocked their authority. It was only because the government guaranteed individual rights that such places were permitted to exist.

People also wondered about the S&A Dry Goods company. That business had been pivotal to the community for so many years. Who would take it over? What would the people do for dry goods? Steve and Albert did have employees, but they hadn't the expertise to run the business. Besides, the four left so quickly. As a result, the business became very disorganized in a short period of time, and never again did it regain its pervasive presence in the region.

Chapter 15
THE TEACHING

One bright morning, Iaman took his Light Team aside. They detected a change, as Iaman's instruction today was directed specifically at them. They were exhilarated to think they would now have the unique opportunity to be with Iaman in a way that they had longed to do since joining the team.

He began sharing, "None of you, if you had an old piece of clothing would patch it with a new, unshrunk piece of cloth. Because, if you did that, eventually the new piece of cloth would shrink, causing a tear larger than the original one.

"Such is the message I bring to you. Each of you knows the power LiarLight has over you. Each of you have been tempted and have failed. Each of you have areas of your mind that you have not given over to the Light. As a result, this is your predicament: you do the things you do not want to do, and do not do the things you want to do. You strive for what you are unable to achieve—freedom from LiarLight. The Old Stories and the messages the Lamplighters proclaim, although good and true, lack the power displayed in a life totally given over to the Light. I will give you that power. The power I will give you, however, cannot be contained within the framework of the Old Stories. The new power would tear the old model like unshrunk cloth.

"Which of you, if he wanted to build a lodge to provide rooms for 100 people, would begin with the framework of his own modest home? The framework and foundation of the old building would be inadequate to support the range and depth of the new. The old, therefore, though it provided comfort for you, is inadequate for your increased needs. True, there is value in what you have learned in building the old. It is the same with the Old Stories, which contain in signs and figures what is to come, and is now in fact among you."

What is he saying? It's a mystery to me, pondered Steve.

"There is great wisdom in the Old Stories. The events they describe were necessary to bring us to the moment in time where we now find ourselves. The Old Stories together lead up to the current events, the arising of this Light Team. They must therefore be interpreted in light of what is happening today.

"For example, the Old Stories say 'an eye for an eye and a tooth for a tooth.' But I say that if you can't do somebody right, don't do him any wrong. If someone wrongs you, don't return the favor. Instead, if somebody slaps one side of your face, turn and allow him to slap you on the other side. If someone takes your shirt, give him your jacket as well. If someone forces you to work for him for one day, work for him two days. If someone asks you for something, give it to him, and more besides; or if someone wants to borrow something, lend it to him freely."

This is crazy—the whole world would be turned upside down if we all did this, Lupe thought.

"The Old Stories say that you should not murder someone. But I tell you that anyone who is angry with a Summa, or anyone who swears at another Sopa or uses racial slurs against a Satie is also guilty. Do you not see that in each of these cases, LiarLight has had his way with you? Do you desire to be free of him? Then consider your brother as better than yourself.

"The Old Stories said that you could 'love your friends and hate your enemies.' Well, I tell you to love your enemies—yes, love them, and seek out opportunities to do good to them. The Light through which all was made causes rain to fall on you and your enemies; He causes the sunlight to shine on you and those who hate you. How hard is it to only love those who love you? Everybody does that. No, the new order requires more of you."

I'm going to have to make friends with people who dislike and misunderstand me. Well, I guess getting to know the other Light Team members has given me a start, reflected Cyrus.

"The Old Stories say to live in sexual purity: to be free from adultery and promiscuity. I tell you that anyone who looks upon a man or woman with sexually impure thoughts is guilty. If something in your life gives LiarLight a foothold, have the sense to get rid of it.

"The first step in fleeing LiarLight is understanding how he works. As the Lone Warrior would say, 'He has no power over you, unless you give it to him.' If your reading material is a temptation, get rid of it. If your entertainment causes you to avoid the Light, don't participate. If your friends imitate LiarLight in their actions and induce you to do the same, find different friends. Practice an examined life.

"The Old Stories say that you should keep all the vows you have made before the Light. Why make vows? Why say, 'I swear to the Light.' Just do what you say you'll do, and do not find a way around it. Likewise, be clear in your intentions, and follow through. When you say 'yes,' mean it, and have the same attitude when you say 'no.'"

"Man, some people are going to have to clean up their acts pretty soon!" hissed Bertrand. Meanwhile, Cyrus bowed his head and whispered, "Light, help me."

"Do not be confused by these words. The standards for behavior as described in the Old Stories are still intact. Power over LiarLight will not come through a relaxation of the standards. Listen closely: until the world ultimately dies, the standards for behavior as described in the Old Stories will remain. Therefore, he who breaks the standards is guilty. But do not use the LampLighters as your performance standard. The acceptable standard of behavior is far above that of the LampLighters.

"To what can I compare you? You are like salt—salt for the world. You make the world palatable. But if salt no longer tastes like salt, what good is it? It's worthless.

"You are also like light. A village on a hill is hard to hide. How many of you would light a lamp and then put it under a barrel? No, you are each lights. You punch holes in the darkness by what you do. When people see the good things you do, they will credit the true Light.

"In your daily lives you should remember that:

> You are fortunate if you know you need the Light:
>> because the Light is close to you.
> You are fortunate if you mourn:
>> because the Light will comfort you.
> You are fortunate if you are gentle:
>> because you will not be overlooked by
>> the Light.
> You are fortunate if your greatest desire is to
>> fulfill the standards of the Light:
>> because the Light will give you your desire.
> You are fortunate if you show mercy to others:
>> because the Light will show mercy to you.
> You are fortunate if you keep your heart clean:
>> because you will see the Light.
> You are fortunate if you are a peacemaker:
>> because the Light will consider you His child.
> You are fortunate if you are persecuted for
>> striving to meet the Light's requirements:
>> because you are part-owners of the Light's country.
> And you are fortunate when, as a result of being a follower
>> of the Light, you are abused, insulted and slandered:
>> because a grand reward awaits you. All who truly
>> cling to the Light will experience such an existence."

Iaman hesitated. "Do you understand what I have said to you?" He looked at each one of them. "I am not here to do away with the Old Stories; I am the fulfillment of them."

Michael recognized, more than the others, the radical change Iaman was proposing. Overcoming his fears of being misunderstood, Michael asked, "But what is the point of this teaching? Why do these things?"

Iaman smiled at him like a teacher would at his best student. "The realm of your experience is limited by your bodies and senses. But there is another realm just as real as this world around you, but not perceived by you now: it is the Country of the Light." He paused. "You can be a master in the physical world, but your mastery is shaky at best. Your wealth can be stolen, your friends turned against you, and your possessions ruined. Even if you can enjoy these things while you are alive, you will definitely leave them all behind when you die. It is much better to store up possessions in the unseen world—the Country of the Light! There, nothing can be taken from you."

They were all puzzled, but Michael spoke up again, "How does one store up possessions in the Light's realm?"

Iaman smiled for he could see Michael's sincere heart. Like a child asking a parent about the facts of life for the first time, Michael had a glimpse of the answer but needed help in seeing it more clearly. Iaman responded, "By devoting your efforts to the things I have taught you; by believing that I am the one to defeat LiarLight, that I am the offspring of the Light."

They were still confused, although Michael seemed to be catching on.

"You see, nobody can follow two conflicting instructions. One command he will follow, and the other he will have to ignore. If one is right, he must choose that one and follow it. If he chooses not to decide, he still has made a choice—not to follow the correct path.

"The best thing to do is not to worry over the things that concern you— or anything else for that matter—but seek the Light in everything you do.

"Your eyes are like windows in a house. The leaders of the LampLighters, among others, sit in the darkness with the curtains drawn, saying, 'I can see fine; I know what is going on.' Yet, do you see that they are in a deeper darkness than the one who gropes around in the dark trying to open the curtains? Open the curtains and let the Light fully in. In that way, no part of your house will be in darkness. Rather, everything will be illuminated. Take caution, therefore, that sitting in darkness, you think you can see."

"Easier said than done," muttered Edward to himself.

"The defeat of LiarLight in your life must take place on two fronts, but these attacks are not mutually exclusive. They are like an intimate embrace. First, illuminate your own house so that you can see and you will better be able to pursue the Light. You will soon find that others will imitate your example. Second, treat your fellow man with love and forgiveness—as you would want them to treat you. In reality, you should treat them even better. Such behavior will frustrate LiarLight's plans for you: his toehold will slip, and you will be free of him!"

Wendell and Seth exchanged glances; others also shifted around uneasily in their places. Clarence spoke up, "You know . . . boy," he shook his head from side to side, ". . . you know this won't be easy!" Without looking at Iaman, he shook his lowered head from side to side. He looked as if he just lost his best friend.

Iaman looked at him unapologetically and shook his head affirmingly. With conviction, he emphasized each word, "That's . . . right!" He smiled. "Another one of LiarLight's lies bites the dust!" He was encouraged; he felt he was getting through to them.

Iaman continued, "LiarLight's road is wide and easygoing. Many follow that path. The problem is that it leads only to him! Many will be shocked when they reach this destination. LiarLight doesn't have to do much when you're convinced to take his road—it's all downhill, and so you perceive it as easy. On the contrary, the way I have described for you is hard. My road is narrow— a rough one to climb. It requires dedication, perseverance, and self-control. LiarLight will definitely resist you if you choose this uphill climb. Few men choose to take the hard way, but it leads to the Light!"

The Light Team reflected in stunned silence upon their leader's words, and no one dared to ask him anything further. They had more than enough to consider. . . .

Chapter 16
WHAT IS THIS?

Iaman continued to gather a significant following and became the latest fad in the region. Some became interested when they heard about the men who left everything to follow him. Many came simply because of the power of his teaching; he spoke with authority, and his message hit home. To those acquainted with the Old Stories, he signaled an intriguing new order. Could he really be the leader of the Light Team? Whatever people were looking for, he always drew a crowd. He was the best show around: he captivated people's attention and held them on the edge of their seats.

Today the intensity seemed to reach an unprecedented peak. Iaman was teaching the people on a hillside in Yucaipa, a town neighboring the Redlands on the east. Suddenly a man burst into the gathering. He was known to be mentally unstable; some even thought he was controlled by an agent of LiarLight, like a wraith or something to that effect. He was homeless and chose to live in a graveyard in east Redlands. On several occasions, the caretakers of the cemetery captured him with the idea of helping him, but he always managed to get away. One time, in frustration, they even bound him head and foot with chains, but he easily broke free from the chains.

Right in the middle of the teaching, he ran up to Iaman and shouted at the top of his lungs, "Why are you bothering us, Iaman of Barstow?" From the same man, a different voice shouted, "Is your plan to destroy us?" Then he screamed in a woman's voice, "Don't punish us!" He settled down and wiped his drooling mouth. He pointed a bony, saliva covered finger at Iaman. Ominously, the rushing sound of a multitude of voices roared, "We know who you are! You are the Leader of the Light Team—come straight from the Light!"

The people were stunned. Albert and Steve got up to protect Iaman. They were ready to pounce on the man if he attempted to do any harm. Instinctively, the rest of the people formed a circle around the men and readied themselves to see a fight. What followed surprised them all.

Iaman rose to his feet. At the mention of his identity, he stopped the madman with a stern glance. Iaman asked, "What is your name?"

The lunatic's face distorted. He answered in a single booming voice, "My name is Mob." The name Mob was echoed by a hundred different voices as they trailed out of the man's mouth.

Iaman silenced him. "Be still!"

Then like a hundred whining children, the plaintive voices begged Iaman, "Do not send us back to our master."

Iaman was unmoved. In a quiet but forceful tone, he commanded, "Be gone!"

The man threw himself on the ground and thrashed around like a rag doll being shaken by a child. Distant screams came from his mouth. Suddenly, he stopped. Regaining his senses, he sat up and held his head in his hands. Gradually, he raised his head. As the circle of men closed in around him, he calmly looked up at them; it was obvious that he was now in his right mind.

The people stared at each other in amazement; they didn't know whether to flee Iaman or embrace him. Stymied, they whispered to each other, "What are we dealing with here?" Others asked, "How is it that a man's mind can be restored with a word?"

The former madman, now fully aware of his new freedom, fell at Iaman's feet. "Please sir, let me go with you!"

Iaman's expression became one of loving care. He took the man by his shoulders and raised him to his feet. "Go home to your family and friends and to all who knew you in your previous state and tell them how LiarLight has been defeated in your life."

He left for home with a joyful spring in his steps. The people who saw him were noticeably moved, and as a result, Iaman's following increased.

Wendell's thoughts, however, were like those of Lupe and most of the others: he knew Iaman was good, but he also knew that following Iaman was no longer safe. He now was a threat to the authorities and their prescribed order of things.

Chapter 17
REAL POWER

Although Wendell, Edward and some of the others became uneasy when Iaman healed the man who was out of his mind, Josh was euphoric. His persistent happiness even annoyed some of the others. In his mind, he was on the winning team. Though the others tried to explain the gravity of the situation to him, he was undaunted; perhaps it was a defense mechanism caused in reaction to his own suppressed fears. But even he would become less confident as events unfolded unfavorably for Iaman. They still were protective of Iaman and loved him, but they did not quite understand his ways.

Iaman must have been aware of what was to come, but he kept it pretty much to himself; only on rare occasions would he reveal his emotions on this matter. During the night and early morning hours, he spoke privately to the Light, who strengthened him. His work had just begun, and many more extraordinary feats would testify to who he was. The amazing thing was that he didn't seem to have to do much outwardly to bring about spectacular results. Take the lady with the health problem, for example: she only touched the sleeve of Iaman's shirt and claimed to have been made well. But because she had had some kind of "female problem," the men weren't overly impressed with what had happened to her—they had no outward proof.

They were astonished when Iaman restored sight to two blind men. But the team had no idea as to why he told the now sighted men not to tell anyone about what had happened. There was a huge crowd around them, and the word would have spread quickly.

It soon did, as LampLighters watched when Iaman helped a man who couldn't speak. The people around who knew him were very impressed when he started talking. Some said, "We have never seen teaching accompanied with power like this before!" Many others agreed, eager to accept it. But the LampLighters in the crowd claimed to be able to explain how he did it. Some had the audacity to say he made the man well because Iaman was an agent of LiarLight.

The incident that really scared them, though, had to do with the daughter of the Summa magistrate. The magistrate governed the area directly east of Redlands. First of all, he came and bowed before Iaman. Bowing was not that unusual, but this man really bowed—to the point of getting down on the ground to do so. If that weren't enough, he was a member of the government and a Summa! The whole situation made the team members very uneasy.

"My daughter has died!" he cried, "But I am confident that if you just touch her, she will come to life again."

The team members looked at each other. The official did not say that his daughter was sick or blind or anything like that—things they were used to seeing Iaman address. This was something new: he said that she was dead!

Edward said what everyone else was thinking, "What does he expect us to do about this? Can't they bury her themselves?" The most startling thing of all was that Iaman got up and went with the man. Disturbed, but at the same time wondering about what Iaman might or might not do, the team followed.

When they arrived at the magistrate's house, everything was in preparation for the funeral. A group of people hurried around politely, in a kind of joyless, dark celebration. They were surrounded on every side by Summa culture. The Summa had a tradition of using "professional mourners" to perform a funeral. Iaman looked sternly at the crowd. "The girl is not dead—she is only sleeping. Pack up your things and leave."

The people became indignant. They offhandedly made cutting remarks about him, with lots of indignant choruses of "How dare he?" and "Well, I never!" These people were experienced with dead bodies. After all, how many funerals had they performed? As they prepared to leave, they shot glares at Iaman and projected loud statements for his hearing as to what kind of fool he was.

Iaman, however, remained focused, unaffected by their derision. He and his followers went into the house and to the doorway of the little girl's room. As the team watched, Iaman entered and approached the girl, who certainly appeared dead to them—cold, white, and motionless. What was he going to do?

Iaman walked around her bed so that she lay between him and the gawkers at the door. With wide-eyed gazes, the team glanced frightfully at each other. Suddenly it dawned on them: He was going to bring her back to life. The realization sent cold chills through them. Each questioned himself, *Who is this man?* Their anxiety was heightened by Iaman's hand slowly approaching the little girl's. An eternity seemed to pass as the comparatively large, blacksmith's hand approached the small, lifeless one.

As soon as her hand was covered by his, normal healthy color returned to her as if she had blushed at his touch. Her hand now reached to stay in contact with his, and with a little effort she slowly arose to a sitting position.

The team members stood awestruck, speechless. There was not a dry eye in the place. The realization hit them: Iaman had just brought a person back from the dead! Steve voiced what others had to be thinking, "What does this mean?" He felt as if a wide gulf had opened up between himself and Iaman.

They immediately opened a path for Iaman and he escorted the little girl out of the room. She smiled at him affectionately, as small children will do for a kind adult. Michael wondered if she had any idea of what had just happened to her.

As the girl left Iaman's side, she skipped out into the crowd. Those who mocked him now gasped in terror. They had decided as a group to remain, claiming that their professional standing was on the line. In reality, they were waiting to jeer him out of the village. They swallowed hard.

Her father saw her and grabbed her, cradling her with tear-filled praises of the Light. She tolerated his hugs for a moment and looked over his shoulder for a friend to play with.

Chapter 18
A VICTORY FOR LIARLIGHT

LiarLight's plan to take care of the Lone Warrior was gradually taking shape. He knew that although the Lone Warrior continued to share his message, his following had diminished. Largely it was LW's own doing, as he consistently encouraged those who came to hear him to follow Iaman instead. LiarLight anticipated this occurrence, as well as the Lone Warrior's corresponding choice of action. He knew that LW would now attack him in a different arena.

At that time, there was a growing movement in Calvada whereby elderly citizens who were deemed no longer able to contribute to society, or who were perceived as having a lower "quality of life," were being put to death. Laws had been recently enacted which made the procedure legal, and death was facilitated in the most humane manner possible. It was a tri-racial movement that preyed on the depression of the elderly, the disabled, and others. This "final solution" was warmly offered in place of counseling or encouragement. In every case, the candidate for death either had to give permission themselves or if deemed incompetent, could have family members give their final assent for the procedure.

The Lone Warrior saw this as an outrage. Now that he had completed his role of preparing the way for Iaman, he decided to speak out against the "death-making." Political battlelines had been drawn over the practice. On one side were the current political leaders and their followers, who advocated for choice. They felt that an individual should be able to choose when to die. On the other side were those in favor of life. They felt that there was a basic intrinsic value in human life—at whatever age—and under any conditions. The first group called itself the Defenders, while the other called itself the Protectors.

The battle had been going on for some time when the Lone Warrior entered the fray. The tactic used by the Protectors movement was to block the entrances of the ironically labeled "Planned-Life" centers where the "mercy-killing" occurred. The government, frustrated by the ongoing dispute over their law—which they felt should have settled the issue once and for all—made the blocking of the euthanasia centers a very serious crime, punishable by lengthy prison time.

These fear tactics had caused some of the Protectors' proponents to fall

69

away. Not that their zeal had faded, but they had families and other responsibilities that they also needed to consider.

The Lone Warrior had no such responsibilities. After his meeting with Iaman who had cryptically told him, "LiarLight will see your demise," he knew that his time was limited. He also knew that his reputation would cause his actions to receive quick public notoriety. After weighing his options, he decided to participate on the frontline of blocking Planned-Life centers.

He was quickly arrested because of the stiffening of the laws against those who blocked such centers. At first the judges were lenient, but ultimately his repeated arrests forced them to send him to prison for the maximum time under the law. He was to be "an example."

In spite of being behind bars, he continued to be an advocate for his positions. He was quoted often, long after his sentencing.

LiarLight relished every step of the process, but it was still not enough. At first, he incited Planned-Life to try to have him silenced. Obviously, this wasn't enough to stop LW. LiarLight wanted him killed, and Planned Life would be the agent. He saw this take-down as a way to further the efforts of the Defenders' crowd. Additionally, if Planned-Life were implicated in LW's termination, he would relish in having contributed to their betrayal. Although there were substantial efforts made to silence him, Lone Warrior's voice continued to be heard.

Finally, LiarLight went with his last resort. It was his last resort because it caused the least amount of anarchy—he would use the other inmates of the prison to kill the Lone Warrior.

The Lone Warrior could see "the events forming around him." He knew that his end was near. Perhaps it was the discouragement of being in prison or of facing his imminent death, but he needed affirmation once more that Iaman was indeed sent by the Light. He communicated to his followers that he wanted to meet with them once again. Some had been following Iaman, while others came back to be with him when the trouble originally began with Planned-Life. He sent these same followers to Iaman with a question. His doubts were largely out of concern for his followers, as he was unsure whom to believe.

A group of the Lone Warrior's followers went to Iaman. He received them warmly, and they briefly discussed how LW was faring, as well as the progress of the Protectors' movement. Finally, one of them asked the question which was their reason for coming.

"Iaman," he stammered, "please tell us if you are the one, or should we expect someone else?"

Iaman smiled sadly at them. He knew that LW was being tormented. He also knew that LW had asked the question mostly out of love for his followers. He reached out to the LW messenger closest to him and put his hands on each of the man's shoulders, looking him directly in the eyes. He smiled warmly, and his eyes moistened as he spoke.

"Tell LW what you have been observing around you. Tell him how people are restored: the lame walk and the blind are given sight; people with every form of disease are healed and the dead are raised." He paused. "Tell him that his message is affirmed. Remind him that even in the midst of his pain, 'Happy is the man who keeps his trust in me.'"

Iaman smiled assuringly at LW's followers as they left. He knew LiarLight's plan for the Lone Warrior was nearing its culmination; LW's voice would soon be silent.

He turned to the team. "What did people hope to find when they went out to hear LW?" he asked quietly. "Was it a regal visitor? Maybe a raving lunatic?" He looked at each one of them. His voice regained its normal volume. "What did you expect to hear when you went out to him—someone who spoke for the Light?"

He looked at them not expecting a reply.

"What can I say about people today? They are skeptics. They are expert at finding fault with each other about anything. They're like spoiled children with their complaining. They say, 'We played upbeat music and you wouldn't dance; we played funeral music and you wouldn't cry.'" He went on, "The Lone Warrior came and disciplined himself by not drinking alcohol and by fasting—they called him a madman, a fanatic! Now I come befriending those who struggle with disobedience to the Light, eating and drinking what I choose. These people now call me a glutton, or say I show a lack of restraint. They say I don't know how to choose my friends and acquaintances." Iaman looked at them and shook his head. "In the end, the Light's wisdom will be seen in it all."

He returned to his thoughts about the Lone Warrior. "In the Lone Warrior, you did indeed hear someone who spoke for the Light, but much more than that! He was the one foretold in the Old Stories who would prepare the way for the new Light Team leader." His voice became louder, "Remember this—the Lone Warrior is the greatest man who ever lived!"

They were shocked at this affirmation. Then his expression lightened and he resumed his gentle tone of voice.

"But also remember that the lowest citizen of the Country of the Light is greater than he is. LiarLight has tried to silence others who have spoken like the Warrior, and has succeeded in violent attacks against past Light Team members. However, winning a battle does not constitute winning the war. In the end, the Light's wisdom will be evident, at every point in the confrontation."

Chapter 19
MIRACLES

Clearly the miracles the team observed had made an impact upon them. The only one unimpressed was Iaman. He recognized that "miracles" were not really miracles at all. Perhaps they exposed a perspective unfamiliar to people, including those on his team; but miracles were simply a reflection of reality.

The adult who can materialize a coin from behind a small child's ear is considered by the child as somewhat of a miracle-worker. With more understanding, the child grows up to be an adult and startles his own child by producing a coin from behind her ear. Iaman recognized that with his team, he was dealing with children for whom he had just produced a coin.

There had been much discussion among the team about what all the miracles meant. Lupe, thinking in terms of political power, saw that Iaman was building quite a following and reputation. He could easily win any election, even against one of the LampLighters.

Steve felt increasingly uneasy around Iaman. It seemed that as he stared into Iaman's "star quality," he became more and more aware of his own personal shortcomings.

Clarence and Albert were uncomfortable; they could not understand Iaman. Typically, they would categorize an individual or an entire group, and then dismiss them, but the ambiguity that swirled around Iaman frustrated their attempts.

Wendell and Cyrus were no better off; they were confused like the others.

Michael was much more quiet than he had been previously. He knew he was in the presence of someone special, but he could not wrap his intellect around who Iaman was. Sure he could spout the words that Iaman was the leader of Light Team, but Michael himself was a member of Light Team, and he didn't even understand what that meant.

Edward was worried as usual, and Bertrand was quiet, but he was always quiet.

LiarLight had begun to sift through the minds of each of the team members to find his agent. The confusion caused by the startling miracles had given him the perfect opportunity to begin his testing. This sifting process occurred unbeknownst to the men, but Iaman knew what was going on.

Iaman met with them under a tree and began teaching again. When he sat down, Seth noticed that the tree was dead. This would not be anything unusual if it wasn't for the fact that yesterday Iaman had been looking for a red on the tree, and having found none, he cursed the tree.

Seth spoke up. "Hey, this is the tree that you cursed yesterday." He yanked off a piece of the peeling bark. "It's dry and withered." The others looked up and realized that Seth was right.

Iaman broke in, "Are you amazed at what happened to the tree? All it takes is reliance on the Light. If you have just a small amount of trust, you could tell the tree to pick itself up, move across the road and be planted over there, and it would do it. If you had trust the size of a red seed, you could say to Mount Gorgonio, throw yourself into the great sea, and it would." The men looked up at the mountain dusted with snow and became thoughtful.

Iaman called them back. "Learning to cling to the Light is like planting a red seed." He picked a red off another tree, pulled off the skin and took a bite. The juice trickled down his arm as he spit a seed into his hand. "To make the most of this seed, you must take it in your hand and plant it." He dug his fingernails into the soft dirt, put the seed in, and covered it over. "Eventually it will grow up, producing seeds of its own." He paused to look at each of them. "If it is your desire to have a full-grown reliance on the Light, like a full-grown red tree, you must take what you have and give it over to the Light. The Light will increase your reliance upon Him. Just as the seed cannot grow itself, you cannot grow your own trust. You can, however, ensure that your kernel of trust is planted, watered and cared for, so that the conditions are good for its growth. You do this by seeking the Light. Doing the things you know you should do—the things I have already told you—will frustrate LiarLight."

The team looked at each other. Iaman knew they wouldn't fully comprehend what he was teaching them until later on. Nevertheless, he continued.

"I am going to give you the ability to cling to the Light, comparable to the size of a red seed. I want you to go to all the surrounding villages and share with them the message you have heard from me. Tell them that LiarLight is on the way out: they must flee him and cling to the Light. As you go to help them, your trust in the Light will enable you to heal the sick, both mentally and physically, and even to raise the dead."

At this, they trembled. Even they didn't believe they would be able to do those things. He continued with some final instructions, "Don't take anything with you: take no money, extra clothes, or food. You need only the power the Light will provide for you through your reliance on Him."

The team members listened intently.

"When you go into a village, stay at any home where you are welcomed." He looked carefully at each man. "In these places, tell the people that the Light Team has arisen, and that LiarLight's downfall is near. Tell them that the power to ultimately defeat LiarLight is very close to them. Support your message by healing people who come to you." Iaman's demeanor then changed, as his brow became furrowed. "Remember, I am sending you out like bulbers into the baola's den. However, you are not unprepared. The Light within you will cause you to be gentle and yet wise. Should the village you visit reject you because of your message, leave and shake the dust off your feet. The Light will cause this act to haunt their memory, and help them recall their rejection of Him."

With that, he sent them out in groups of two.

Chapter 20
GARY AND THE LAMPLIGHTERS

With his team gone on their mission, Iaman decided to celebrate Lightday by going to Bernardino for the LampLighters' Lightday meeting. By this time he was well known to the LampLighters, so there would be little chance of repeating the scene that took place in Barstow. He went to the meeting because that was where the people were on Lightday.

Dislight had been hard at work on the minds of the local LampLighter leaders, stirring up their resentment toward Iaman. Iaman's popularity among the people proved great fuel for jealousy, and Dislight had their anger raging by the time Iaman entered the meeting house door.

The LampLighters hoped Iaman would come because they had schemed up a way of tricking him into breaking the Lightday rules. Their plan was to get him to heal a man on Lightday. Everyone knew that any work was strictly forbidden on Lightday. One could go to the LampLighter meeting but little else. The original traditions for the observance of Lightday had been handed down from the Old Stories. Lightday grew out of the original creation of the world by the Light. The Old Stories said the Light created the world in six days called the "creation days," and then rested on the seventh day, which became known as Lightday.

Like most things the LampLighter leaders touched, the original understanding of the observance of Lightday had also been distorted. The Lamp-Lighters had orchestrated a complicated system of rules that were too cumbersome for the average person to follow in their daily lives, and Lightday was no exception. The LampLighters themselves made a great public show of their accurate commemoration of Lightday. They became "Lightday police," backing their proscriptions up with threats and punishment.

In his teaching, Iaman tried to make the point that the Lightday described in the Old Stories was a weekly time for people to rest and to refresh themselves; a day to put their work aside and enjoy family; and time to spend reflecting on the Light and thanking Him for His provision. Iaman said, "Lightday was made for people; people were not made for Lightday." The interpretation of the LampLighters was just the opposite. To them, Iaman's perspective on this issue was simply unacceptable.

The LampLighters' trap began several weeks earlier, when they made friendly overtures toward a mentally disabled man. Although they had habitually ostracized him, they now tried to reach out and befriend him. Even with his diminished mental faculties, the man thought this quite strange at first, since they had never acted as if he even existed in the past. Society had typically hidden people like him from the public eye; and when seen, they were shunned, mistrusted, or at best misunderstood. In spite of how he was treated, the man was a very accepting person. His attitude could have been partly due to his condition, but nonetheless, he enjoyed the newfound acceptance he was receiving from the LampLighters.

The key to the LampLighter's plan was inviting him to their meetings. He had been attending the meetings now for several weeks, much to the chagrin of some of the members, although other rank and file LampLighters felt it signaled a new flexibility on the part of the leadership—a wonderful development. Everyone, however, struggled with the inappropriate questions or comments he would sometimes make during meetings. Additionally, his social skills and hygiene were found wanting at best. He had received many angry glares from others at the meeting, and the complaints to the leaders had been numerous. The LampLighters knew, however, that they only needed to wait, and sooner or later (hopefully sooner) Iaman would show up at one of their meetings.

They felt their plan was foolproof. Iaman always paid particular attention to the people among his followers with disabilities; he seemed to be drawn to them. People brought those with varying handicaps to him, and his typical response was to heal them. If the LampLighters could only get Iaman to heal the man on Lightday, they would have something substantial against him—he would have violated the prohibitions of Lightday.

As they had hoped, Iaman came to one of the meetings when the mentally challenged man was present. The LampLighters felt that all they needed to do was watch and wait.

Iaman picked the man out of the crowd right away. He was sitting off by himself, focusing on some small detail on the wall that no one else had noticed—perhaps it was an insect or a crack in one of the blocks of the wall. At the same time, he rocked back and forth with most of his right hand shoved into his mouth. Now and then he would stop and try to engage the person closest to him with eye contact, or a friendly observation, but no one would respond. He didn't know it, but most of them did not want him there.

The people knew how the leaders felt about Iaman. His entrance was like the turning on of a switch, igniting tension in the room; it was heavy and oppressive. Iaman seemed unaffected by it, however, and moved to the front of the room.

Iaman called out to the man in a loud, friendly voice, "Gary!"

The man immediately stopped rocking and looked up.

"Come up here so everyone can see you."

"All right!" Gary said in a loud and chuckling voice. He smiled broadly, "Do you know that I am a hard-working man?"

Iaman shook Gary's wet, white hand and looked back at him warmly. "I have no doubt that you are."

Through his squinty-eyed smile, Gary asked, "What's your name?"

Iaman looked on him lovingly, "My name is Iaman, and I am going to help you—"

"Yeah," Gary interrupted, "you know that I lost my job, but the men here have been very nice to me. You know, I want to be a LampLighter, 'cause there's no lights where I live."

The LampLighter leaders rolled their eyes, and a few sighed in desperation. They sat impatiently listening to the conversation that for them was already too long. People in attendance looked at the leaders as if to say, "What's going on?" It seemed to the leaders that Iaman knew exactly what was on their minds and was deliberately putting them through agony. He did, and he was.

He and Gary talked about Gary's home and Iaman's mother. The conversation turned to every health problem Gary had ever had and each girlfriend he could remember. Iaman listened as if it was the most interesting conversation in which he had ever participated.

After a while there seemed to be a lull in the conversation. Iaman and Gary stood together before the assembly. Gary reached over to him, and they hugged like long lost friends renewing their acquaintance. Iaman kindly broke the embrace and turned to the leadership sitting in the front row of benches— the honored place at the meeting.

"Please tell me: is it right to do good or evil on Lightday?" He paused, but they would not answer. He questioned them again. "Is it right to help someone or to kill him?" Gary leaned around Iaman to also look at the leaders, as if echoing Iaman's questions, although he hadn't a clue as to the dynamics that were developing. Iaman waited to allow sufficient time for a response. As they stood there waiting, Gary lost interest, and went back to his staring and rocking.

Iaman looked at the leaders and shook his head disgustedly. His anger began to grow at their hardheaded, obstinate attitude. The room was silent except for Gary's shuffling feet. Iaman stared at each leader in turn, riveting them with his eyes. Each squirmed but lowered their eyes and refused to speak. The LampLighters knew their plan was now set in motion.

Iaman relaxed as he turned back to see Gary staring, sucking, and rocking his way through his own world. Iaman looked on him and smiled, loving him as he was, ignoring all the acrimony that wracked the LampLighters' hearts.

The room could not have been more tense. Every clenched muscle held its owner still. Every eye focused on the pair, afraid to blink. Finally Iaman said calmly to Gary, "Your mind is restored."

In an instant, he stopped rocking and took his fingers out of his mouth. He carefully wiped the saliva from his hand on his shirt. A different demeanor came over him. Gradually he turned and looked at Iaman. He was a different Gary.

Before the people had even realized what had happened, the LampLighter leaders rose up and stormed out of the meeting in a huff. As the people stared in amazement and wonder at the miracle performed in their midst, a very different meeting began in the adjoining room.

The LampLighters burned with anger. One of them sputtered out, "How dare he do that on Lightday!"

"He is in direct violation of the Old Stories."

"We are losing our influence over the people."

"He is an enemy of all that is right!"

"We must find a way to get rid of him."

"He must be destroyed!"

* * * * * * * * *

Meanwhile, the 12 bewildered Light teamers set out with their "red seed trust." Clarence was the first one to break the silence. "You know, he didn't really tell us what he wanted us to do."

"He said: 'first tell the people the Light team has arisen; second, that LiarLight is on the decline; and third, to flee LiarLight and cling to the Light,'" responded Cyrus. He hesitated to tell the rest of what he knew.

Lupe filled in the blanks for him. "He also said we will be able to heal the sick and raise the dead!" He was excited about the possibilities.

"He also told us to break into groups of twos," Steve reminded.

None of them really wanted to break up; there was strength in the larger group. They were grateful that at least they were able to go in parties of two.

They paired up in the manner that might be expected: Josh and Seth headed toward Cabazon; Clarence and Scott decided to go south to Riverdale, while Steve and Albert went off to Running Springs; Michael and Bertrand went to Hesperia as Edward and Cyrus went to Pomona; and Lupe and Wendell headed off together to Fontana.

Chapter 21
SOMETHING IN THEIR MIDST

Iaman left the LampLighter meetinghall and started walking back toward home. Soon he was in the center of Bernardino where four men headed towards him. The woebegone looks on their faces gave away their tragic news: the Lone Warrior was dead, apparently murdered in prison; there were no suspects. Iaman appeared sick at heart over his loss.

As he sat on a park bench, a group of people brought yet another person who seemed controlled by one of LiarLight's wraiths. Life goes on. He thought again about his mission. He had much still left to do, not the least being to heal the people who waited before him.

Those around Iaman talked among themselves. "Do you think he could be the descendent of Paso-Lomon?"

"Well, they say he's from Barstow!"

"So! Couldn't a descendent of his come from there?"

"Can you imagine Paso-Lomon living there?"

"I guess not. But I don't know, maybe? A descendant of Paso-Lomon could live there even though he never did."

Two leaders of the LampLighters, also in the crowd, overheard the conversation of the men and began to converse with one another in loud, confrontational voices.

"How is he able to cure these people of the apparent wraith domination? I just can't understand it," the first said loudly, setting up his friend for the answer.

"Well, it's as plain as day: who could have power over wraiths, except one given the power to do so by LiarLight himself? He must be in cahoots with him." The people standing around were shocked at the suggestion that Iaman was an agent of LiarLight. They turned toward Iaman, awaiting his response.

Without looking up, Iaman responded. "Can an army fight against itself and defeat its enemies at the same time?" He paused. "Will a divided family last very long?" He appealed to the crowd, "If LiarLight's minions are fighting amongst themselves, it can only mean that we will soon see his downfall." He then walked calmly over to the men who had made the accusation. "You say that my power to heal comes from LiarLight. I tell you it is the Light which gives me power over the followers of LiarLight. Do you understand

79

what this implies?" He waited for a moment. The men were quiet. He reached out and lightly touched one of the men on the chest. In a hushed voice he said to them, "What it means is that the Light is among you."

The two men were silent.

Iaman turned to the crowd and reasoned, "Could any of you break into the house of a strong man and steal his things without first tying up the strong man? Would he willingly allow you to pillage his belongings?" He waited for a moment, then turned back to the men, inviting them, "Think about it."

The people looked at each other befuddled while Iaman continued: "Likewise, anyone who is not my ally is really against me. If you aren't helping me to build up followers of the Light, you are actually breaking them down."

The LampLighters who originally confronted Iaman stood with arms folded across their chests, incredulous. Finally one of them blurted out, "Show us a miracle!" Most of the people there were hoping for the same thing, but no one had the nerve to request it, let alone demand it.

Iaman exhaled loudly as he shook his head. "You know nothing about the Light. You say you want a miracle? The only sign I will give you is Ghozman's miracle." The crowd was puzzled, so he explained, "Just as Ghozman spent three days in the stomach of a great fish, so will the Leader of the Light Team spend three days in LiarLight's domain. After being spewed forth by the fish and washed onto the shore, Ghozman completed the task that the Light had prepared him for, and as a result, many people turned from their evil ways and returned to the Light."

Iaman studied the crowd. "I tell you that there is something in your midst which is greater than Ghozman. For centuries, people have traveled the world to find wisdom. The Old Stories tell how many traveled to sit at the feet of Sapient to hear his wisdom. Well, I tell you that there is something in your midst greater than Sapient."

Chapter 22
RED SEED TRUST

When Clarence and Scott arrived in Riverdale, they walked through the heart of the city. Although well known for its commerce, the city also had a large university.

They surveyed the scene. Surrounding them were large stone-front buildings, and hundreds of people bustling past. As they looked out toward the street, the traffic slowed because of the sheer number of vehicles. Ayugas occasionally reared up, but this must have been a common occurrence as the passersby barely noticed.

Clarence spoke first, "What now, Scott?" He was overwhelmed by the sights of the big city.

Scott smiled, "I don't know. There are lots of folks to talk to. I'm not sure how we should get their attention. I guess we could just start by shouting out the message."

"Do you think they might have heard of Iaman here?" Clarence asked.

"I don't know, but anyone familiar at all with the Old Stories would know about the Light Team. We've passed two or three LampLighter meetinghalls, so they're here." He paused in thought, scratching his head. "There's no guarantee they've heard about Iaman, but Redlands isn't that far away."

Clarence decided to "test the waters" with a passerby. One of the first people he noticed was a man, wearing the characteristic LampLighter leader coat, who walked by without greeting him. Clarence touched him on the arm to get his attention. "Excuse me, sir; we are looking for someone. Do you know a guy named Iaman?"

The man pulled his arm away testily and gave him a dirty look. Obviously bristled, he proceeded briskly on his way.

"I guess the LampLighters know about him here."

Undaunted, Clarence approached a younger man, about 22 years old. He wore a brown suit with a black bow tie and carried several books. "Excuse me! Have you ever heard of the Light Team?"

The young man brightened up. "Sure. We talked about the Light Team when I was a kid going to Twinklings."

Clarence looked at him puzzled.

"You know," the young man responded, "Twinklings, the kids' program the LampLighters run."

Without the experience of growing up as a LampLighter, Clarence was unfamiliar with the Twinklings. He responded with a question, "Well, the people around here—are they LampLighters? Have most of them been through the Twinklings?"

"Well, I can't really say about the Twinklings, but most Sopas do attend LampLighter meetings. Some really believe the stuff, and others just feel pressured to," responded the young man.

"What about you?" asked Scott. "Have you ever heard about a guy named Iaman?"

The man paused thoughtfully, and then shook his head from side to side. "No, not that I can remember."

"He's been teaching over in Bernardino," Clarence interjected. "He says," he counted to three on his fingers to be sure to get it right. "'One, the Light team has arisen; two, that LiarLight is on the decline; and three, to flee LiarLight and cling to the Light." Clarence smiled proudly at Scott; he had gotten it right!

Scott smiled back, impressed by Clarence's initiative. Additionally, he noted the man's interest in what Clarence was saying, in spite of how he said it. "Hey, if you'd like, we can talk about this further; but as you can probably tell, we're from out of the town. Do you know of some place where we could stay?"

The young man became excited. "Heck, I'm house-sitting for a guy, and there's plenty of room; why don't you come and stay with me?"

They left with the young man, and along the way they explained further about Iaman and the Light Team. It turned out that the man had heard quite a bit about Iaman after they described him more fully. He was a student studying philosophy at the university, where students were encouraged to present any new ideas they had heard about to the class. A classmate had been in Bernardino and had talked about Iaman. He had even gone to one of Iaman's "lectures," as he called it.

Finally they got back to the young man's house and settled in. The plan was that they would join him for his class the next day.

* * * * * * * * *

Josh and Seth headed for Cabazon. On approaching the city, they came across a Satie settlement.

The Satie people knew little of the Light, but rather followed the leading of many spirits. They saw spirits in everything—animals; the clouds, wind and sky; mountains and waters; and various other geological formations of the earth. Josh and Seth knew they would have to address these issues when they reached Cabazon.

As they approached, Seth saw a man lying in the middle of a field. A group of people dressed in black were walking away from him. Each one had approached him with quiet reverence, looked on him for a moment, and then walked away solemnly.

"I've heard that these people leave their dead out for the animals to devour them—something about the spirit of the man going back to nature and living on through the animals," Josh observed.

They walked quietly up to the man. His clothes were torn, and his form emaciated. Additionally, either his body was decaying, or he had terrible body odor.

"Maybe these people put something on the body to draw the animals?" Seth wondered. Josh motioned with his hands as if to say, "Could be."

They couldn't tell if the man was breathing or not, but he looked dead. Having the same idea, the two men nodded in agreement. They looked around to see if anyone was watching and Seth leaned over, put his hand on the man's head and called out, "In the name of Iaman, I command you to arise!" Nothing happened. Undaunted, Seth grabbed the man's shoulders with both hands and said, "By the power of the Light, I command you to arise!"

With that, the man shook himself and stood up. Seth smiled proudly at Josh. The man, however, was angry. "What do you want? I ain't got no money!"

Perplexed, Seth responded, "We represent Iaman, the Leader of the new Light Team, and by his power, we just gave you back your life!"

"What are you talking about?" the man replied exasperated. "I was sleepin'!" The man shook his head and lay down again. "Damned Sopas!" he muttered, and settled down to go back to sleep.

The two men swiftly made their escape and sat down under a tree. Immediately Josh broke out laughing. "Good job, Seth! You healed a man of his nap!" With that, even Seth could not restrain himself. They both fell down laughing so hard that tears of laughter spilled out of their eyes, and their sides ached. They'd do better in the future. This experience encouraged them to step out boldly in the name of Iaman, while at the same time not taking themselves so seriously.

* * * * * * * * *

Excitedly, Cyrus and Edward looked around Pomona. They had both caught the vision of what Iaman wanted them to do, and committed themselves to follow through on his request. They had entered Pomona a couple of days earlier and were moving about the place to get the lay of the land.

In the center of the town there was a kind of a gazebo area surrounded by a well-kept lawn and trees where people liked to relax. Sometimes, concerts were performed there and public meetings held. The locals called it the "Free Speech Area." Edward convinced Cyrus that this might be the best place to start. There was a diverse group of people milling around, just enjoying their day. Cyrus went and stood on the "free speech" platform. Doing his best to turn on his charm, he attempted to strike up a conversation.

"Greetings, friends!" he began.

Several of the people cautiously replied, "Hello."

"My friend and I have recently come from Redlands. There is a man who lives there. His name is Iaman, and he is making an amazing impact on people." Cyrus paused and smiled. "Not only is his teaching incredible, but he has been performing many—well—I guess you would call them 'miracles.'"

One of the women in the group came rushing forward, "We don't want to talk about this! Leave us alone, stranger!"

Cyrus was taken aback at first. He thought over what he had said. "Did I say something to offend someone?" He slowly approached the woman. Sheepishly, he started to say, "I'm sorry if I . . ." when suddenly a large man came up to him from the group.

"Leave us alone!" he threatened.

"I don't understand," Edward said as he moved slowly up alongside of Cyrus.

"Don't come around here causing trouble, talking about religion and teaching and such. We've been doing jus' fine here without your interferin'. Besides, religion has only caused us more trouble than we know what to do with."

"But I'm not really talking about religion as a set of rules, but about a man who is a real person. He has been doing such amazing things in Redlands. He is the one predicted in the Old Stor—uuh." Air escaped his chest as the blow knocked him to the ground.

The large man loomed over him menacingly. "I don't want to hear about this—I don't want to know nuthin' about it!"

The others standing around agreed.

At that, a lawman came walking up. He looked to the people he knew and asked, "What's going on?"

"These strangers are tryin' to force their religion on us. We told them we weren't interested, but they keep insisting." The lawman eyed Cyrus and Edward. "One of them even threatened my wife!" the large man lied.

"You two aren't from around here, are you?" Not giving them a chance to respond, the marshall grabbed Cyrus by the arm. "Why don't you just go back where you came from?" He winced as he grabbed Cyrus's arm, aggravating an old knife injury he had sustained years back. He quickly released his grip and grabbed his own wrist.

Cyrus saw this as his window of opportunity. *These folks must have been expectin' us,* he thought. He knew he had to act quickly. As the lawman grabbed at him with the other hand, Cyrus spoke up, "I can help you with your arm."

"Yeah, right—what are you going to do?"

"The man in Redlands that I started to tell the people about—Iaman— has given us the power to heal people, to demonstrate that the power of the Light is with us."

The brawny man and his wife broke in, "Shut him up and send him on his way!"

With a pained look on his face, the sheriff hesitated for a moment. He had been suffering with this wrist injury for years. He also knew that, should his supervisors find out how difficult it was for him to just hold on to a suspect, he'd be out of a job. He grabbed Cyrus with his good hand and moved him gruffly along. After a couple of blocks, he stopped. He spoke, but his initial defensiveness had eased up. "This town doesn't have much time for religion. The LampLighters are pretty active 'round here, and there's not much room for anything but the LampLighter party line." He looked around. "Those people back there might have seemed angry, but they were mostly scared—you being Sopa strangers—after what just happened with Elie. You never can tell who's watching, and who'll report back to the LampLighter leaders."

Cyrus and Edward listened intently. They never expected the hostile reception they had received and now were equally confused by the somewhat friendly manner of the lawman.

Cyrus spoke up, "Would it be all right if I give you a gift in the name of Iaman from Redlands?"

Edward readied himself for the worst. How many beatings did Cyrus need before he'd finally give up?

The lawman hesitated.

Cyrus smiled and said, "I'll take that as a 'yes.'"

He reached out and touched his arm. "In spite of the lack of hospitality we've been given, Iaman wants to be known to your people and to you. It is in his name that I restore your arm."

The marshall felt foolish. *These guys don't know when to quit,* he thought angrily. He reached out with both arms and grabbed Cyrus. He raised him and threw him into Edward. Together, they slammed to the ground. For a second, he looked at them on the ground. Taken aback, he realized what just happened to him. *My arm is as good as new—maybe even better!* He looked at the two dazed men gratefully. Then he realized the quandary he was in: if he accepted them, he would be an outcast in his own town; if he rejected them, he would turn away the men who had just healed him.

****

Lupe and Bertrand headed for Hesperia. To get there, they had to go through the Cajon Pass. Along the way, they met many wayfarers. The Bernardino mountains formed a barrier between the high and low desert areas of the region, so that the pass was the best way to get from areas like Barstow down to Riverdale. As a result, quite a variety of life could be seen. Families traveled on all sorts of transportation—some journeyed with more elaborate carts smacking of refinement and distinction; others were more simple, barely holding it all together to manage a straight line, but making it just the same. Business people carefully transported their supplies and equipment, merchants hauled their wares, and distributors conveyed their cargo in the direction of vendors in the region.

At the height of the pass, there were several places to stop and rest, as well as a few lodges. Some people stopped simply for the beauty of the surrounding mountains. The elevation was in the 10,000 hands-width range, and the mountains were snowcapped for much of the year. It occurred to Bertrand that this might be a better location to meet with an ample cross section of the population, rather than going directly on to Hesperia, so they stopped there.

Because Lupe had a lot of experience in public speaking before meeting Iaman, he had no trouble addressing crowds. Additionally, he saw the pass as a prime opportunity to speak with many different people. Most of the travelers would be resting before continuing on their way. Bertrand figured the people wouldn't mind a little entertainment, so he encouraged Lupe to "go for it."

Although a little nervous—due primarily to the message he would deliver— Lupe stood up on a rest stop bench and began, "Do you know where you are going?"

The people nearby gave him a glance, and then continued their own private discussions. Bertrand shouted, "Hey!" The people got suddenly quiet and looked in their direction. Then he started again, this time in a louder voice.

"Do you know where you are going? I have some facts that will influence the direction you might be taking." He hesitated momentarily while he sucked up his courage. "The Country of the Light is at hand." The statement seemed totally natural to him. The words encouraged him, so he repeated them. "The Country of the Light is at hand. The Light Team has arisen, led by Iaman— the one predicted in the Old Stories. He will lead us to a new day. A time of prosperity and peace is at hand, once we remove the yoke of our oppressors!"

86

He cringed. *Wrong speech!* he thought to himself, but he quickly made the connection. "Yes, our worst oppressor—LiarLight—will be defeated by Iaman. It is predicted. Freedom from our hateful oppressor has come to us!"

The people began gathering around Lupe. Some laughed with each other. "There are always great street entertainers up here. Maybe this one can do some juggling or something while he speaks. Let's see!"

Others more acquainted with the Old Stories shouted back, "How many times have we heard this before? Why not just ask for money like the other charletons! No need to sully the Light with your pandering!"

"We don't want anything from you," Lupe replied. "We'd just like to let you know about something happening in your midst."

At that moment, a young Sopa woman came forward, her body crippled with muscular hypertension. Her hips flung forward with each laborious step. Her hands were embarrassingly poised like the forelimbs of a praying mantis. Her face was contorted for no apparent reason, although she looked as if she was in physical agony. She was traveling with her parents to Riverdale to get medical attention. She labored to draw speech from her mouth. "I w-would-d . . . lo-ve to be fr-ee . . . of L-L-Liarrr . . . Ligh-t's . . . con-trol of m-my . . . m-mind." Staring with an expression distorted by twitching facial muscles, she looked back at Lupe and Bertrand and smiled crookedly but with sincerity.

Bertrand was amazed. She was not concerned about her body—the physical prison she was living in. Instead her main concern was with being able to effectively fight the same battles in her mind that he did. But she was afraid to let the Light help her in her daily life.

Lupe sized up the situation. Probably 40 people were watching. He had caught their attention with his words. *Do I dare believe what Iaman said . . . that I could heal people?* He found that his heart went out to the woman. He recognized that she was asking only to be free of the torment she endured because of her fearful resistance to letting the Light transform her mind; what she experienced in her body was secondary.

Taking the biggest risk of his life, he reached out to the woman. "You desire to be free of LiarLight's control of your mind? By the power of Iaman, the Light chooses to demonstrate your freedom in your body." With that he reached out and touched her. At the moment of his touch, her facial contortions ceased. Her trembling subsided, and her legs and back immediately straightened.

She looked down at her knees—they no longer pushed against each other! She looked at her hands—her fingers no longer strained to touch her elbow! She looked at her parents. Their tear-streaked faces affirmed what she now suspected: she was free!

Bertrand squinted in disbelief. The woman had definitely appeared disabled. But Lupe healing someone? Lupe, who not an hour earlier had been droning on and on about his political aspirations? Bertrand stepped back and groaned, "It can't really be happening like this."

The woman fell at Lupe's feet, but he took her hand and insisted she stand.

"This has happened to you through the power of the Light. His messenger, Iaman, walks among us to signal the coming of the Light. LiarLight is on the decline. The Light Team has arisen. A new age is dawning."

For the first time since he left everything and followed Iaman, and in spite of Bertrand, Lupe believed.

Chapter 23
RETURN TO REDLANDS

The Team had been gone nearly four weeks now. Group by group, they returned to Redlands. They were eager to report to Iaman what had happened. He was in Yucaipa but was to return any time. In the meantime, they swapped stories about their incredible successes, as well as their failures. They had healed people of many serious diseases, even of mental disorders that seemed to be caused by wraiths. One after another, the stories of healing flowed. Although their experiences were similar, each contained a unique element of wonder.

Cyrus, wondering whether any of the others experienced any persecution, waited for a break in the discussion. He wanted them to know that his and Edward's trip had not gone smoothly.

"We met with a lot of hostility at first," started Cyrus. "We were roughed up a a bit—"

"A bit?" Edward broke in, "I wasn't sure we were going to make it out of there alive! I think that law officer could have killed us on the spot, and the people wouldn't even have blinked an eye!"

"Well, that's history," replied Cyrus. "As it turns out, their anger was pretty much out of fear—even the law enforcement people are afraid of the Lamp-Lighters."

"It might have had something to do with that Elie they're looking for, too, you know," Edward interjected. "Here we were, a couple of strange Sopas walking into the town."

"But when they saw what happened to their man George, they eased up on us," said Cyrus. "We healed him of the aftereffects of a nasty knife wound. Everyone on the force knew and respected George, but were hesitant to be partnered with him because of that injury. They also got tired of being bullied by the LampLighters and were lookin' for a way to get out from under 'em." He smiled. "However, the change that came over George's friends was a surprise. Overall, our success was minimal, but we did give 'em somethin' to think about. I think whoever goes back there in the future will at least be less likely to be bullied." The others agreed.

"You know, we took a beating, too," started Clarence, "but not physically. We went over to Riverdale, just over the hill, and straightaway found out they knew Iaman. One of the first people we met was a LampLighter—a very unfriendly type—he gave us a look that could have fried an egg. Then we saw a youngun' and asked him about the Light Team. It turns out he heard about them when he was a Tinkling."

"A what?" asked Steve.

Clarence looked confused. "A Tinkling!"

"He means he heard about him when he was a *Twinkling*," inserted Scott.

"Even better!" a few snickered and then erupted into hilarious laughter.

Scott shook his head, recovering from his laughter, and attempted to restore order. "You mean the LampLighter kids' group?"

Again they lost it.

"What are you laughing for, Seth?" Josh asked. "Why don't you tell 'em what you've done?"

With a smirk on his face, Seth lowered his head. In a barely audible tone, he mumbled, "I healed a man of his nap."

"What was that?" Lupe shot back, looking at Josh.

"I thought a guy was dead, and I tried to heal him!" Seth admitted in a loud voice.

Josh smiled broadly. "In other words, he healed a man of his nap!"

Once again, they were beside themselves.

Seth playfully pointed an accusing finger at Josh, "You thought he was dead, too!"

"Well?" probed Lupe.

Looking up, Josh laughed and shook his head to the affirmative.

"What's Iaman gonna' do with us?" chuckled Scott.

"Hey, we had a woman who wanted us to heal her dog!" said Albert.

"The funniest thing was, the dog's name was Lilly," added Steve.

Again the laughter erupted and slaps on the back rang out. Anyone could see that they were jelling as a team.

Michael called them back. "But what happened in Riverdale, Scott? You said you guys were knocked about."

"Well, the young guy we met was a TWINKLING," he pronounced carefully, with glances and grins at Clarence, ". . . and a student at the university. The following day, we went with him to his Philosophy class. He had related to us beforehand that they enjoyed interacting with new ideas, and at first we were welcomed. The instructor introduced us, and we began telling our story about Iaman and the Light Team and such." He paused to think. "Everything was going well until we got into a discussion of the truth and what it means. The teacher took the position that there were many forms of truth, and that as we get closer to the ultimate truth, our own thoughts kind of fall away. I responded that if lesser truths are shown to not be truth, then they weren't true in the first place. The person believing in them had been deluded."

Clarence shrugged. "This is where he started to lose me."

"I went on to make the argument that there is only one true truth. I said that I knew what it was, and it was Iaman. Therefore any truth—be it an intermediary or final truth—in conflict with the truth of Iaman becomes a lie." Scott paused again. "In order to be truth, an idea cannot be fallible. Fallibility implies incompleteness—a lack of total and complete understanding. Real truth will refute all challenges to its authority."

Albert and Steve looked on in amazement. "I told you he lost me," said Clarence, giving voice to what Albert and Steve were thinking. *Where did Scott get the ability to develop such arguments?* A short time before, Scott was hauling dry goods. Now he was debating the nature of truth with college professors.

Scott looked back at them knowing what they were thinking. "Hey, I don't know where the ideas came from, I just got 'em."

Iaman had slipped in unnoticed and spoke up. "A follower of the Light will find that he can do many things through the power of the Light inside him. Don't be surprised by this. Go on!" They all greeted him excitedly with cheers and fist-bangs and laughter.

Scott started again, "The professor took my statement about being deluded as a personal insult. The students also picked up on it following his lead. You see, they held the position that there are many ways to the truth, all equally valid. I guess I told them that there was only one way, and I found it—and that was very offensive to them. To them, it's fine to be searching for the truth, just don't claim to have found it. I guess those kind of claims are initially greeted with accusations of lunacy, followed by anger."

"I'll say there was anger!" said Clarence. "They were on us like baolas on a bulber. At first they discussed, then they argued, but when they couldn't answer Scott's questions, it got ugly. Everybody was sure that he thought he was right and that everybody else was wrong. They had all talked about freethinking, but when push came to shove, they really didn't believe it. And push came to shove. They couldn't put down what Scott said, so they attacked his integrity, his race, his appearance. Anyway, it didn't take too long for us to see that this was going nowhere fast—I mean nowhere! But somehow we got out of the room pretty much unnoticed."

"That was a miracle in itself," Scott observed.

"What ever happened with the young man?" Michael asked.

"We don't know," said Scott. "I'm sure he had a lot of explaining to do for bringing us in there."

"That's for sure," responded Clarence emphatically.

"Don't get the wrong impression of our time away: we did experience some great successes. The Light used us to heal many—some of whom have followed us back here and have joined the larger group following Iaman. We might not have gotten off on the right foot at the university, but overall we felt we were very successful."

"By the way, we shook the dust off our feet when we left that university," Clarence added solemnly. There was silence as they realized the gravity of his statement.

Iaman interrupted the silence. "Much that is hidden from the 'wise' or educated, has been revealed to the unlearned."

After a while, Wendell spoke up. "Michael and I started off for Fontana— no particular reason. As it turned out, when Steve and Albert heard about our plans, they decided to come with us, rather than go to Running Springs." The four nodded at each other.

"Anyway, our going together turned out to be a good move. I'm sure our friendship was an example to the people there. It helps to see others different from themselves acting in an honest and friendly manner with them. After all, Iaman's message is not just for one group." He reminisced, "One Satie woman hesitated to have me touch her ill, beloved daughter. Some Summas distrusted Steve and Albert at first. Albert even admitted that he felt uncomfortable among people of different races; prejudice runs deep in us—even though we're members of the Light Team."

Iaman laid his hand on Wendell's shoulder as he sat down at his right. "It was my intention to use you all as messengers to get the Light's story out to people. It was also my intention for you to learn about yourselves, just like Wendell, Scott, and Albert did. In order to clean a spot out of a dirty shirt, you have to first see the spot. You walk around thinking your shirt is clean, while the eyes of others are drawn immediately to the spot. It is even worse when you point out the spot on someone else's shirt while yours is splattered. First clean the splatter off your shirt, then you can begin to help others to see the dirt they need to clean."

"I, too, learned about myself," began Lupe. "One of the people that Bertrand and I healed was a disabled woman. I would have thought that the challenges she faced because of her disability would be the most trying difficulties in her life. But I found that I had underestimated her. Or perhaps, I projected my thoughts onto her. She shocked me when she said that in spite of everything she had to contend with, her toughest struggle was in doing what is right. She too was in a battle with LiarLight over her mind."

"LiarLight does make many inroads into people's thinking, and it takes a lot of encouragement to get them to see things clearly," observed Iaman.

Lupe nodded his agreement and continued, "Bertrand talked with her later, and found out that LiarLight really used her disability to confuse her. She said she would accuse herself of having done something wrong which resulted in her disability. She would then ask the Light to heal her. When she wasn't healed, she accused herself of not having enough trust in the Light."

Lupe shook his head in disgust. "Friends who weren't disabled agreed with her self-accusations. At times her trust was shaken by the notion that the Light couldn't be fair. Ultimately, she came to accept her disability."

He looked at Bertrand. "I think she was the most shocked by the healing." Bertrand pointed at Lupe as if to say, "You're right on that count."

Lupe went on, "She had come to a point of maturity where her life no longer revolved around her physical body and a constant quest for wellness." He put both hands on his head and then raised them in disbelief. "The request she made to Bertrand and I was to help her to defeat LiarLight in her life. But all I could see was her disability." His eyes glistened. "She was exactly like me on the inside." He looked on them with a tearful stare, "I never will look on a person with a disability the same way again."

Iaman looked at his team. For a moment he thought about the difficult times ahead, but quickly set them aside when he saw the contented faces of his men. He seemed pleased, thinking of what they would do in the future.

Descriptions of this interchange reached the crowds. Over the next week, people were abuzz with the results of the Team's first venture out on their own.

Iaman was now prepared to expand his outreach. From the throngs who followed him, he selected a group of 70 men loyal to him, who had a good grasp of his teaching and sought a greater involvement in his work. He brought these promising candidates together and gave them final instructions.

He began with a smile. "The world is like a red tree in harvest season: its branches are weighed down with fruit just waiting to be picked. Like the tree, the world groans for relief, but the fruit pickers are few and far between. Ask the Light to send out more harvesters into the orchards."

His demeanor then took on a more serious tone. "Once again, you are being sent out on a dangerous assignment. As I said to the Team when they were sent out, you are like bulbers in the baola's den. However, don't despair, for the Light is with you!"

He paused to make sure they were with him in their minds. "Take nothing with you other than the clothes on your back. When you enter a dwelling, offer a greeting of peace. Should people of peace live in that dwelling, stay with them. Enjoy what they will give you, as you will have earned your pay. Then go out among the people of that place, talk to them, and heal those who are sick. Explain to them all you have learned about the Light. Help them to understand that the Country of the Light is within their grasp. Tell them the Light team has arisen, and that LiarLight's defeat is at hand." He paused. His demeanor was very serious, almost somber. "If, however, you are rejected, go into the streets among the people. Get their attention and warn them something like this, 'You have made your choice. We want nothing of you to remain with us. Even the dust of your streets we shake off our feet to remind you of your rejection. Nevertheless, the coming of the Country of the Light is imminent. Be warned: things will not go well for you upon its arrival.'"

Chapter 24
THGIL UNLEASHES THE WRAITHS

LiarLight enjoyed his victory over the Lone Warrior. It was true that LW was now under the Light's protection, and therefore unassailable by LiarLight. But at least, he thought, he was out of the game!

The Lone Warrior's death had been brutally carried out by one of LiarLight's human followers. The reports were that LW had been decapitated in a bizarre manner, but the press did not investigate. Among Protectors groups it was assumed this was due to political like-mindedness between the Defenders and those who managed the news.

While orchestrating Lone Warrior's death, LiarLight also continued to sift the Light Team members for his potential operative. He recognized that Iaman had indeed chosen well. thgiL reported that LiarLight's wraiths or "thgiLers" experienced extreme difficulty influencing the men in the presence of Iaman. They were still present, but they had to be vigilant as their power became more shaky. The wraiths tried to influence their hosts to leave Iaman's presence on occasion since they could not survive being in constant close proximity to him.

As thgiL studied each man, she found one in particular who surfaced as the best potential agent for LiarLight. She reported back to LiarLight with her intended choice.

The team member was a total skeptic, although he didn't verbalize his thoughts. He felt he could see through Iaman's "tricks," as he would label them to his friends, who weren't followers or members of the Light Team. thgiL used the combination of this man's skepticism and his growing disdain for Iaman to cause him increasingly to draw away from him. Being a quiet individual in the first place, this change was hardly noticeable. The only real indication that something unusual might be going on with him was the constant disappearance of money; he was in charge of the Light Team's meager funds. Because all of the group had been handpicked by Iaman, they seldom second-guessed each other. This resulted in little accountability, at least as far as the money went.

In his earlier instructions, LiarLight told thgiL to remain vigilant and seek out opportunities to corrupt both the Team members and Iaman himself, should the opportunity arise. When she reported that she thought the Team would scatter if Iaman could be taken out of the picture, her master seemed satisfied. However, LiarLight became increasingly distracted with Iaman and the Lone Warrior. Although the Lone Warrior was now out of the way, LiarLight had not devoted sufficient time to secure thgiL. As a result of his laxity, thgiL began to lose control of her mind. She found it increasingly difficult to focus her thoughts on her mission. At times, her mind went on forays uncharacteristic of her in the past. She became disturbed, as questions that never would have occurred to her in the past now drove her to distraction.

The team continued to be largely confused about Iaman and what was happening to each of them. They loved the trips they had made and the power they were able to wield, but this was all new to them and they didn't know what to make of it all, nor were they aware where it could lead. thgiL contributed further to their bewilderment by prompting their thinking with questions such as, "What did their own gaining of power have to do with anything? Who among them held the most power? Who would be the ranking official when Iaman set up his kingdom? Why did Iaman spend so much time with Steve, Clarence, and Albert?" By provocative suggestions and instigations of every kind, thgiL purposed to quickly turn the power the team members had to her master's purposes. If she could distract their focus from Iaman and the Light, they would begin to look at themselves as the source of their power and only guide, and would thus be in LiarLight's domain.

Chapter 25
SEED OF THE TRAITOR

Like the others, Bertrand enjoyed the time out among the people. The power he felt was intoxicating—something he could really live with! Additionally, Lupe was entertaining at times. They talked a great deal, although mostly about Lupe's favorite subject—politics. Lupe didn't know what to make of everything that was going on. He certainly didn't know why Iaman would trust him with great abilities. Power was just what Lupe wanted, but it was given in a way that was unfamiliar to him, one that started him thinking of questions he had never conceived before. Bertrand had similar mixed emotions, but was sure he didn't want to change if it came down to a choice. Occasionally they would put their ambivalence aside, dreaming together of the land they would own and the responsibilities they would have in Iaman's new order.

Lupe did most of the talking during the dreaming sessions. His plan was dramatic. He would make the world a better place, beginning with kicking the current political regime out of office. They would start a new government—one that favored the people's needs. Lupe would prohibit the LampLighters from continuing their bullying in the new regime. He felt confident that such a move would appeal to Iaman, based on the way he dealt with the Lamp-Lighters. Lupe, Bertrand, and the others would then assume their places of power. At least that was the way Lupe envisioned it.

Lupe watched Bertrand for an outward reaction that would reveal his opinions, but he observed none. Bertrand just listened and participated mildly in these conversations, but Lupe could never "get inside his head."

Really, Bertrand thought to himself, *what could a poor guy from Barstow offer the people that would make any difference in their lives? Weren't the LampLighters the ones who made life profitable? What Lupe says means nothing—life in Calvada needs no significant improvement. Iaman's activities will do little more than stir things up needlessly. I am surrounded by rather unenlightened individuals.*

Bertrand continued to feel a loyalty to the LampLighters that withstood even all he had seen and done. Deep down, he resonated more with their perspective and their sense of order than he ever did with Iaman's. He knew that if he had his way, he would be a LampLighter.

Like Michael, Bertrand often removed himself from the group. On one particular day, he walked several stone's throws away, but decided not to join his friends in the town, or to go to meet with the LampLighters as was his custom. Typically, he would tell the group he was leaving to perform some money-related duty. When the team became suspicious, charging that he was meeting with the LampLighters, he would shrug them off, saying, "They need the truth, too." Eventually the team stopped asking where he went. Even when he was with them, he was reserved. Only Lupe could draw him out sometimes.

Finding a large placilla tree, and few people around, Bertrand sat down in the shade and closed his eyes. The sunlight sparkled on the leaves, producing a fluttering shadow below. He sorted his scattered thoughts. *Can Iaman's teaching really be trusted? How can he be from the Light? What am I doing here? I hate this team! I'm alone, with no one to rely on—not that I'd change it if I could. Am I the only one around here to see things with any clarity? Why are the others so slow and unperceptive?*

Undetected by Bertrand, thgiL moved alongside him. Bertrand was thgiL's choice to betray Iaman. thgiL saw Bertrand's moody actions as the perfect opportunity to begin a program to corrupt Bertrand's mind. She found it fertile for the planting of her own ideas. thgiL knew, however, that she would have to act subtly. Under Iaman, the team learned to recognize more quickly LiarLight's indirect assaults, which tinkered with their thought patterns. thgiL began by listening to Bertrand's thoughts.

What have I gotten myself into? Bertrand thought to himself. *How can I follow him when I don't want to follow him?*

thgiL perked up. Perhaps it was LiarLight's lack of attention to her, but her own mind suddenly flooded with questions. Bertrand's words hit a nerve in her. Such musings were not uncommon in the mind of a victim, but this time the words caused her to stand back and think. She remembered LiarLight's comment about her being an object. *Am I really an object? I want to do my master's will, don't I? Do I really have no desires at all? LiarLight said I'm not able to desire.* She continued to listen.

Bertrand's thoughts traveled in the same disturbed stream of consciousness. *The others have bought into the whole package. They say that they choose to follow him, but in reality, they can't. At least they can't wholeheartedly. No one ever gives himself completely over to the Light. No one ever chooses to totally surrender himself, his entire will.*

Yet, Iaman's healings and teaching are powerful and convincing. He does claim to be the leader of the Light Team. Don't the Old Stories say that he will in fact defeat LiarLight? If LiarLight were defeated, would there even be any temptation? I guess one really could obey if there were no temptation. But then there wouldn't be any need for obedience.

thgiL thought to herself, *I could try to exercise free choice. I could try all I want, but what's the point? I have no option but to follow LiarLight. But what do I lose? What don't I have, that this fool has, by having a free will? I have no desire and no choice; LiarLight has told me so. Or, like this man, do I have a desire, but not the ability to act upon it?*

Bertrand's thoughts called thgiL back again. *He is deluding them. He's got to be deluding them. But why? They haven't the ability to follow the Light, even if they were to choose to follow Iaman. We are all under LiarLight's control. It is only through obedience to the Light that we have any hope. The LampLighters understand this fact, as their system does give structure to life, something to count on.*

"I wish I didn't have a choice!" Bertrand shouted out loud, then quieted down. "I wish I would follow the Light of the LampLighters even when I desired not to." He paused for a moment and verbalized under his breath, "How different—how much better this world would be—if men could only do good and never evil. There would be no suffering, no hate and no delusion."

thgiL reacted harshly to Bertrand's words, *You have no idea what you are asking!* thgiL shook her head. *What a paradox. People have no ability to follow the Light, even if they choose Him? I am compelled by some inner source to follow LiarLight. Would I choose LiarLight if I had a choice? It is indeed a great gift, this free choice.*

Bertrand shook his head and pondered, *Iaman can't win. And yet he seems so sure of himself and so . . . good? The government or the LampLighters will bring him down for certain. Better it happens sooner than later—he prolongs the agony of this team of fools. He gathers more naive followers all the time.*

thgiL stared far off distantly, as if receiving a revelation. *In creating, the creator chooses free choice and relationships or blind obedience in his creations—creating either a world of chaos or a world of order. LiarLight's world of order is based on influencing what was already created by the Light to think and act just like him—to give him control over their free will in exchange for a feeling of power and an air of invincibility. What chaos he is wreaking on the Light's human scene!* The thought jolted her to her senses, causing her to shake all over and shriek, "I have been created for obedience!"

The fallout of his plan will be disastrous if not successful, Bertrand mused. *Even Lupe told me that. Is it better to allow him to continue, or to stop him now? In sacrificing one, wouldn't many be saved?*

Refocused, thgiL smiled at that thought. She flooded Bertrand's mind with seemingly sensible reasons for treachery, deception, and betrayal. Bertrand saw his path increasingly laid out before him. He vowed that he would carry out his plan.

thgiL's eyes squinted behind her sadistic grin. *You have given me access to your mind through your duplicity. You will be corrupted, but blame only yourself.* Maliciously she cooed, "You had free will—look what you have done with it!" With that, her wicked laughter resounded, delighting the twisted unseen world of wraiths.

Chapter 26
HARD FACTS

Iaman sat down among his followers. Seated in the circle nearest to him were the Light Team members, and then the rest of the people encircled them. The throng represented every group of people found in the region. There were also a good number of women—some having accompanied their husbands and some having come on their own. As a result, there were children of all ages present. His following developed into somewhat of a community, where the people looked out for each other. In this situation, as in any place people were being taken care of, there were many who tagged along because they were able to get an occasional good meal, or who felt safe among the group.

And, as always, there was a group of LampLighters who huddled together. At times they shot questions at Iaman or the group, trying to trip them up on some point of luzology (the study of the Light and his ways). Iaman often interacted with them. Depending upon who was among the group, there were often stimulating discussions. Some of the LampLighters were truly interested in seeking the truth. When Iaman would discover one like this, he would engage him cordially. He could also be ruthless in putting down ideas that in no way represented the perspective of the Light.

These confrontations made the Light Team uncomfortable at times. Iaman responded by quoting the Old Stories. "These people talk a good talk, but their hearts—as evidenced by their actions—are far from me. Although unable to keep even the most basic rules laid down by the Light, they encumber others with their contrived rules, ascribing them to the Light Himself."

The team came to Iaman and chided him, "Offending the LampLighters isn't in your best interest."

"If a plant was not planted by the Light, it must be removed, roots and all. Don't worry about them, but also do not be influenced by them. It only takes a small amount of yeast to cause a change in bread. Beware of the yeast of the LampLighters."

On this day, the LampLighters were out in full force. For some reason, though, most of the friendly LampLighters were absent. Iaman began to address the group. "Why do you devote so much time to working for things like food that spoils? Rather, work for the food that lasts forever. This is the kind of food that the Leader of Light Team can give to you, because the Light endorses him."

One of the group spoke up, "What does the Light want us to do?"

"The Light wants you to trust in the one He sent you."

Another LampLighter addressed him, "The Old Stories tell that the Light provided food to his followers for a long time during their exile in Maxima. The food became known as 'what do you know,' as the people were surprised to find it. The leader, Heston, said this was a direct provision of the Light. What type of amazing feat will you do?"

"What Heston provided for you was not the true food the Light offers," said Iaman. "For the real 'food' is the one who comes from the Light to revitalize and sustain the whole world."

The people became enthused and called out, "Give us this kind of food!"

"I am am sent by the Light to be the food that supports life. If anyone comes to me, he will never be hungry again. I will never turn anyone away who comes to me because that is the reason I came: to do the Light's bidding. It is His desire that I shouldn't lose anyone with whom He has given me a relationship. It is His desire that all who see His offspring and trust in him shall see LiarLight's downfall, and live forever in the Country of the Light."

The LampLighters and the people began grumbling amongst themselves. "What's he talking about? He's the food sent by the Light? For Light's sake, he grew up in Barstow. We know his family! Where does he get off saying he came from the Light?"

"No one can join me unless the Light draws him to me. This is the truth: I am the food of life. Anyone who eats this food will not die. The food I give is my own flesh: I will give this so that the world may live. LiarLight will have no control over those who eat my flesh."

The people were taken aback and began vehemently cursing. The Light Team members themselves simply shrugged their shoulders when questioned about what he said. A LampLighter rose, pointed threateningly at Iaman and shouted, "How can this . . . this . . ." he paused, thinking better of his original choice for a word, ". . . man give his body for us to eat?"

Iaman did not back down at all, but looked directly at the man and replied, "If you haughtily decline to eat my flesh and drink my blood, you will not have the Light within you, and you will be in LiarLight's domain. But I desire that you see LiarLight's downfall, so you can live forever in the Country of the Light and be brought back to life on the final day."

All were shocked, but Iaman calmly continued, "For my body is the real food and my blood is the real drink. Because I have been sent from the Light, the Light is in me. And if anyone eats me, they will have the Light within them. I am the food sent from the Light. If you eat this flesh and drink this blood, you will live forever."

The LampLighters stood all at once and remained silent, glances of concern passing among them. It seemed as if they had made a fateful decision, having gotten what they wanted from him. By drawing him out, they had finally showed Iaman for what they believed he was—a raving lunatic. Some of the people turned to them for answers. The LampLighters welcomed them with cynical words of encouragement like, "We knew it would come to this," and "At least now we know for sure."

Even the Light Team members murmured discontentedly among themselves. "This is insane," said Lupe.

Bertrand listened but said nothing. Iaman's words had already set Bertrand's feet firmly on the path he would choose.

"Who can listen to this?" Edward responded.

Michael felt that they must have misunderstood Iaman's meaning. He looked appealingly into Iaman's eyes and said, "Teacher, this is a hard teaching." He wanted to understand.

Iaman addressed his team. "Does it make you want to quit the team?"

They looked down, occasionally glancing at each other. "This lesson I have given you is about the power of the Light in you, and about life. Don't you see that your bodies—your flesh and blood—profit nothing? The Light must give you His life. . . . It's clear that some of you do not yet trust me." Iaman knew that LiarLight, through thgiL, had chosen the one who would turn traitor. "That's why I told you that no one can find his way to me unless he is prompted by the Light."

The team members looked around and saw people leaving in droves. They felt depressed and disillusioned. Finally, Iaman spoke again, "What about you? Would you like to leave as well?"

Steve spoke up out of his depression. He held out his shaking hands, desperate that they would be filled with hope. "Leader of the Light Team, where would we go? I don't understand, but I know that only you possess the words that lead to the life without end." He shook his head. In spite of his apparent weakness, he looked at Iaman, and in a voice shaking with emotion declared, "We know now that you are the Leader of Light team, sent from the Light!"

The trace of a smile formed on Iaman's lips. He said to Steve, "The Light told you that—remember that He is your source." He looked on the men for a moment with satisfaction. "Did I not choose each one of you? I chose well." A sober expression now quickly replaced his smile as he uttered, "But one of you belongs to LiarLight."

Chapter 27
HEIGHTS AND DEPTHS

The team hardly had had a chance to relax since returning from their trips. The lack of opportunity to fully unwind, coupled with the unrest resulting from Iaman's recent troubling teachings, created low morale among the team.

Several days elapsed while they were busy teaching and helping the people who followed Iaman. The number of followers, which had dwindled, had now swelled once again, due in part to the outreach the team had done at Iaman's instruction. Toward evening, the larger group of followers broke up to prepare for an evening's rest. The team surrounded Iaman, conversing with him and each other. After a while, the conversation died down, and Iaman went off by himself. He would often take time to privately talk to the Light, and lately, even more so. Sometimes he would leave only briefly; at other times, he would be gone all night.

This evening, for some reason, the team followed him. Their overall intent was to get more information about some of his recent teaching. When he noticed them, he turned to them and smiled. They sat down together and began talking again. Unknown to the team, thgiL moved amongst them.

"Your following has become great!" started Lupe. The large following caused Lupe to wonder if Iaman would start talking about political or governmental strategy. He didn't know what the others were thinking in this regard, but he would be ready for a revolution.

Iaman simply smiled, "Thanks be to the Light for the following we enjoy!"

They sat in silence for a moment. Iaman asked them, "Who do these followers say that I am?"

"Some think you are LW," Scott replied.

"Hmm!" Iaman responded with raised eyebrows.

Michael spoke up, "Others say you are Antibol or Te-ars, or another member of a past Light team."

"But what about you?" Iaman asked. "Who do you think I am?"

Without hesitation, Steve rose to his feet and spoke up, "You are the Leader of the Light Team, and the Son of the Light."

The others looked utterly bewildered. First, could there be an offspring of the Light? Did the Light have children? If he was a child of the Light, would he not actually be the Light Himself in a different form?

Iaman rose and enthusiastically stood beside Steve and grabbed him by the shoulders, laughing joyfully as he spoke, "Steve, you are amazing! You didn't learn that from any person. The Light Himself put this fact in your mind. Steve, you are like a firm foundation. On this foundation, I will build the spectrum of the Light. Death itself will not darken this Light." Iaman paused and made eye-contact with each of them. "Now is not the right time for this information to be public knowledge: tell no one what you have heard."

Iaman continued in a grave tone of voice. He had been waiting for the right moment to tell them. For the first time, he gave them a prediction about what would happen to him.

"Shortly, we will be going on to Camden. There I will experience great suffering from the LampLighters, city elders, and governmental leaders. Ultimately, I will be put to death. Three days later, I will arise to life again."

They all looked at him strangely. They wondered where this assertion came from.

thgiL probed each man's mind. Most were too fearful to raise the questions formulated in their minds. thgiL settled on Steve, sensing his courage. In an instant, Steve's mind was not filled with questions, but rather with assertions. thgiL encouraged Steve's thoughts, *I will never let this happen. I love him! Haven't we just performed great miracles? Clearly we can defeat any challenger. I have got to stop him!*

Steve got up and pulled Iaman aside. His mind was filled with the thoughts thgiL had encouraged, which were amplified with the force of his emotions. Steve grabbed him by the arm. With their backs to the rest of the team, he whispered sharply in Iaman's ear. His words were meant for Iaman, but his voice projected so that they could all hear him.

"May the Light Himself forbid this!" he hissed. "This must not happen to you!"

Indignantly, Iaman shook off Steve's grip. He glared at the team and then back at Steve. He looked right through Steve and shouted, "Get away from me LiarLight! You will not block my way!" With that, thgiL fled. Iaman then focused on Steve. His severity diminished, but his expression was still intense. "These thoughts are the thoughts of men manipulated by wraiths. These are not thoughts prompted by the Light."

Steve was shocked, as were the rest of the team members, who rose to their feet. Iaman knew that thgiL was working on their minds.

"Understand this clearly," Iaman started again, speaking slowly and deliberately. "If any of you—or anyone else for that matter—wants to follow me, he must forget himself." He paused for a second. "No, he must renounce himself, choose my path, and then follow—even if it leads to his death. If you live to protect your life, to live for yourself, you will lose it for sure. . . . However . . . if you will freely relinquish your life for my purposes, you will just as

103

surely find it." He motioned for them to sit down again. Pointing at Steve, he went on, "What would be the use in gaining the whole world, if you lost your own life in doing it? You could not enjoy your gain, and there would be nothing you could give to regain the life you lost!"

Changing his tone of voice again, Iaman looked up. As if describing a picture right before his face, he said, "The Leader of the Light Team is about to be given honor directly from the hand of the Light. Surrounded by the original members of the Light Team, he will judge all . . . according to what they have done." He looked back at them. "Those who are ashamed of me or my teaching will experience shame. Those who have known me will be welcomed into the Country of the Light with past Light followers, Light Team members, and the Leader of the Light Team himself."

The team members were stunned at first. They felt enthused and filled with wonder, but at the same time were also very confused.

Chapter 28
IAMAN REVEALED

About a week passed before things started to get back to "normal." The men got over their original shock resulting from Steve's confrontation with Iaman, as well as the talk about "eating his flesh." They laughed again, and began to let down their guard.

Steve, Clarence, and Albert were called aside by Iaman. He wanted them to accompany him to the top of one of the larger hills at the foot of Mount Gorgonio. Leaving after breakfast, they hiked all day, reaching the summit about the time Heart Red was setting. The new moon resulted in the stars appearing especially bright. The hill seemed to thrust them up into the heavens; the lights of the city seemed far below. At the summit, they paused together for a light meal. Finishing quickly, they sat back and rested from the day's hike.

As was often his custom, Iaman removed himself a short distance from them and began to speak to the Light. Sitting carefully on a mound of dirt, the three men casually observed him although by now they could barely make out his silhouette. Iaman sat quietly for several minutes while the three casually talked among themselves.

"What's the point of coming up here?" asked Albert.

"I don't know," replied Clarence, "but look at the view!"

Steve felt uneasy. The occasional chills that darted up his backbone told him that something was about to happen. He had no idea what it would be, but he definitely felt anticipation in the air.

The soft snapping sound of the dry brush prompted them to look in Iaman's direction. To their surprise, as he got to his feet, his appearance began to change.

At first, they began to see him more clearly. It was as if a dim light shining on him was gradually gaining in intensity. The light, however, was on his body alone. To their disbelief, they saw that the light radiated from him. Its brightness increased slowly from that of a candle, to a lantern, all the way to that as brilliant as one of the suns. The three fell to their knees in astonishment and fear. Shielding their eyes, they squinted in his direction. His clothing shone with the purest white, like a blinding light reflecting off of silver.

If this weren't strange enough, two men emerged from the radiance and began conversing with Iaman. Clarence looked wide-eyed at Albert and Steve.

105

Fascination was etched in his furrowed forehead and gaping mouth. He knew the two resplendent men! Albert and Steve also recognized the two men as Heston and Antibol.

Steve's excitement at seeing the renowned members of past Light Teams overcame his dumbfounded tongue. His cracking voice called out in fear and awe, "Leader, it is fortunate that we are here! I'll . . . put up three tents: one for you, one for Antibol and one for Heston!" The other two looked at Steve and then the three brilliant figures and nodded their heads.

While Steve stammered the words, a cloud moved above them. The glow of the three reflected softly off the billowing ceiling. A booming voice shook them where they stood, "This is my treasured son: hear and obey him!"

At the instant the voice thundered, Steve, Clarence and Albert hit the ground, their faces smashing the brittle brush and their gaping mouths filling with dust. With hands outstretched, they lay prostrate and shook uncontrollably. Albert grabbed his head, as if expecting to be struck down at any moment.

When the roaring voice subsided, the light dimmed and they laid there in the dark. After a moment, they heard the rustle of someone approaching. Iaman crouched down to them. "It's all right, friends. Don't be afraid." He touched Steve on the shoulder, and Steve fearfully looked up. He saw Iaman's reassuring face against the background of a cloudless starry sky. Steve reached out to the other two men, and at his touch, they looked up as well. Sensing they had recovered as well as could be expected, Iaman broke the silence. "What you saw was for your eyes only. Keep this vision to yourselves until the Light's offspring returns from death to life."

A question welled up in Steve. Motioning toward the place where the two visitors had been standing, he asked, "Why do the Old Stories say that Antibol has to come first?"

Iaman welcomed the question. "You're right! The Old Stories do say that Antibol must come first . . . to get everything prepared." He smiled and pointed at them, "But," he paused, "Antibol has already come. Of course, no one recognized him. Instead they treated him cruelly, according to their nature. In the same manner, the Leader of the Light Team will be mistreated by them."

At last they understood something: the Lone Warrior was Antibol.

Chapter 29
A TEST OF TRUST

The suns rose, silhouetting Gorgonio's dramatic peak. Although it was morning, they were still in the mountain's shadow. In spite of their dramatic night and the long hike the day before, the three men didn't feel tired. They hadn't spoken to one another throughout the evening, but with the light of morning their conversation sputtered to a start.

"What do you think that was all about last night?" Albert started.

"You know, I've been trying to figure it out. I guess he brought us up here to see the vision of him and Antibol and Heston," Clarence responded.

Steve stared straight ahead and shook his head as if still in thought. "Why only us? Why not the rest of them?" He thought some more. "And what was the purpose of the whole thing? He said not to say anything to anyone until the Light's offspring is raised back to life."

"He did say that he was going to die, you know."

Steve glared at Clarence. "I won't soon forget that."

Steve continued, "So many times, he doesn't give us the whole story. . . only bits and pieces."

"It's almost like he doesn't trust us," said Albert, "but at the same time, I feel like he does."

"I don't think it's a matter of him trusting us, but of us trusting him. It's as if he only tells us what he wants us to know for the moment. We have to rely on him, and trust that he knows what he's doing," Steve concluded.

Albert picked up on Steve's comment, "Yeah, I always want to know 'why' up front—not later on."

Clarence agreed. "Ever since I've been with you and the team, I've been confused. You know, his stories have so many hidden ideas, it's hard to know exactly what he's talking about."

"But it's not just the stories," Steve replied, "its everything about him. He's like a mystery man. He says we are to keep last night's vision a secret until the offspring of the Light comes back to life. Well, what does that mean? In the next life, will I even remember anything of a vision? Who would I tell at that point, anyway, and who would care?"

Albert laughed, suggesting, "You could always shake hands with Antibol, and tell him you were the guy who offered to put up a tent for him!"

They all grinned at that advice.

"There is so much I don't understand," said Steve. "Maybe I never will. It's hard to trust him when your mind cries out for specific answers. I know the answer is to trust him, but it's still hard."

The men packed up their things and were down the mountain in about four hours. As they approached their camp, they observed an argument in process. It seemed that Lupe and Edward were having somewhat heated words with some LampLighters while a helpless man stood nearby. Behind the group, a boy was sitting surrounded by a large number of people. Michael was trying to settle everyone down, but he was having little success.

When the people saw Iaman walking toward them, they ran to him. With a concerned look on his face, he went straightaway toward the confrontation.

"What are you arguing about?" he inquired sternly.

The helpless-appearing man ran up to Iaman. Looking at him with eyes streaked with concern, he pleaded, "Sir, I brought my son to your followers because LiarLight has control of him. He throws the boy to the ground, where he shakes and foams at the mouth. I asked your followers to drive the wraiths out, but they couldn't do it."

Iaman was visibly angry. "You have no trust in the Light! How long must I remain with you?" He shook his head in disgust. "Bring the boy to me," he ordered.

The boy seemed to ride on the crest of a wave of people. Finally, he stood before Iaman. He was barefoot, wearing suspenders, with his pants cut off at the calf. As soon as the boy saw Iaman, he fell into another convulsive fit. He shook violently, grinding his body on the stony ground.

"How long has he been like this?" Iaman asked the father.

"Since birth," he responded. "It seems the wraith sometimes tries to kill him by throwing him into a fire or into deep water. Please help us, if you are able!"

Iaman looked sternly at the man. "If I am able!" replied Iaman to the man, who was filled with fear. "All things are possible if one has trust in the Light!"

The father shouted back in frustrated desperation, "I have trust! I have trust! But help my lack of trust!"

Iaman turned to the boy. "LiarLight, release this boy. Wraith, remove yourself from him and never trouble him again."

With a wailing shriek, the boy was thrown to the ground. The crowd recoiled from the boy when they noticed the him lying still on the ground. *At last he is free,* the father thought to himself, *even though it was through death.*

Iaman reached down to the boy and took his hand. The boy rose and stood for the first time in his right mind. A look of consummate relief shone on the boy's face. Exhausted, he went to his father and hugged him.

With Iaman and the crowd looking on, enjoying the miracle, the boy walked to Iaman and hugged him. Holding his face in his hands, Iaman stooped down and kissed him on the forehead. The father could only breathe a thank you through his tear-filled eyes. The crowd parted as the two left for home.

Later, the team was alone with Iaman. In spite of his angry words about "no trust in the Light," the team felt comfortable approaching him; they were sure he wasn't talking about them. Michael asked, "Leader of the Light Team, why were we unable to defeat this wraith?"

"The power of LiarLight is strong, his minions many and varied. This wraith could only be driven out by a direct appeal to the Light evidenced by fasting. Nothing else could remove it."

Iaman then took them away from the crowds so that he could instruct them further.

* * * * * * * *

When together, the team talked about very common things. After all, they were common men. In addition, because the team was made up of men, they discussed the things men discuss when they are together. They talked about the local political happenings, of ayugamanship, and family. They bragged good-naturedly about their own past riding or business successes. Apparently, Steve had been quite an athlete in his youth. Scott had had little success in that area, but knew business better than any of the others. Lupe could discuss the nuances of politics with aplomb—from his own unique perspective, of course. Josh and Seth would tell about the times they had growing up. Josh was also an avid reader, so he would talk of the latest and best in literature. Bertrand basically kept to himself in spite of efforts by the others—particularly Seth—to involve him. Michael was perhaps the greatest thinker of the group. As time went on, he became quieter. He, perhaps more than the rest, realized that they were a part of an important historical moment.

Often when people are in the midst of a particularly pivotal time, they do not realize the full ramifications of events. All the team members now knew about all of the predictions in the Old Stories, and even participated in the miracles. On the surface, they understood what was happening around them. Michael ruminated on the events constantly. He even made occasional notes, as he felt that the story of what was happening to them—and for that matter the world—was worth writing down. He was often found off by himself with a twig in his hands, gradually breaking it into pieces and looking into the distance at nothing in particular. When approached, he was always friendly but distant: he was consumed with his thoughts. He would join the group from time to time and ask an astute question. The group became accustomed to his custom and looked forward to Michael's probing questions. At times, they would ask him to join them just to talk about what he was thinking. Iaman was also quick to join the group when Michael was sharing his thoughts. To Iaman, Michael was a kind of a barometer of how things were going. He acted as a catalyst for stimulating discussion that helped to focus the group's thinking. Although Iaman enjoyed the discussions, their real benefit was for the team.

The group had been talking about the local geography. Cyrus described his travels south into Maxima. This led to a discussion of the desert. On this particular occasion, Michael walked over to the group. He had been slightly apart from them, sitting under a tall and broad puncella tree. He interrupted the discussion with a question.

"When the father of the boy whom Iaman just healed told him that we could not help him, Iaman said two things. First he said, 'You have no trust in the Light' and then he questioned, 'How long must I remain with you?'" Michael paused while his finger tapped his lips. "Was he speaking about us when he said 'these have no trust in the Light?'" The others just looked at him, as he continued, "It seems to me that if he was talking about us, it was a relative statement. No trust compared to whom? Obviously we have some trust, which increases with our time with him. Additionally, our time with him immediately after that incident gave no indication that he was angry with us. Thus, he must have been talking about the other people or the wraiths themselves. However, since his goal is always to increase the trust of those who are watching, why would he attack them with criticism? Therefore, he must have been talking about the wraiths."

The group looked at each other and nodded in agreement.

Michael went on, "Next he expressed how tired he was of the status quo, saying, 'How long must I remain with you?' At first I was dismayed, thinking he was talking about us, but I now think he was disgusted at being in contact with the wraiths themselves."

The expressions on the faces of the group indicated that these thoughts had never even occurred to them. They enjoyed Michael's analysis and listened with rapt attention.

"The part I can't figure out is about seriousness in following the Light being evidenced by fasting. That doesn't make sense to me."

"You know, he said the commitment to the Light was evidenced by abstinence from food," Clarence interjected. "The point was not about seriousness, but evidence."

"Aren't they the same thing?" asked Lupe.

Michael was deep in thought again.

"What if someone could not fast because of health reasons?" Edward said, partly to justify his own corpulence, but the comment was taken seriously by the others.

110

"I guess one can only be expected to do what he is able to do: no more, but certainly no less," Steve reasoned.

"I think there is another aspect of it as well," Michael slowly went on. "Not all are expected to deal with wraiths, therefore not all would have the ability to do what is required; they would be expected to work in other areas. If, however, those who are able to attack the wraiths do not do so, many will remain ensnared. On the other hand, if everyone attempts to be a wraith slayer, there would be many charlatans about."

Shaking his head knowingly, Lupe said, "I see your point."

The others agreed. They were satisfied with the conclusions reached. The discussion proceeded in the direction of the charlatans they had seen.

Michael sat there for a moment, but was distracted by the questions that continued in his mind. *Are we expected to do battle with wraiths? How do we know what we're expected to do? How did Iaman develop such an obvious disgust for something like wraiths, when they exist largely in the realm of the spirit? Where was Iaman ultimately going to go, where he would no longer have to be with them?* Quietly he picked himself up and got a drink of water. He looked casually back at the group but remained unnoticed, except for a wink from Clarence. He returned a smile and went back to sit in the cool shade underneath the puncella.

There was suddenly a clamor among the larger following who had been resting as well under a nearby clump of trees.

Lupe rose to his feet, demanding, "What the heck is going on?"

"You know, the men Iaman sent out are due back anytime," Josh responded. "Steve and I were just talking about when they would be back. Maybe it's them."

Sure enough, several groups were returning amidst shouts, knocking fists and congratulatory slaps on the back from the larger following. They beamed with excitement. The crowd got silent with occasional choruses of laughter or applause arising randomly from the bands that surrounded each group of men. The team jerked themselves back and forth to look, as the bands around them responded with noise.

The excitement was different from when the team had returned. Sure, there was excitement then, but the team members were a bit distant. They were not as personally familiar with each other. The 70 were more of the rank and file brand of followers. They were husbands and fathers. They, like the team, had also left everything to follow Iaman, but they didn't enjoy the close day-to-day relationship that the team had with him. The selection of the 70 and their sending was an affirmation for them and their families. The jubilant reception at their return was therefore a reflection of both their wonderful success and the honor of their initial selection.

Iaman came on the scene unannounced. He, too, was exulting with the energizing news he heard as people ran up to him. Gradually, the 70 and their followings formed around him and got quiet. One of the 70, Jeff, could not restrain himself, but charged forward in excitement. Tripping on the way up, he landed hard on his right knee. The crowd cringed and then grinned. Jeff was known for his enthusiasm. He was a sincere follower, who led with his heart. Regaining his composure, he said to a smiling Iaman, "Leader, it was incredible, amazing, awesome! We healed the sick, and even the wraiths obeyed us when we commanded them by the name of the Leader of the Light Team!"

Iaman broke into joyful laughter. His expression lit up as he helped Jeff to his feet. He turned partly to the crowd and declared, "Thanks to you, LiarLight fell flat on his face." The people cheered, and Jeff smiled tearfully. Grabbing the closest members of the 70, the crowd encompassed them. The team themselves joined the crowd, participating in the celebration.

After a few moments of hoopla, Iaman raised his hands. The crowd slowly became quiet. A few blasts of laughter and whoops of joy lingered, rumbling before becoming quiet.

Iaman continued, "Power was given to you men over all kinds of danger, but the lesson to remember is this . . ." The people stilled a bit more, as Iaman, still jubilant, paused and then continued, "The wraiths obeyed you, but don't be glad for that reason. Be happy because your names are known to the Light! Be happy that you are citizens of His country." The people hesitated, stunned for a moment. Iaman turned to Jeff and hugged him. As they talked together, the din arose again as they people rejoiced at being claimed by the Light as His own.

The team had been enjoying their time together and alone with Iaman. Since the 70 had returned, the public attention temporarily shifted away from them. Today they had enjoyed nearly a full day away from the crowds. It was such a relief.

Iaman spent much of the day alone, apart from the team. They assumed that he was talking to the Light as he always did. But when he was absent for unusually long periods of time, they knew a time of particular importance had come. While he was thus occupied, they took care not to disturb him, only leaving his daily meals a short distance away from where he was. Sometimes he would eat, and sometimes he wouldn't. Michael wondered whether his eating behavior was at all related to what he was about to do. Perhaps he was abstaining from food to demonstrate his seriousness. The whole notion of not eating to gain power was still a riddle to the team.

That evening, as the team sat together for dinner, Iaman returned to their warm welcome. Small talk filled the air for several minutes as they finished the evening meal. Something was about to happen, they were sure about that.

After a while, they quieted, anticipating that Iaman would start in on his teaching. They gave him their whole attention, but his instruction was brief.

His face took on a look of concern that alarmed them. Pausing for a moment, he looked at the ground and then brought his gaze back up to them.

"Remember, the Leader of the Light Team will be given over to men and subjected to their power. They will kill him. But, three days later, he will be raised to life!"

They were heavy-hearted because of his once more sharing that discouraging and incomprehensible statement with them. He was the one who always lifted their spirits; they found themselves unable to help him. They couldn't understand what was going to happen, how it would happen, and why it had to happen that way. They didn't understand because the time had not yet come for them to comprehend. The Light was keeping full understanding from them. They wanted to talk to him about his assertion, but none could bring themselves to frame the questions. They also remembered Steve's confrontation when the subject was first breached. In despondency they sat, afraid to ask what their hearts could not understand.

Chapter 30
LIARLIGHT'S REMINDER

Another performance at the graveyard had just concluded. LiarLight's generals waited to meet about the growing problem of the Light Team. The dance had been very angular and coarse tonight. The thrusting, jabbing movements had made the entire throng uneasy. The generals knew something was bothering LiarLight.

In a tirade, LiarLight began. "I am sick of Iaman's self-righteous teaching! I know our plan must work itself out, but Iaman must also know that he hasn't won. His great Light Team," he said disdainfully, "must be given a dose of reality. I control this world: nothing happens unless I allow it."

"My creator," thgiL stammered. She looked toward LiarLight. She knew LiarLight had to be aware of her brief period of questioning while she worked on Bertrand's mind. LiarLight waved his hand, giving the permission. thgiL restarted, "My creator, as you know, Iaman's theme has been the importance of surrendering one's self to the will of the Light. He helps people to understand the desires of the Light so they can act upon them. In this way, he has attempted to mimic your followers in their complete dedication to you."

LiarLight paid little attention to thgiL. With a sidelong skeptical glance, he muttered, "Go on."

"If it is my creator's desire to remind Iaman of your control of his puny team, perhaps an attack on their allegiance to the Light would be useful."

LiarLight stared at thgiL. "Their allegiance, you say?"

thgiL became uncomfortable.

LiarLight became a bit interested. "What are you suggesting?"

"Perhaps my creator would enjoy seeing the followers of Iaman fighting amongst themselves over which of them are the greatest in the kingdom of the Light." thgiL looked for interest from LiarLight. She received no indication that he was disinterested, so she continued, "Perhaps we can remind Iaman of our control if we cause dissension among his beloved team. They could easily fight about who is the greatest among them. Their disregard for the purposes of the Light would be a slap in the face for Iaman. True, it would be a minor, almost insignificant set-back, but it would remind Iaman of my creator's power."

"A minor, insignificant setback. . . . A slap in the face." LiarLight moved toward thgiL. "Would you slap my face, thgiL?"

thgiL looked away nervously.

LiarLight enjoyed the discomfort of his general. "I don't worry about you. Have your dalliances of thought, because I own you!"

LiarLight was amused. It was an unexpected delight to have a general who entertained thoughts of leaving him, but was irrevocably bound by loyalty and obedience to him. What an interesting twist—to find a glimmer of ambition in his automaton! A wistfully evil smile found his face. "Make it so . . ." LiarLight paused. He grabbed thgiL and drew her up so closely that their noses nearly touched, ". . . my choiceless object!"

thgiL winced inside at her innate predicament. At the same time, she was relieved to be out of the situation. She disappeared and went back to working among the team.

* * * * * * * * *

The team had been traveling from Yucaipa to Colton. It was quite a menagerie: there were ayugas and a few carts, and of course there were the packs of stray baolas that seemed to congregate among groups of people—especially those with food.

People passing by watched with curiosity. The diverse group moved slowly, but with direction. There was much discussion among the people, except near the front where the people quietly listened as a man in loose jeans and a billowy tan shirt spoke to them.

As often happened when they were traveling, the team would get separated from Iaman. He tended to lead the throng of people as they walked along the road. The team members occasionally found their way up to Iaman to determine whether he needed something, but the people crowded around him so thickly that the team would fall to the back.

thgiL moved among them. The men were discussing a variety of issues as they walked along. The general theme of the discussion was the nature of Iaman's new regime—what would it look like, and what types of people and skills would be critical to the new government. thgiL tweaked each one's thoughts toward self-importance. Each one began to think of how he would hold a place of particular prominence. Lupe was the first to state his thoughts out loud.

"It's obvious that Iaman will need someone who understands politics to head his government. He needs someone who knows what the people want and is not afraid to push his political agenda. . . . Someone who can put the right people in the right political positions . . . who can orchestrate the passing of the kind of laws that can bring this republic back to following the Light."

"And I guess that person is you?" Edward asked.

"What Iaman needs is a leader," Steve interrupted, "a proven individual who can rally people around him. Business experience will also be an advantage, as there will be financial concerns."

Scott became indignant. "You think you know business? You know nothing. The dry goods company would have been nothing if I hadn't brought some sanity to your business practices."

Steve only shook his head and muttered, "Get serious."

Josh then spoke up, "Iaman needs someone who can understand the culture. He'll want someone with the intelligence to make compromises. What he won't need is some political zealot, self-proclaimed leader, or money-grubber. People have to live together."

The discussion went on this way, becoming more and more heated. Michael didn't participate in the bickering only because he didn't want to lower himself to their level. *What a bunch of fools*, he thought. *What Iaman will need is someone with half a brain—a commodity that is severely lacking among this group.*

Their banter created such an uproar that the people around them began to take notice as the argument intensified. thgiL continued to prompt the minds of the group. *Light Team, indeed*, she thought to herself. *How easily their minds are manipulated. They are a joke.*

About that time, Iaman approached. The people had called his attention to the group as they were walking. He caught Clarence's final comment, "You know, I was the first to figure out who he was!" Scott wanted to respond, but the group went silent as they caught sight of Iaman. thgiL quickly departed.

Iaman knew what they were bickering about, but he asked anyway, "What are you arguing about?"

The team began to regain their senses with the departure of thgiL, but would not answer.

"Don't you recognize that in order to be the greatest, you must be the lowest? You must be the servant of all as you submit to the demands of the Light." He looked briefly at the group of people surrounding them. He walked over and took a child by the hand; she followed willingly. "If you would be great in the Country of the Light, you must become like a child. Accepting this child is like accepting me, and accepting me is accepting the Light Himself."

Iaman had their attention; they felt like fools. Iaman understood that their minds had been manipulated. LiarLight's reminder through thgiL came through to him loud and clear. In an instant, he reflected on how far he had come, yet how far he still had to go with his team.

All the men of the team looked at him guiltily.

"It is the least among you who will be the greatest." Iaman paused for a moment. The people were silent. He moved to the front of the group and started to walk on again.

Chapter 31
THE TEACHING

When they arrived in Colton, they rested. The people milled around, waiting for something to happen. They wondered whether Iaman would have anything further to say about the conduct of the team back on the road. Finally, Iaman called them together and began to instruct them again in the ways of the Light.

"People will always make mistakes in their behavior: it is the way of a world controlled by LiarLight. It is sad that circumstances occur and situations arise that cause people to turn away from the Light they had been following. Yes, there will be a penalty to pay for those who fall away from the truth. However, the greatest penalty will be for the one who causes another to fall away: there will be no escape for that person."

Iaman got up and began to walk among the people. "The way to be free of LiarLight begins with coming to the Light. The Light will then enable you to live according to his standards. Understand that this is serious business. I would go so far as to say that if your eye leads you into trouble, get rid of it! It would be better to enter the Country of the Light with one eye than to live with LiarLight, seeing everything. The same goes for your hands or feet. What is the point of being physically complete when you are only a pawn in LiarLight's game?"

Iaman came upon a group of elderly men and sat among them. "One of the most powerful bonds to keep you ensnared is your lack of forgiveness toward one another. In reality, you enslave yourself when you cling to an offense committed against you."

Steve, Michael, and Clarence had been casually following him as he moved among the crowd. Steve spoke up. "Leader of the Light Team, how many times should I overlook a wrong done against me?" He hesitated in thought. "Seven times?"

Clarence was dismayed, thinking to himself, *How could someone allow themselves to be abused in such a manner. Seven times!*

Iaman's answer surprised him all the more.

"Seven times? No, not seven times. . ." Clarence was relieved. Iaman continued, ". . . but 70 times seven times."

Even without a quick calculation, Clarence knew that Iaman was talking about a lot of times—even an unlimited number. He winced and looked at him in disbelief.

Iaman explained, "Let me illustrate the standard for you. There was once a man who, through poor business judgment, lost about 1,000 credits of the magistrate's money. The magistrate called him in and said to him, 'Pay me the money you owe me.' The man sank into his chair before him and said, 'I haven't the money to pay you!' The magistrate ordered that the man be sent to prison, and that his family be stripped of all their possessions down to the shirts on their backs. The man begged the magistrate, 'Please allow me time to pay off my debt to you. If you have patience with me, I will pay back the money I owe you.' The magistrate knew that the debt was far beyond the man's ability to pay, but he had compassion on him. He then forgave the debt and set him free."

Clarence swallowed hard.

"The same man then went back to his home. He saw a neighbor who owed him a comparatively small amount of money. He grabbed his neighbor by the throat and began to choke him. 'Give me the money you owe me!' he bellowed. The man replied, 'I don't have the money right here; give me a week, and I'll get it together' (he owed him about 120 credits). The first man replied, 'Forget it! I'm calling the officers of the law and suing you in court for everything you have!' Others who knew both of the men were angered by what they observed. They knew of the kindness the first servant received, and couldn't believe his flagrant disregard for the other man. One of them reported to the magistrate all that had happened. When the magistrate heard of the situation, he grew furious. He had the first man physically dragged in to meet with him. 'You worthless, hypocritical scoundrel! How dare you behave in such a manner! I canceled your entire debt simply because you asked me— a debt you would never be able to repay in your best dreams. Yet you treat you neighbor as you did. At the very least, you should have forgiven him! I now bind you to your entire debt. You will remain in prison until every last credit is paid back!'"

Iaman directly addressed the men around him, "The Light will treat you in the same manner if you don't reconcile with your neighbor. Additionally, it is LiarLight's sick desire to see you faced with this dilemma—to be in the presence of the Light only to face His wrath. LiarLight's hope is to enjoy the punishment of those he has fooled."

Michael addressed Iaman, "Teacher, what is the standard?"

Iaman turned to Michael and waited as he clarified his question.

"I mean, as a man in LiarLight's world, I cannot help but fail," Michael continued. "I have no hope to meet the standards required by the Light. Additionally, I have come to this realization too late in my life. When confronted by the Light, my past will condemn me."

Iaman, seemingly pleased with Michael's sincerity, pursued the matter further. "There was once a red grower who needed to hire workers to pick his fruit. He went to the place in the town where workers waited to be hired for work. He gathered the men and said to them, 'I will pay you a full day's wage if you come with me and pick reds.' The men were pleased with the arrangement, went with him, and began picking. Several hours later, he went out to the hiring area and found some more workers. He offered them the same deal as the earlier workers, and they followed him to his red groves. At noontime, he was back again. Some more men were just arriving at the hiring place. The red grower approached them, saying, 'Are you just now getting out of bed? Come and work in my orchard.' Offering them the same deal, the men went to work in his orchard. Finally, there were only a couple hours left in the work day, when he went into the town once more. Again he saw some men milling around at the hiring place. 'Do you waste all your time doing nothing? Come and labor in my orchards for the remainder of the day.' Again he offered them the same deal that he had offered each of the other groups he had hired.

"At the end of the work day, the last who were hired were called forward. Each was paid the full day's wage, as was promised to him. Each of the remaining groups were then called and paid the same wage. When the group who had worked an entire day were about to be called, they discussed amongst themselves, 'We will undoubtedly get more money, as we worked the entire day!' To their dismay, they received the same wage as all the others. As they turned away from the orchard owner, they complained to each other, 'We worked the whole day, and look what we got!' The orchard owner responded, 'I have given you what I promised I would. Have I cheated you in any way?' The grumblers would not answer, but only looked at him angrily. 'It seems to me that I can spend my money as I like. Would you begrudge me the right to be generous?'"

Michael pondered the answer to the owner's question, as Iaman studied him for his reaction. He thought he saw the lesson, but he still didn't know how he could conform to Iaman's standards from this day forward. No one said anything further to Iaman at this time.

* * * * * * * * *

The middle-aged woman approached the crowd cautiously; she didn't know if she'd find her sons there or not. Friends had told her that they were involved in following a new leader. "The Leader of the Light Team" was how they referred to him. Additionally, the friends said they heard that her sons were selected to be members of the Light Team—the team described in the

Old Stories. She had little understanding of what that was all about, but she got the impression she should be proud of them. She moved her way through the people, looking for her sons. Finally, she was directed toward an area where it was thought her sons would be found.

Albert and Clarence chuckled at their mother's approach, particularly because of the basket she carried under her arm—that could mean nothing less than butter cake! It was a family treat as much associated with their mother as her smiling face. Their father had died several years back, but Mom was still the same.

Albert introduced her to the other members of the team and then related all of what had been happening: the teaching they heard and the healing and other miracles they observed and participated in themselves. They also told her how Iaman was going to establish a new order called the "Country of the Light." He would be in charge of things, and each of the members of the Light Team would play a critical part in the process. They talked about the power they had been given and the plans for the future. They were going to defeat LiarLight, although they weren't exactly sure how.

Their mother listened attentively, but was filled with a healthy skepticism. She had not seen the events they described and had not had any contact with Iaman. Although impressed by her sons' enthusiasm and the respectful crowd that was milling around, her response was no more than a motherly, "That's nice, dears." Her reaction was quite a letdown for her sons.

Albert wouldn't let the trite comment pass. Hoping for more enthusiasm on her part, he pleaded, "Don't you see, Mom, Iaman is an important man! His coming was predicted in the Old Stories."

"Yeah, Mom, he's going to set up a new government . . . a totally new way of doing things!" Clarence added.

"You mean he is going to be like a new magistrate or something?"

"Yeah, that's it, Mom," Clarence affirmed.

"Well, where do you two figure in this arrangement?"

Albert hesitated, "Well . . ." he thought and looked at Clarence, "We aren't really sure how we'll fit in yet. We know we'll take part, but we don't know what our exact role will be."

"Are you your father's sons or not? Confront your leader: ask him for what you want. Do you want positions of leadership next to him?"

"You know, that would be really great, but we don't feel comfortable asking him about it right now. We had a big talk about this whole thing a couple of days ago. . . . This might not be a good time." Clarence hoped his plea would dissuade her from what he knew was about to happen.

"Well, let's go talk to your leader. I would like to meet him," she insisted.

Looking around, Albert saw Iaman a short distance away, conversing with the rest of the team. As the three approached, Albert could see that they were engaged in a lighthearted discussion, but Iaman rose to meet them. He assumed correctly that the woman with them was their mother.

Albert approached Iaman with his mother in tow. "Mother, I would like you to meet Iaman. He is the man I have told you about."

"It is a pleasure to meet you," said Iaman courteously. "I am pleased to have your sons be a part of our group. The Light has great plans for them."

She bowed before him. "Sir, if my sons have found favor in your sight, would you grant me a request?"

"What is it that you'd like?" Iaman responded cordially.

She stared directly into his kind eyes. "Please promise me that my sons will sit at your right and left hands when you come into power." The sons shrunk while anticipating his answer.

"You have a good desire, but you really don't know what you are asking me for," was Iaman's solemn reply. Turning to the brothers, he reached out his hands toward them, holding each one by the back of his neck. At Iaman's touch, Albert felt some of the anger toward his mother leave him. He asked them, "Are you prepared to drink with me from the cup that I must drink?"

Clarence and Albert had no idea what he was talking about, but their hearts burned with loyalty toward him. Their trust in him welled up within them; they would willingly do anything he asked. Responding boldly, they affirmed, "We are!"

As he slowly nodded his head, Iaman's prophetic stare struck fear into them. "You will indeed participate with me in the cup I must drink; this I promise you." His gaze mellowed slightly as he continued, "But the determination of who will sit at my right or left is not mine to make: it is the Light Himself who will decide. Those who have been prepared for these positions by Him will occupy them."

With that, they moved away from him awkwardly. They were unsure of what had just transpired. The assurances they received were not what they had anticipated. If only their mother had known what future she had ensured for her sons, she would not have been so bold.

* * * * * * * * *

When the rest of the team heard what had transpired, they were irate. Even Steve and Scott were irritated with their friends. They were irked because of the lecture they had all received a few days prior, which apparently had no effect on Clarence and Albert; but they were also infuriated because, deep down inside, they desired to do the same thing, but did not have the nerve to ask first. Sensing the tension within the group, Iaman called them together.

"The magistrates like to lord their power over their people," said Iaman.

"This, however, is not how you should act. If you would be a leader, you must be a servant of others. If you want to be first, you must be last. Even the Leader of the Light Team did not come to be served." He gestured to the people around him. "You see no servants here. Rather, he has come to serve you. He has come to lay down his life to defeat LiarLight."

As it turned out, the team learned that nothing was really promised to Albert or Clarence concerning sitting at Iaman's right or left hand. Additionally, they weren't sure, but what Clarence and Albert were going to participate in didn't sound very positive. The men of the team did not soon forget the request of the mother of the sons of Thunderhead; but remembering Iaman's other lessons about forgiving, they tried to move on.

The team and its following continued on their way toward Camden. They arrived at the city of Serenity, about ten miles outside of Camden. Pausing there, Iaman continued his teaching, and many who were sick or disabled came to him for healing. The people there remarked, "As great as he was, the Lone Warrior never did the amazing things this man can do. Everything we have heard about him is true!" As a result, many came to have trust in the Light, and the numbers of his following increased.

While he was engaged with the people, a man charged through the crowd to Iaman. The group parted as he fell on his knees out of breath. Everyone waited tensely for him to speak. Breathing heavily he said, "Iaman!" He puffed some more. "Iaman, you need to come right away." His chest heaved some more. "He's sick, deathly sick. You've got to come right away!"

Iaman recognized the man as a servant of his friend Jay. He and Jay had grown up together; they were playmates and lifelong friends. Jay followed Iaman's movements, and they met together on several occasions. Kathi and Amy, Jay's sisters, were also good friends of his.

The servant finally recovered and gave Iaman the complete message. Jay was very ill; he had been so for several weeks, and was now at the point of death. The sisters sent the servant to Iaman, hoping he would come and help their brother. Jay and his sisters only lived about eight miles down the road in Temple City, so a quick trip could be made.

Alarmed, Steve quickly spoke up, "The last time we went through there, the LampLighters wanted to arrest and kill you!"

"In the end, Jay will not die from this disease. This has happened to bring recognition to the Light, and his messenger, the Leader of the Light Team." Yet, after saying this, he went on about his business in Serenity. He remained there for two more days, teaching and helping those who came to him. Finally, he told the team, "It's time to go to Temple City."

"Are you really going back there?" asked Steve.

"Aren't there 12 hours of light in a day?" Iaman replied. "If someone walks in the light, he won't trip and fall. Yet if he goes during the night he will fall, as he has no light in him." Steve was puzzled by this response. Before he could ask a question about what he meant, Iaman spoke, "Jay has fallen asleep, and I am going to wake him."

"If he's sleeping, he should get well," Clarence objected.

Iaman turned to Clarence and Steve and announced gravely, "Look, Jay is dead. I'm glad I wasn't with him for your sake. Let's go on to Temple City."

Under his breath, Edward said, "Let's follow our leader, so we can die with him." They all heard the remark.

As they came to the outskirts, a servant approached them. Iaman learned that Jay had been dead for about three days. The servant then ran back to get Amy, who hurried out to meet him. Kathi, however, stayed home.

Amy ran up to Iaman and threw her arms around him. "Leader, if you had been here, Jay wouldn't have died." Amy sucked up her courage and said, "But I still have confidence that the Light will give you whatever you would request of Him."

"Your brother will be raised to life," Iaman responded.

She smiled her assent through her tears. "I know that he will rise on the last day."

"I am the rising! I am life! Anyone who trusts in me will rise, even though he dies. Whoever entrusts himself to me will never die!" He stared at Amy. "Do you believe this?"

Unhesitatingly, Amy replied, "I believe that you are the offspring of the Light Himself, and that you are the Leader of the Light Team come into the world to defeat our enemy!"

They talked some more, and Iaman sent Amy to get Kathi. The sisters arrived in tears. Choking back her sobs, Kathi pleaded, "Iaman, had you been here, my brother wouldn't have died." Iaman was moved, as he loved the sisters as if they were his own.

"Where have you placed your brother?"

They took him to the tomb, a simple cave cut into a rocky hill. A large whitewashed boulder, cut like a wheel, rested in front of the entrance. Looking on the place, Iaman wept. The hearts of the team went out to him as he knelt down alone, heedless of the rocky terrain; but no one made a move toward him, for they could tell he was talking to the Light.

By this time, a crowd had gathered. They were touched by Iaman's love for his friend. One person remarked quietly, "I wonder why he couldn't save his friend? He healed that blind man."

"Many others as well," another responded.

Iaman appeared to have gathered his thoughts sufficiently and walked directly to the tomb. In a bold voice, he ordered, "Take the stone away!"

Amy hurried up to him. Concerned, she whispered, "But Leader, won't there will be a bad odor?"

Iaman sternly replied, "You will see the glory of the Light, if you have trust!"

Josh and Seth stepped forward and moved the stone away. The air was filled with the scent of spices mingled with decay. Some in the crowd covered their faces with a cloth or their sleeve, trying to fend off the odor that a breeze blew towards them.

Iaman remained still. Looking up, he lifted his hands to the sky. "Thank you for hearing me. I know that you always listen to me, but I say this for those around me, so that they might trust you."

He then turned his attention to the tomb. The chalky white stone lay on the ground. The interior of the cave was dark, and the stench of syrupy corruption filled the air.

Iaman's voice boomed, "Jay, come out!" Instantly, the air was scented with the fragrance of the spices alone. The aroma of death, which the spices had fought to cover, was gone.

A figure like a mummy—bound head, hands and feet—was compelled forward from the darkness into the light. The crowd was aghast. Several dropped to their knees blubbering.

The sisters raised their hands to their faces with gasps. They bolted for their brother and removed the wrappings from his face. He looked confused, as if he were fighting off many layers of sleep. Upon recognizing his sisters, he smiled faintly.

Iaman, glad to see his friend again, told them to unbind him. Hearing Iaman's voice and seeing his surroundings, it began to register in Jay's mind what had happened to him. He looked at his friend gratefully.

Michael thought to himself, *Three days dead . . . and look at him! Only the Offspring of the Light, or the Light Himself, could do that.*

A marvelous time of rejoicing followed; trust in the Light was at an all-time high.

In the crowd were many of the LampLighters. Some came to comfort the family and others to monitor Iaman. Upon seeing what transpired, a few believed and became his followers. Others returned to the leaders in Camden and reported what Iaman had done. A council was quickly formed to discuss the issue. The LampLighter president at the time was a man named Dermod; he convened the meeting. "Gentlemen, what is the latest on this Iaman?"

"He just brought a man back from the dead in Temple City," one started.

"I saw the man after he died, and he was definitely dead; a couple of us examined the body ourselves." Several heads nodded in agreement.

"This is not the only amazing thing he has done. Remember, he healed that blind man, and that guy who was mentally handicapped. He did that right in the middle of a meeting on Lightday!"

"You know, if we keep ignoring him, and let him go on with these activities, well . . . everyone will be following him!"

"Hold on!" Dermod could take the hand-wringing no more. He sighed and shook his head. Slowly and deliberately he said, "You don't know anything!" They became quiet. He shook his head again. "Did you hear that the authorities captured Elie—the leader of the radical group who murdered the seven in Rialto?"

"They got 11 of his followers as well," one of the leaders threw in.

"Did they? Well, I suspect it won't be long before we hear from the governor's office. They will be seeking the death of a LampLighter in fulfillment of the Justice laws," said Dermod.

One of the men became distressed. "Could they come after your—"

"Huh, I suppose they could . . . but it's not likely. In that regard, I have a plan. The government knows they got away with murder in the case of the "Sopa Seven" killed by the police. If not for the quandary of the jury over how the Justice Laws should be applied to our tripartite government, we would have had justice. But there is still the possibility that that decision can work to our advantage. I think there is a sentiment among government leaders that they owe us something. Bring Iaman to me; I have a plan."

They each left for their homes. As they left, they also discussed among themselves what would be done with Jay. They decided to have him killed as well, since because of him, many were leaving the LampLighters and following Iaman.

This occurred about a week before the Celebration of the Deliverance, the yearly festival that commemorated a time in the history of the LampLighters when the Light protected them.

Chapter 32
THGIL'S CHOICE

"Our plot is coming together perfectly, my creator. Like a fly, the fool approaches your web. The spiders are also prepared to bite." thgiL reveled in her success. Although still keeping her typical subservient posture, she exuded self-congratulations.

"Is he in the net yet?" LiarLight glared at thgiL. "Is the spider upon him?"

thgiL's confidence quickly faded. Before she could respond, LiarLight was on her again.

"I will tolerate no mistakes this time. Should you fail, you will experience the same fate as CounterLight." LiarLight paused. "Do you know what happened to CounterLight?"

thgiL would not so much as raise her head. With her face pressed against the floor, she responded, "He is no longer with us; you banished him."

"Is that what you and my . . . great generals . . . say behind my back?" He was disgusted. LiarLight's face took on an evil smile. "Perhaps you would like to . . . find out?"

In an instant, thgiL found herself somewhere in the dark, although she didn't know where she was. She found she was in a body, one like a human body but with significantly more senses. Besides the five senses, she had a sense of knowing about the future. She had a sense of seeing parallel events. She became aware of senses for perceiving stimuli she didn't even know existed. She had a knowledge of spirits. She felt an unhindered sensitivity to the Light. She even felt she had the power of choice, but there was nothing to choose.

Then, like a bolt of lightning, all her senses went into a hyperactive state. Fear swept over her. There was nothing around her to fear, but it consumed her. Her eyes saw things she couldn't bear, but was powerless to shut out. Her ears heard sounds even grotesque to a wraith, but she couldn't cover them. Every pain receptor in her body surged and pounded. At the same time, her future senses saw her painful doom replayed over and over. It was a doom orchestrated by her own hands: she felt she could have avoided it. Each attack on the senses was perceived as if for the first time, with undiminished fury and sensory pain. With each moment, she thought her existence would be over, but an equal amount of strength to live was given with the sensory attack so that the cycle was unending. She bore this cycle for what seemed an eternity: fear upon fear, pain upon pain, with no escape.

Without warning, she was before LiarLight again. LiarLight smiled. "Has this been instructive?"

Although her mind was suddenly clear, she couldn't answer. She wouldn't answer. She wouldn't answer—the free choice given her remained. For a split second, she beamed! *She could choose not to follow LiarLight!* Then she remembered her situation.

LiarLight smiled again. "Yes, you have your choice. It will remind you of your visit to 'pain land,' and help you with your newfound ability to prioritize. Do you still choose to follow me?" thgiL didn't answer, because she didn't know, but LiarLight knew her thoughts. "Sometimes choice is a painful gift, especially . . . when you have no choice."

thgiL quickly recognized her dilemma. *If I choose LiarLight, my condition would be no different than it has been. If I choose not to follow LiarLight, I'll be back in pain land. I have no other choice. Would the Light accept a reformed wraith?* That thought even disgusted thgiL herself. *No, I am trapped; LiarLight has designed a new form of torment.*

LiarLight listened to thgiL's thoughts. He savored her dilemma. "Now that we understand each other, continue on with your plan. Harbor no confidence regarding your adversary. The Light is a clever foe. I want your, 'spiders,' to be so filled with malice that they'll do anything. I want them blind with hate. This Iaman must die—and die brutally. People must fear me. As a bonus, my human agents will bear the guilt!"

thgiL left LiarLight and pondered anew this "choice" she had been given. *What good is choice, if there is no choice?* she thought to herself. For a moment a thought broke through to her. In the midst of her pain, the only hope she harbored came an unimpaired glimpse of the Light. Thinking back on her pain, it seemed that the only sense that did not bring agony was the channel that opened access to the Light. As she thought, she recognized that she received a glimmer of the appeal of her enemy. *Why was it that people—those who could choose—would choose the Light over LiarLight? How would she choose if given the opportunity? Wait, I do have the opportunity!* she thought. *Would the Light really reject me as LiarLight has always told me?* She thought again about her situation. Practically speaking, she felt she still had no choice, but she would file this information away. Perhaps it would prove useful later.

Chapter 33
A CHANGE IN DIRECTION

The next day, there was a stirring in Iaman's following. A rumor circulated that they were to prepare to relocate. In the past, they had moved around quite a bit. This wouldn't be one of the simple local moves they had been used to. They were to prepare to go to Camden—why Camden, they weren't sure. The Light Team members had simply circulated among them, indicating they were going to go to Camden.

Camden was a major city: masses of people, and everything that goes with masses of people. There were diverse ethnic groups, the government had a major regional office there, and the LampLighters' national headquarters was also in Camden. LiarLight had a strong presence there; it was a town famous for being superficial.

At times, the team felt almost as if they were in a dream. The events that enveloped and swept them along seemed detached from them. A lack of understanding surrounded them like a moat. Lupe was the only one who thought he knew what was happening. When he was away from Iaman, he would excitedly tell the others, "We're going to Camden so he can set up the Country of the Light! I can feel it!" He would grin contentedly. "All this time with him is finally going to pay off. Don't get me wrong! The teaching has been excellent, and I feel like I am in the presence of the Light Himself when I'm near him; but now comes the reason why he brought us together!"

Michael looked at him skeptically. "What might that be?"

"Isn't it obvious?" Lupe had a quizzical look on his face. He chuckled, "We are going to Camden so that he can set up the Country of the Light. I bet Camden will be its capital. After he takes over, the first order of business will be to shape up the LampLighters. What better place to do it than from their national headquarters? It's all finally coming clear to me now."

"I'm not as sure that that's what this is all about," Clarence responded. "You know he keeps talking about the fact that he is going to die. How does that figure in?"

"I agree." Michael hesitated. "Lupe, you could be right! Much of what he's said points to it. Yet, there are other things, not the least of which Clarence pointed out, that don't go along with your scenario. I'm still not sure."

Edward just shook his head and muttered, "This is ridiculous!"

About that time, they stopped in Eagle Rock, a small city just on the outskirts of Camden. Iaman called the team together. Addressing Josh and Seth, he said, "The next city north of here is called Cherry Hill. Go up this road, and there you will see a kaamen and its colt in the front yard of one of the homes. Go through the gate, untie them, and bring them back here. If a neighbor should ask you what you are doing, tell her 'The Teacher needs them,' and she will let you take them. Meet us with the animals back on this road, just before it enters Camden."

Josh and Seth went on down the dusty path. After a while, they came up on a group of two-story clapboard buildings. The buildings formed two parallel lines which faced each other. Just before they entered the town, there was a cottage with a split-rail fenced yard on the right hand side. They saw the two animals just as Iaman had described them.

"Does he want just the mother, just the colt, or both?" Seth asked.

Josh jumped the fence and untied them. "Better be safe," he advised, and they walked them toward the gate.

Suddenly, the cottage door burst open. A large, overweight woman burst through the door. Her clothing was old and washed out. "Where you goin' with Conrad's animals?" she bristled. "They're Conrad's animals."

Josh and Seth looked at each other. "The Teacher needs them?" Josh replied half-questioning.

"'The teacher needs them': are you talking about Iaman?"

"Yes!" was Josh's encouraged response.

"Have a good day," she said, as the door closed behind her.

Seth sighed. "Sure glad we didn't have to tussle with her!"

Josh could only smile and shake his head.

Josh and Seth arrived at the Camden road with the animals where the people were gathered. Iaman had apparently given the team instructions while the two had been away. Albert immediately took the animals, and the others put some clothes on their backs. Iaman sat up on the colt and gave it a 'click' and kick. The larger kaamen stirred and began walking ahead. The colt followed.

Steve and Clarence started to cut down palm branches and throw them on the ground in front of Iaman. Spontaneously, the followers who had come along began to cheer. The team members also got caught up in the celebration, cheering and dancing along as Iaman rode slowly on the colt. People along the road or in their homes strained to see what was going on.

Occasionally someone would ask, "Who is that guy?"

Wendell's joyful, out-of-breath response was, "He's Iaman, the Leader of Light Team—the one who will defeat LiarLight!"

Some, upon hearing this, followed along, dropping everything. Others just shook their head disgustedly at the deluded followers. A large throng gathered as people were caught up in the celebration. People took the team's lead and threw down their outer clothing. A colorful carpet of many textures muffled each step of the colt. Others cut more palm branches and threw them down in front of the animals. The road became a pattern of stripe and color.

Shouts arose from every quarter of the procession.

"The Light has remembered us!" one shouted.

Three young girls choraled together, "Iaman!"

Recognizing their voices, Iaman turned and smiled broadly. They giggled and turned away.

"Paso-Lomon's son is with us!" another called.

"Hail to the Leader of the Light Team!" someone screamed.

Another group began to chant rhythmically, "Fall on your face, LiarLight! Fall on your face, LiarLight! Fall on your face, LiarLight! Fall on your face, LiarLight!"

Iaman beamed at the throng; the joy they exuded delighted him. He reached out and touched the followers. Occasionally, a child would ride with him briefly. People sang songs about the Light. The tumult freely expressed their joy.

This went on for over an hour as Iaman made his way into the city. Neither the team nor the throng had any idea where he was headed. Some of the followers who had joined the group tried to talk as they reveled. The noise was deafening.

Michael approached one of the people who had just joined the group. "I've never been to Camden before. Where do you think he's headed?" he shouted.

Mishearing him, the man held out his hand and shouted, "My name is Richard."

Michael shook his head and shouted back "Where does this road go?"

"What?"

"The road! The road! Where does it go?"

The man pointed ahead and shouted his response. "It leads into the business sector. It ends at the Camden LampLighter's headquarters!"

Inaudibly, Michael mouthed, "Thanks." Both understood the meaning, though neither could hear the word over the noise.

The crowd was getting even louder, if that were possible. The occasional bursts of shouting became more frequent and finally merged into a single continuous roar. Michael found he was having difficulty thinking; he was trying to process everything that had happened. *Iaman surely wouldn't mind if I ducked around the corner for a moment,* he thought. He continued to be troubled by Iaman's redundant predictions. He wondered if Iaman would really be killed in Camden. At that moment, someone came up and put an arm around him. It was Lupe.

He shouted, "Hey, what did I tell you?" Realizing it was quieter, he grimaced and lowered his voice. "What did I tell you! The city is going nuts! Look at all the followers! There must be 5,000 people following him. Look at them: they're trampling one another!" He chuckled, "Now the fun begins!" He smiled at Michael, and raised his hand to his mouth as if sharing a secret, his eyes darting side to side. "The LampLighters are going to get what's coming to them!"

"You didn't have anything to do with this crowd—did you?"

"Well, I told a few people that Camden was probably going to be the center of his political power, but no—this was his own doing. People are excited. You might not agree with me politically, but we agree he speaks for the Light." Lupe pointed a finger at Michael. "Heck, this is the Light's doing!" With that, Lupe bolted off to join the rest of the crowd.

Michael just stared as the crowd continued to pass by. *Is my beloved leader about to go to his death?* He joined the parade again. Soon the answer to his questions about their destination was affirmed. They arrived at the LampLighter's Headquarters, and Iaman jumped down from the kaamen.

Those inside the LampLighters' headquarters hardly noticed the hubbub of the crowd following Iaman; they had a cacophonous throng of their own they were dealing with. The headquarters building was designed according to specific plans outlined in the Old Stories. There was an inner secluded section that was exclusively for the LampLighter leaders. The LampLighters considered it the most hallowed part of the structure. Attached to it was the regular meeting place of the rank and file LampLighters. This room was separated from the inner sanctum by a thick curtain almost like a rug. The curtain was stationary, however, and was more like a wall between the two areas. Outside there was a large, enclosed courtyard. The LampLighters reserved this area for foreigners who would come to hear about the Light, or to honor the Light to the best of their knowledge. It was an expansive area, equal in size to the rest of the building. The walls that bordered each side had several large rainbow-like archways that allowed for free movement in and out of the courtyard. Over the years, the courtyard had become a place where followers of the Light who came from outlying areas could exchange money to give to the LampLighters in support of their activities. The LampLighters would only accept local money, so there were money traders in the courtyard.

Additionally, there were animals for sale, specifically sheep, cattle, and pigeons. The Old Stories described an elaborate system whereby the death of an animal could satisfy the Light's need for justice in relation to wrongs done by an individual. The animal was bought, taken to the LampLighters, and killed. The LampLighters then cooked the animal over a large fire pit. The sweet aroma of the meat cooking was thought of as pleasant to the Light, particularly when associated with a repentant Light follower. People found it difficult to

131

bring animals all the way to Camden, so the LampLighters sold them in the meetinghall courtyard. In some ways, the LampLighter's sacrificial practices were not unlike the recently developed Justice laws. In fact, the LampLighters saw a logical connection between them and their own religious practices.

The impact of these activities were many. These ranged from the presence of animals in the Light's meeting place, to unethical money changing, to simply making it difficult for foreigners wanting to honor the Light to do so in the midst of the noise, odors, and movement. It was onto this scene that Iaman came.

The crowd still chanted as he moved up the steps into the outer courtyard. Walking through the gate, he surveyed the courtyard. There were those selling penned up sheep and cattle. Others had caged pigeons on stools; these were for the poorer of the pilgrims. There were also money changers with the animal sellers. As he looked around, anger welled up in him. Some of the reveling throng had spilled into the courtyard with him. They loved the carnival atmosphere.

Iaman looked around him and saw some animal lead lines, used to bring in the larger animals. He grabbed three of them and formed a fist around their ends. He quickly moved to the first money-changing table and flipped it over. Coins jingled everywhere. The men operating the table shouted angrily, "What are you do—" when the cords came down on their backs. As they darted off, Iaman knocked down a fence that corralled eight sheep. He jumped in among them, and the whip came down again. The sheep bolted, knocking down another money-changing table.

The people's immediate reactions were of outrage. "What's wrong with him? Has he lost his mind?" one remarked. "What does he think he is doing?" another demanded.

At about this time, Lupe came through the archway. At first, he was puzzled at the chaos. His eyes then moved to where Iaman was creating havoc. "Yes!" he shouted, "They had this coming!"

The others nodded, but did not share Lupe's enthusiasm. As they stood there, people and animals ran wildly everywhere. The followers who came with Iaman into Camden wondered what this all meant. Some began shouting the same praises they had along the way to Camden. But Iaman persisted in his tirade. Suddenly, there was a flutter of white feathers, as the air filled with pigeons. The crowd applauded. The raining of loose feathers only added to the spectacle. Merchants began to gather up their money and organize their animals in an attempt at a quick exit. Any notions they might have had of attacking Iaman disappeared when they saw the huge throng that had arrived with him. As the merchants crossed the courtyard, Iaman would stop them, bringing the cords down on the pavement with a loud crack. The animals would bolt and the men would follow, heading for the closest exit.

The crowd noticed that Iaman was shouting. The destruction of commerce continued, but the sounds changed. Only the animals and an occasional disgruntled merchant could be heard, punctuated by the chinging sound of an overturned money table. Iaman's voice boomed, "The Old Stories say that the House of the Light should be a place where He is honored. A place for communication with Him! But you have made it a hideout for thieves!" Iaman carried on his work until the last of the merchants were gone. People scurried over the floor, picking up the scattered coins as the merchants hastily departed. The excitement continued, with people madly snatching up the money wherever it could be found, no matter what the effort.

While the two groups rushed in and out, Iaman moved to the side of the courtyard. Sweating and out of breath, he threw his bundle of cords aside and sat down. No one dared to approach him. He hunched over, panting, and gradually caught his breath. With a final deep breath, he looked up at the people who surrounded him. His now calm demeanor assured them he was all right. He reached out his sleeve and wiped the sweat from his brow. An audible sigh arose from his friends; they looked relieved. The courtyard regained a sense of order. There was only the chattering of a few excited followers, occasionally punctuated by "Great is the son of Paso-Lomon!" or other shouts of approval.

With the release of tension, people who were debilitated or infirm began approaching Iaman. The scene was reminiscent of a line of children waiting to receive a new plaything. But only Iaman gave them what they needed. The healings were proceeding for about half an hour, when the LampLighter leaders arrived on the scene. Headquarters security men pushed their way through the crowd. The burly guards knocked the people aside without an afterthought. As they burst through to the place where Iaman sat, they spread out and pushed the people back. Behind them came the incensed LampLighter leaders. Motioning to the crowd, one shouted at Iaman, "Do you hear what they are saying?"

Iaman was unruffled. "In fact, I do."

Another leader could only blurt out indignantly, "Well?"

"Aren't you familiar with the Old Stories?" This reply of his made them angrier than ever, as they were experts in the Old Stories. Iaman continued, undaunted, "They say, 'You have taught infants to proclaim praise that is perfect.'"

Upon hearing these words, his questioner's face had reddened and his jaw tightened with seething anger. He only managed to shake his head in disgust, and quickly looked away. Iaman was aware of the wraith standing behind the man, maintaining his blindness to the Light and inciting him to hatred. The wraith left with the man, pleased at what had taken place.

Another LampLighter shouted at Iaman, "What gives you the right to destroy our headquarters? Can you perform a miracle to justify yourself?"

Before Iaman could answer, voices from the crowd shouted out, "What do you think he's been doing?"

"Afraid you'll lose your graft?" another accused.

"He healed me!" a young man fired back.

An elderly man, moving cautiously around one of the huge guards, motioned pleadingly with his arms. "He restored my vision!" With a jerk of his elbow, the guard dashed him to the ground.

At that, Iaman arose. Looking piercingly at each of the LampLighters, he challenged, "Destroy the Light's meeting place, and I will rebuild it in three days."

They laughed mockingly at him, "You are a lunatic! It took 46 years to build this place." They turned to the crowd. "Did you hear what he said? He's insane!"

The crowd reacted, "He is the son of Paso-Lomon!"

"The Light Team has arisen, led by Iaman."

Finally, someone shouted, "You are the crazy ones, if you think we will let you get out of here alive."

With that, the leaders motioned to the guards to leave. They once again pushed their way through the crowd. This time, it was the people who jostled the guards in their hasty departure. As they moved past the team, Steve overheard one LampLighter say to another, "He's a dead man!"

* * * * * * * *

The next morning, Iaman, the Team, and the following went back into Camden. They had spent the previous evening at Anthony's home in Pennsauken. On one of his business trips to Redlands, Anthony had heard Iaman speak and became a Light follower. Although Anthony lived a good distance from Redlands, he had struck up a relationship with Josh and had continued to correspond with him by way of mail couriers.

Upon entering the LampLighter's meeting place—the same area he had cleared the day before—Iaman sat down and began to teach as the people gathered around him. He had hardly begun when several of the LampLighter leaders approached him.

"By what authority do you do the things you are doing? Who gave you the right to do these things?"

The people in the crowd bristled; Iaman, however, was unmoved. "Let me ask you one question. If you will answer me, I'll tell you what you want to know." Not waiting for a response, he asked, "Where did the Lone Warrior get the right to do what he did? Was he sent by the Light, or did he come of his own accord?"

134

The crowd rumbled as the leaders huddled together. They whispered to each other. "If we say his authority was from the Light, he will say, 'Why didn't you follow him?' If we say his authority came only from himself, we'll have a riot on our hands, as many of the people think he spoke for the Light." Finally, they turned to Iaman and said, "We don't know; we can't tell."

Iaman shook his head, "Well, neither will I tell you by what authority I do these things." As simple as that, he turned back to the crowd and resumed his teaching.

"Let me tell you a story." Iaman began, "Once there was a landowner who had a ranch. He put a fence up around the property and built a barn and all that's necessary for raising ayugas. He rented his ranch to some tenants with the agreement that, at a future time, he would come to take his share of the profits. After a couple of seasons, he sent some of his hired hands to the ranch. The tenants roughed up some of them and threw them off the ranch, and others they killed. So the landowner sent some more men, and they received similar treatment. Finally, he thought to himself, 'I will send my son to them. I'm sure they will respect my son.' The tenants saw the son and conspired to kill him, reasoning, 'If we do away with the son, we will gain his inheritance.' So they killed the son and tossed his body off the property."

Iaman then asked the crowd a question, "What do you think the landowner will do to the tenants?"

A flurry of voices responded,"He will throw them out."

"He will kill the evil ranch hands."

"He will lease the ranch to somebody else."

". . . Somebody who will keep his part of the agreement."

"Do you recall what it says in the Old Stories? It says that the stone rejected by the builders ended up being the cornerstone for the building. This stone is the great stumbling block. Those who fall on this stone will be cut to shreds, and those on whom this stone falls will be crushed to dust."

He turned to the LampLighters with an ominous stare and warned them, "And I say to you, that the Country of the Light will be taken from you and turned over to those who will keep their part of the contract—those who produce the desired ends."

The LampLighters bitterly resented his criticism and wanted to arrest him, but feared the crowd, which now was spilling outside the meeting place. Instead, they made plans to trap him with an argument.

One of the leaders stepped toward Iaman and addressed him, "Teacher," he gestured to the LampLighters around him, "we know that you teach the way to the Light with truth and integrity. You aren't influenced by men, and don't care if you offend them. Help us with this question. Is it right to pay taxes to the government or not?"

Iaman saw through their scheme. "You charlatans! Why are you trying to trap me? Show me a coin."

One of them produced a coin.

Iaman asked him, "Whose picture do you see on the coin?"

The man responded, "The governor's."

Iaman answered, "Then give to the governor what belongs to him, and give to the Light that which is His due."

Impressed with the wisdom of his answer, some of the deriders went away.

Another group of LampLighters addressed him. "Teacher, Heston taught that if a married man has no children by his wife and then dies, his brother must marry the woman. What if there were seven brothers? The oldest married the woman and died before having a child with her. Then the next eldest married her and died, leaving her childless, and so on with each of the seven brothers. Finally the woman herself died. On the day when the dead are raised to life, whose wife will she be, if all of them had been married to her?"

Iaman answered, "You have it all wrong! I think it is because you need a better understanding of the Old Stories. When people are raised to life, they will be like creations of light, like original Light Team members. These beings don't marry. Regarding the dead being raised to life, have you not read what the Light has said?" Iaman looked at the man, who was silent. "He says He is the Light to Maharba, the Light to Caasi and the Light to Bocaj. Now, is He a Light to the living or a Light to the dead?"

"A good answer!" one of LampLighters responded. The other leaders looked at him and rolled their eyes. With each attempt to trip Iaman up, the LampLighters became increasingly frustrated. At the same time, the people watching him became more and more convinced that Iaman spoke the truth.

"Teacher, what is the greatest commandment of the law?" questioned another LampLighter.

Iaman responded, "To love the Light with all your heart, and with all your mind and with all your being." They nodded in agreement. "The second command is similar to it. You should love your neighbor as much as you love yourself. The entire teaching of the Old Stories can be summed up in these two commands."

The leaders stood quietly together, not knowing what to say next.

Iaman addressed them, "What do you think about the leader of the fifth Light Team? Whose descendent is he?"

"He will be Paso-Lomon's descendent," they answered.

"Why, then, do the Old Stories depict Paso-Lomon as referring to his offspring as 'My Master'? Don't the Old Stories quote Paso-Lomon as saying, 'The Light said to my Master, sit here at my right side, until I put your enemies under your feet?' If Paso-Lomon called him 'Master,' how could the leader of the fifth Light Team be Paso-Lomon's descendent?"

None of them were able to answer his questions, and from then on, no LampLighter ventured to ask him anything further.

But Iaman pursued his course, "Calamity awaits you LampLighter leaders. You hypocrites! You've taken away the keys to knowledge of the Light. Not only do you remain distant from the Light yourselves, you keep others from approaching Him.

"Calamity awaits you, LampLighters. You are like unmarked grave sites. People stumble over you without realizing it.

"Calamity awaits you, LampLighters. You set aside a tenth of everything you have for the Light, but ignore justice and service to the Light. You should have persevered in honoring the Light with your things, while also focusing your attention on justice and service.

"Calamity awaits you, LampLighters. You load people down with burdens impossible to carry, and refuse to even lift a finger to help them.

"Calamity awaits you, LampLighters. You love the most important places in the meetinghall, and the respectful greetings you demand in public.

"Calamity awaits you, LampLighters. You build tombs for past Light Team members whom your forefathers killed. Your actions testify that your fathers were murderers, and that you approve of their actions. You kill agents of the Light and persecute His followers. I assure you, this generation will be accountable for it all."

Iaman stopped his diatribe and looked at the crowd. They were silent as stones. No one had ever addressed the LampLighters in such a fashion. The LampLighters themselves stood there immobilized. Looking down, Iaman shook his head slowly from side to side, and began again. "O Camden, Camden." His eyes glistened. "You kill the Light's messengers, and beat and disgrace those sent to you. How often I have desired to gather you up as a paloma gathers her chicks under her wings. . . ." Looking up, he said quietly, "But you were not willing." His voice gained strength. "So, see now the situation you are in. For by no means will you see me from now on, until you say, 'Fortunate is he who comes in the name of the Light.'"

Most of the LampLighters retreated, except for the few who either believed his message, or were genuinely interested in finding out more.

Iaman turned to his team, as the crowd listened. "Be careful of the Lamp-Lighters. They like the respect they receive in the community, and always choose the seats of honor at feasts and Lightday meetings. They make a great public display of their monologues to the Light, while taking advantage of widows and robbing their homes. They will receive punishment commensurate with their behavior."

Chapter 34
AN EXTRAVAGANT GESTURE

As the moon rose behind the men and gradually made its way over the city, the dark sky was dotted with tiny flecks of white light. From the hills just outside town, the Team could see the city lights. That evening, they retreated back to Anthony's home. They sat together in his large living room, resting from their day of traveling together, listening to Iaman, and teaching the people in groups. The confrontations with the LampLighters seemed to be intensifying. The leaders had become bolder in their attacks against Iaman while Iaman sharpened his indictments of the lack of substance behind what they taught. The people looked to Iaman as to how to respond to the Lamp-Lighters' affronts, but his peaceful demeanor indicated they should simply listen, taking no direct action. Observing Iaman during this time, their trust in the Light increased.

As they sat together, some finished up their dinners, while others sipped cool drinks of fermented reds. The mood was light and the conversation casual; all were in a relaxed frame of mind. Amy had been their hostess, and as was typical for her, she had prepared an excellent board. To her delight, the men praised her, one by one, as she poured refills of the drinks. Jay sat at the table with Iaman, and they quietly laughed over the good times they had shared together. Clarence and Edward sat at the table with them, enjoying learning about their leader's youth. It seemed that Iaman used to be very good at wood sculpting. Jay said that he was the best in town, although Iaman shrugged the compliment off. They talked of their times swimming together, riding ayugas on Race Day, and working for Iaman's father.

About that time, Kelly walked quietly into the room. She had been a follower on the fringe of the group ever since Cyrus left to follow Iaman. Before she came into the room, she hesitated for a moment at the door, as if unsure whether she should enter.

Clarence leaned over to Edward. "Who's that?"

"I know her," said Cyrus. He smiled warmly at Kelly. The rest of them did not put together the fact that she had been one of 'his girls.' The connection of Cyrus with a bordello seemed a distant memory.

Finally, she gathered courage and walked across the room to Iaman. She was carrying an ornately decorated porcelain jar. As she came alongside him, the conversation dropped off.

Iaman turned to her, "What is it, Kelly?" He could see her distress.

Without answering, she knelt down by Him and carefully removed the lid from the jar. Instantly, the room filled with a beautiful, light, fresh fragrance. Tears began to flow freely down her face.

Iaman pushed his chair out from the table and turned to her. She nervously looked in his eyes, trying to hold back her tears. He looked at her reassuringly and leaned his head forward. Kelly raised the jar and poured a generous amount of perfume on his head. The perfume rolled across his head, down his face and onto his neck and clothing. She paused for a second to be sure the liquid would not get into his eyes, and then poured the rest of the contents over his head.

Several of the team became angry. The perfume must have been worth over 100 credits. Edward rose to his feet and spoke up first. "Why would you waste money like this? Don't you realize its worth?"

"This could have been sold, and the money given to the poor!" shouted Bertrand indignantly. Others agreed.

Iaman turned to them. His head glistened with the perfume, his face streaked with its purple color. "Why do you bother this woman?" he calmly asked. He turned to Kelly. "She has done a generous thing for me." He smiled at her, and she lowered her eyes. "You will always have poor people around you, and there will always be opportunities to help them. But what this woman has done is to place perfume on my body in preparation for my burial. What a beautiful thing she has done!" He looked back at the Team. "In the future, when our story is sung among the nations, the tale of her kindness to me will be told in memory of her."

* * * * * * * * *

Later that evening, Steve and Michael sat with their backs to the fireplace in which only glowing embers remained. Seeing them together, Albert walked up quietly, studying the fire. The rest of the team were asleep. Steve grabbed a stick and began to stir the embers. Michael turned and looked at him.

"His burial—he said she prepared him for his burial." Lupe looked at Steve, wanting to hear what he thought about that.

"Do you have any idea what he meant?" was Steve's reply.

"Well, do you remember that old LampLighter chant?"

Steve shook his head. "I never was much of a LampLighter."

"Well, it's from the Old Stories. I committed it to memory many years ago, because it always seemed so strange to me. The LampLighters expect the coming of the greatest Light Team Leader, but they anticipate a political leader . . . something along the lines of what Lupe is always talking about. But listen to the words of the old chant. . . . It's about the coming of the Light

Team Leader." Michael looked up for a moment. Then, with concern in his eyes as he thought through the words he was repeating, the chant tumbled forth.

He was like a Lamb led to the slaughter,
Yet he did not open once his mouth.
Like a sheep before the shearers, silent,
Still he did not open once his mouth.

See my servant, raised up:
Beaten beyond recognition, is he still a man?
See my servant, man of grief:
He will be raised up in glory, shrouded now in pain.
See my servant, kings shut their mouths.
Seeing mystery, understanding what they have not heard.
See my servant, no desire he brings,
Like one from whom men hide their faces,
No esteem is spawn.

He was like a Lamb led to the slaughter,
Yet he did not open once his mouth.
Like a sheep before the shearers, silent,
Still he did not open once his mouth.

Still my servant, despised:
Stricken by the Light himself, he carries our sorrow.
Still my servant, eyes in pain:
Crushed for our iniquity, pierced for our rejection.
Still my servant, man of sorrows:
His wounds heal us, punishment escapes us; we have peace.
Still my servant, lamb led to the slaughter:
Straying sheep should all face judgment—
Not the shepherd man!

He was like a Lamb led to the slaughter,
Yet he did not open once his mouth.
Like a sheep before the shearers, silent,
Still he did not open once his mouth.

The Light's offspring, alone:
His descendants: are there any? He leaves only blood.
The Light's offspring, afflicted:
He was cut off from the living, stricken by the Light.
The Light's offspring, caused to suffer:

His descendants? There are many; I owe all to him.
The Light's offspring, shrinks not from his task:
Sacrifice for us, no less; we prosper at his hand.

He was like a Lamb led to the slaughter,
Yet he did not open once his mouth.
Like a sheep before the shearers, silent,
Still he did not open once his mouth.

As Michael related the chant, the gravity of the words struck him. One moment, he felt he understood a truth he hadn't seen before; the next moment, he just shook his head as he spoke, not quite sure of its connection to Iaman.

"That's incredible!" Steve replied. "Do you really think it's talking about Iaman?"

Albert, who listened intently, suddenly spoke up, "The first time I met Iaman was on my Barstow run."

Michael nodded since he'd heard this one before; the other men were familiar with the story as well.

Albert continued, "Iaman talked a lot about the Old Stories, but one thing that stuck with me was that he said the next Light Team leader would be 'a man of sorrows, acquainted with grief.' Sounds a lot like the chant to me."

"It has to be about Iaman," said Michael. "I wonder if we have come to Camden just so he can be killed?"

"'Beaten beyond recognition,' and 'leaves only blood'—is that what lies ahead of us?" Steve replied.

"It's obvious it would come at the hands of the LampLighters," said Albert.

"His confrontations have stirred them up like a stick in an ahshaker's lair," Michael replied. "The attack has got to come from them."

"We need to be watching for them," cautioned Steve. "Obviously, he sees it coming."

"Yeah, but he seems reconciled to it. In the chant, it says he didn't even open up his mouth. Seems that's his current posture." Michael shook his head with regret. "I see no fight in him, if you get my meaning. He's been battling quite a bit with words—but no physical fight." Michael paused. "Remember he even taught us that if somebody hits you, you should let him hit you again!"

"He said himself to 'turn the other cheek.' Sure doesn't sound like fightin' words to me." Steve shook his head. "I figure he means to let it happen."

"Well I've counted four times now that he's talked about dying: the time you tried to stop him, two times along the way, and now tonight," said Michael.

"Well, right or wrong, I'm not going to let it happen. I've been carrying my knife for about two weeks now—ever since we started toward L.A." Steve looked at Albert and Michael. "Will you back me up, if it should come to it?"

141

Albert shrugged and gave him a quizzical look.

Michael looked back at him, puzzled. Steve could just make out his eyes as he turned toward the dying embers of the fire. "I don't know for sure. I guess so: it depends on what Iaman does. . . . No tellin'."

Steve looked back at Michael, his set jaw accentuating the muscles of his face. Through clenched teeth, he vowed, "Well, I won't let it happen. I would die before I would let him be taken."

Chapter 35
PLANS FOR BETRAYAL

thgiL knelt before LiarLight. "The time is at hand for your triumph. The LampLighters fume with rage: they have been humiliated before the people. The betrayer has made up his mind, and at this moment seeks out the Lamp-Lighters, asking, 'What will you give me if I hand Iaman over to you?'" thgiL was nervous as she spoke. She would no longer be resigned as before. Her mind waffled as to the rightness of what she was doing—rightness in the sense of what was right for herself. Nevertheless, she steadfastly held to LiarLight's plan; she feared being detected of any wavering.

"Iaman would set himself up against me?" LiarLight gave no indication that thgiL was even present. "The fool! Perhaps I cannot corrupt him, but those around him haven't the ability to resist me."

thgiL said nothing. Statuesque she knelt, moving not a muscle. In the past, she hadn't really feared LiarLight. Her existence caused her no fear, for she lived only to serve her master. With her free choice, came fear. Now, she could be corrupted by the other side. There was also the possibility of experiencing LiarLight's wrath for disobedience. In some ways, the free choice obstructed her view of LiarLight's desires. thgiL found she often could not distinguish her own desires from those of her master; this realization only heightened her fears.

LiarLight surveyed thgiL's disoriented mind. He delighted in her new-found fears. He wondered about the Light's reason for instilling free choice in humanity. Knowing the Light as he did, it was certainly not to drive them to fear. *What other reason could there be? Could choice also drive someone to love? That seemed to be what the Light desired from His followers. Were those really the two sides of the coin: fear and love? How interesting.* His mind moved back to his servant before him and the events at hand.

"See to it that the man carries out the plot. The betrayal must continue as I have planned."

"As you have planned?" was thgiL's reply.

thgiL departed from LiarLight's presence and went to the scene of the betrayal. Several of her thgiLers reported to her before prompting Bertrand to hand Iaman over to the LampLighters. *His payment—30 credits—is a small price,* she thought.

Bertrand walked away with the money in his pocket. When asked at what time the betrayal should occur, he mentioned, "We're often alone in the evenings—that could be the best time. There wouldn't be many people around, and they would need to use stealth."

Evening it would be.

thgiL smiled as she read Bertrand's thoughts. All that remained was for Bertrand to accomplish what he intended to do.

Chapter 36
A FINAL MEAL TOGETHER

The following morning, Josh and Seth approached Iaman. Seth spoke up, "We've been wondering: where do you want to celebrate the Deliverance?" The Deliverance was a time when the Light saved His followers from the Government of Maxima. The Light followers were taken into a form of slavery. Heston had attempted to get the leader of Maxima to release the people. With a variety of plagues, the Light punished the Maximan people, but ultimately the leader refused to let the Light followers go. Finally, the Light killed all the firstborn males of the nation. They celebrated Deliverance Day as the time when the Light saved the Light followers who put vatellor's blood on their front door. Original Light Team members carried out the Light's punishment, but those with the blood on the door were "delivered" from the destruction. The Light followers celebrated this occasion on a yearly basis with a special meal.

"Go and look for Anthony," directed Iaman. "Tell him, 'My team and I will celebrate the Deliverance at your house tonight.'"

Josh and Seth left and did as Iaman instructed, making arrangements for the evening meal.

* * * * * * * *

When evening came, the team gathered again at Anthony's house. They sat down to the meal traditionally served on Deliverance Day. The gathering was quiet, almost solemn, as the Team could sense a marked difference in Iaman's demeanor: his face was pale, his attention seemed elsewhere, and he said very little. Occasionally, they said something to one another, but everyone waited for him to share what was on his mind. Finally, he spoke up.

Iaman cast a glance around the room. "One of you here, eating with me, will betray me to the LampLighters."

Shocked, they echoed their replies, one after another. "Leader, it can't be me?" Each response was half-assertion and half-pleading to not be the betrayer. There was a brief pause, upon which Bertrand looked up and wiped his mouth. "Surely, you don't mean me, Leader?"

Iaman's piercing gaze caught Bertrand's glance and held him captive. "Is

145

this your response?" There was no question as to which blinked first: truth probed falsehood and found it wanting.

Silence that was hard to bear came over the group once again.

thgiL had been observing the scene. She quickly began to work on the minds of the team. *I bet I know who it is*, thought Edward, *that big talking Lupe.*

Albert looked at Edward. *That worthless rascal. What has he contributed to our work!* he thought.

Prompted by thgiL, others thought similar things. At their corner of the table, Josh began arguing with Bertrand. "What a worthless member of this team you've turned out to be!"

"Like you've contributed so much?" countered Michael.

"At least Josh and I have given ourselves wholly over to Iaman," responded Seth, coming to Josh's defense. "All you do is sit around and think."

Bertrand sat up, "What have you guys actually done?" There was silence. "Yeah, I thought so. At least I've kept on top of the money matters!"

"You know, I've been wondering what's been happening to the money," Clarence answered. "When I kept the books at S&A Dry Goods, the accounts always balanced."

"Gimme a break!" Lupe interjected. "I'm the only one who has any clue as to the Leader's plans—"

"You mean your plans!" Michael interrupted. "You are always trying to make Iaman's plans fit your plans. I am the only one who has been discerning enough to follow Iaman's plans."

Steve couldn't take it any more: he expected Iaman to come to his defense, confirming to the team that he himself was the most important member, based on what Iaman had said about him.

Iaman, however, remained silent.

But before Steve could speak up, Albert said loudly, "What a bunch of losers!"

Iaman waited no longer. Without saying a word, he got up from his seat and stripped to his undergarments. Instantly, the room was silent. He then wrapped a towel around himself and filled a bowl with water. One by one, he went to each team member, removed his shoes, and washed his feet.

Steve was still fuming by the time Iaman got to him. Some of his anger spilled out as Iaman knelt before him. "Are you going to wash my feet?" he blurted out.

"Right now, you don't understand what I am doing, but later it will become clear to you."

"There is no way you will ever wash my feet!"

146

Iaman responded seriously, "If I do not wash your feet, then you can no longer be a member of my Light Team."

Steve became flustered. "Well then, don't just wash my feet—wash my head and my hands, too!" he pleaded.

"The rest of your body is clean, as you have bathed today. All of you are clean—except for one," Iaman replied.

Iaman finished washing Steve's feet and moved on to Bertrand, who would not look at him. Bertrand thought over what he was about to do, and couldn't wait to leave. A feeling of loathing came over him as he looked down on Iaman barely clothed, kneeling before him. His hands wet in the dirty water, the towel hanging over his shoulder. *What kind of leader is he?* Bertrand thought. *Is this any way for a leader to act?* The image of servitude repulsed Bertrand.

Iaman moved on to Josh and washed the final team member's feet. No one moved or even looked at each other. When he was finished, he rinsed his hands in clean water, dried them, and put on his clothes. At last, he took his position at the table again.

"Do you understand what I just did for you?"

No one spoke or looked in his direction.

"You refer to me as the Leader of the Light Team, and you are right to do so, because I am. Consider this, however. If this same Leader—even the one who will defeat LiarLight—would wash your feet, shouldn't you also wash one another's feet? No servant is greater than his master; no messenger is greater than the one who sent him. Now that you know these things, you will be fulfilled if you do them."

The men's minds went back to the fact that one of them would betray Iaman. Michael leaned over to Steve, who was at Iaman's right hand, and whispered, "Ask him who'll betray him to the LampLighters."

Steve leaned to Iaman and asked, "Who is it that will betray you?"

Loudly enough for all of them to hear, Iaman answered, "It is the one to whom I will give this bread, once I have dipped it into the dish." He then took a piece of bread, dipped it into the dish and handed it to Bertrand. As soon as Iaman handed the bread over to him, LiarLight himself entered Bertrand's mind.

"Do what you are going to do quickly," said Iaman.

Bertrand took the piece of bread from Iaman, ate it as he stared into his eyes, got up, and left. But the men didn't understand what was happening. The Light Himself dulled their understanding. They watched as Bertrand went out the door, thinking that perhaps he was getting something else for the dinner.

Iaman turned back to the group, anguish all over his face. His eyes looked at the rest of his team with an appealing pride and love. He had worked with them for a significant amount of time now. He wanted to be confident in them in spite of their foibles. Much would be given over to them, men with very human limitations. Still this was the plan that had been in place since the beginning of time; it was the Light's plan and so would prevail.

With a sad smile, Iaman addressed them, "I have looked forward to sharing this meal with you all. Because I will not eat the Deliverance meal again until it is celebrated in its completeness in the Country of the Light."

He picked up a loaf of bread and passed it to Steve on his right, indicating that he should break off a piece and pass it on to Michael. "This bread represents my body, which will be broken for you. Whoever eats this bread will live forever in the Light. Whenever you break this bread, remember me, your friend, who allowed his body to be broken for you, and I will be present with you."

When all of them had taken a piece of the bread and eaten it, he picked up his glass of fermented red. Once again he passed it to Steve, and indicated that he should take a sip. "This red signifies my blood, which will be shed on your behalf. My shed blood will be the weapon by which LiarLight is defeated. Whenever you drink this red, remember me, your friend, who allowed his blood to be shed for you, and I will surely be in your midst." Once they had all had a drink, they sat together quietly for a few moments, to thank the Light for His deliverance.

Iaman then took a deep breath, as if something were weighing heavily upon him. "The time has come for the Leader of the Light Team, the Offspring of the Light, to receive renown. I will not be with you for much longer. You will look for me, but I won't be found, as you cannot go where I am going."

The words shot through Lupe's brain like a knife. He felt his body suddenly go cold. What of his political plans? *What about the Country of the Light?*

"Why can't we go where you are going?" Steve questioned, distraught.

"No, you cannot follow me where I am going, but later you will follow," Iaman replied.

Iaman then dropped another bombshell, "Tonight, you will all desert me. The Old Stories predict, 'The Light will smite the vatellorman, and the vatellors will scatter.' But after I rise to life, I will go back to Bernardino to meet with you there."

Steve thought back to the argument over who among them was the greatest. *Desert him!* he thought. His thoughts broke into voice, "I would never!" Standing, he waived his hand, gesturing to the rest of the team. His voice cracked with anger and loyalty. "Even if these guys desert you, I'll never do so! Never would I leave you!"

Iaman stood and looked him straight in the eye. His look alone filled Steve with fear. "Mark my words: before the paloma crows tomorrow morning, you will disown me. Three times, you will say you don't even know me!"

Steve's mouth dropped open, and his hands shook. Through gritted teeth, he doggedly affirmed, "I would never say I don't know you." He poked his own chest with his finger. "I would die with you."

The others stood by him and echoed Steve's words. Iaman paused for a second and sat down again, leaving them standing. After a moment, they joined him. Iaman watched as each returned to his seat.

"Be calm, and don't be worried. Trust in the Light, and trust in me. The Country of the Light contains many places, one of which I will prepare for each of you. I wouldn't tell you this if it weren't true. If I leave you to prepare a place for you, then I will also return to bring you there with me. And you know how to get to the place where I am going."

The whole evening had weighed heavily on Edward. First, Iaman was leaving, and they couldn't go with him. Next, he said they would follow him later. Then, he was leaving, and they knew how to get there. His childlike trust was stretched to the limit.

"Leader, we don't know where you are going," he admitted. "How will we know the way to go, if we don't know where you'll be?"

Iaman looked at him kindly. "I am the way to go, for I am the truth. No one will find his way to the Light except if he goes through me. Because you know me, you know the Light. From now on, you do know the Light, and have seen Him."

Seth was confused. "Leader, show the Light to us; then we will understand."

"I have been with you for all this time, Seth, and you still don't know who I am? Anyone who has seen me has indeed seen the Light. The Light is in me, and I am in the Light.

"My words are not the words of a man, just as the things I have done are not the works of a man. I am in the Light and the Light is in me: the Light will fill those who trust in me as he has filled me, and they will do even greater things than I have done. Anything that you ask the Light for in my name, He will do for you. In this way, the power of the Light will be demonstrated through the Offspring of the Light."

The team stared at him, astonished. Iaman now had a captive audience; they waited for him to continue, like students cramming for a final exam.

"I won't ever abandon you without providing for you. I will come back to you after a while, but then I will have to leave, and the world will never

149

see me again. But the Light will send another to you, one who will help you and be your guide. He will teach you what you need to know, and help you recall what I have said and the things we have done. But remember, because I live, you will also live. You will live in me, and I in you, in the same way that I am in the Light, and the Light is in me.

"I want to leave you with peace. My peace isn't the same kind of peace that the world gives. The peace I give you will build your confidence, so don't be afraid. I am leaving you, but I will see you again. If you love me, enjoy the fact that I am going to be with the Light. You have heard this now, before it happens, so that you will remember my words with understanding, and will trust in me."

Then Iaman's face took on a serious tone. "The king of this world is coming. In reality, he has no power over me. However, the world will understand that I do the things I am about to do because of my love for the Light; I do all that He commands me to do. . . ." He allowed his words to sink in a bit. "It's time for us to leave."

Iaman arose and walked toward the door. Dazed, the men moved outside with him. The stars burned through the blackness of the night. Leaving Anthony's house, they made their way east across town to Cinnaminson Garden, to a place known to all of them. As they went, Iaman began teaching them. He had told them this time was coming and prepared them for it the best he could in the brief and busy time they had spent together. However, the men felt like they were definitely not ready for this exam, and they anxiously accepted any last minute instructions their teacher would give them.

Tonight Iaman used an easily remembered analogy of a tree.

"I am the true tree. The Light is the gardener who tends the tree. He cuts away any branches that will not produce fruit and tends to those that will. He prunes and cares for these branches; whereas the branches that are cut away, die, as they are not connected to the tree. But those that remain, produce fruit; and there is no fruit without attachment to the tree. Just as I am the tree, each of you are the branches. You bring honor to the gardener—the Light—by producing fruit, and you bring honor to me—the tree—by producing fruit. Branches do not choose the tree: the tree chooses or produces the branches. You will remain with me, like branches from the tree, if you keep the commandments of the Light. The greatest commandment of the Light is that you love one another."

It was late and few people were out; most were at home with their families, celebrating the Deliverance. The team continued walking through the town, their pace steady but not hurried. Iaman walked amongst them, at times beside them, at times in front, at times walking backward, but always continuing his instruction.

"Don't be surprised if people hate you. If this world hates you, remember that they hated me first, and no student is greater than his teacher. But also remember that I chose you from this world, to be apart from it. You no longer belong to this world. The time will come when you will be forbidden to enter LampLighter meetings. Those who conspire to kill you, or who do kill you, will be praised as working on behalf of the Light. But these acts are evidence that they know neither the Light nor me. I tell you this so that when these things occur, you will remember that I told you.

"I know that when I told you I was going away, it made you dejected. But don't grieve for me, as I am going to the One who sent me. It is better for you that I do go away, as the helper and comforter will come to you. He will be closer to you than a brother, and you will find no finer advocate than him.

"There is so much more that I would like to tell you, but you can't be expected to take it all in right now. Much of what I have told you has been in the form of stories, but understand this now: I came from the Light, and I came into the world. The Light will do what you ask of Him because of your love for me."

His words clicked with Clarence. "Now you are speaking clearly. It's obvious that you understand everything. You know, this makes me believe that you came from the Light!"

Iaman looked on them as a parent knowing the limitations of his children. "Do you trust me now, Clarence? Shortly, you all will scatter. You will run for your homes and leave me. But I will not be alone: the Light Himself is with me. Once again, I have told you this not to make you downcast, but so that you will remember, and know what to do when the time comes. This world will surely cause you to suffer." Iaman took on a look of determination that gave them hope. "But don't lose heart: I have overcome this world!"

Iaman stopped where he stood. They found that they were on the outskirts of the garden. He raised his arms up to the sky and began to speak to the Light.

"The time has come to bring honor to Your Son. Please give me the same honor in Your presence that I had together with You before the making of this world. I have made known to these men the message You gave to me. They belong to You, as You gave them to me. They have grasped Your message, and know that it is true that I came from You. They trust in me as the one You have sent.

"I ask that You would care for them. I do not ask for the entire world, but for those You have given to me, for they are Yours. Now, I am about to come to You. Although I will no longer be in this world, they will remain. Please keep them safe by Your power. Make them one: give them unity, just as You and I are one!

151

"I ask that You would care not only for them, but also for those who will trust in me through their message. May they also be united. May I be in them and You in me, so that they can be completely one. Their unity will show the world that I came from You and that You love them as You love me!

"You have given them to me, and I ask that they may be with me where I am going. May they see the honor that You will give me as a reward for their trust.

"Dear Light, although this world does not know You, I know You, and they trust that You sent me to the world. I have made You known to them, and I will continue to do so, that Your love for me might be in them, and I might be in them."

Iaman stood silently, with his hands raised for several moments. Slowly, he lowered them to his side. He turned to his team, who were standing together behind him. His demeanor changed to one of concern and distress. "Speak to the Light!" he pleaded, "Ask Him to strengthen you for the ordeal you are about to face."

Moving away from them to a lonely place, Iaman fell to the ground, his demeanor changed, seemingly frightened. Beads of sweat began to form on his brow, and large droplets began to course down his face. It didn't take long for his shirt to become totally soaked. His face was anguished as he spoke to the Light.

"Oh, dear Light, I know that I have come for this moment." He paused, as if to pluck up his courage. "I ask that what I am about to face be removed from me, yet . . . I am here to do Your bidding. Therefore, it is Your desire that I fulfill . . . not my own."

At this time, one of the original members of the Light Team appeared to him and strengthened him. Iaman continued on for some time, asking that he might complete the Light's plan. After a while, he got up and went back to the team. To his dismay, he found them sleeping.

He roused them vigorously. "Wake up! Why are you sleeping? Ask the Light to protect you from LiarLight's trap!" Startled, they sat up and looked sheepishly at each other.

He withdrew from them several paces, fell to his knees and held his head in his hands. In a low voice, he spoke, "If it is within Your plan, remove the suffering I am about to face." He slowly pulled his hands away from his face and extended them upwards. "Still, it is You who are in control: I will obey Your commands." He did his best to completely resign himself, laying aside the emotions that waged war within him.

After a while, he again went back to his team. Their emotional ordeal had exhausted them, and he found them sleeping again. This time, he grabbed Steve by the shoulders. "Wake up! Won't you keep watch with me for but one

152

hour? Ask the Light to protect you from the trial that is ahead! It is LiarLight's desire to sift you like flour. Be on your guard."

Steve, shocked out of his sleepy stupor, nodded his head. "I will, Iaman; I will."

Once again, Iaman left them. A short distance away, he stopped, his body tensed and hands raised to the sky. His open hands now clenched into fists as he lowered them to his chest. After a moment, his body relaxed. He had made his petition before the Light, and the Light had given him his answer. Relaxed, but with renewed courage, he went back to the team. They were sleeping again. Resignedly, he said to himself, *"Are you still taking it easy? Can you still be sleeping? Well, never mind: the time has come for the Leader of the Light Team to be turned over to LiarLight's agents."* He turned to find a crowd of men with torches approaching. Looking back to his team, he raised his voice. "Get up! The betrayer is coming!"

It was around two o'clock in the morning. Clouds had rolled in and a few stars fought their way through the haze of the Camden evening. A smear of light stood in place of the moon. At Iaman's prompt, the men staggered to their feet and tried to shake off their weariness. For a moment, they were disoriented, wondering what the commotion was.

In the distance a group of men was approaching. They moved forward like an oozing mass with red flames. Interestingly, they were dead quiet. They had been instructed by the LampLighter leaders to call as little attention to themselves as possible. As much as they could, they had kept to untraveled roads, so the light they were carrying and their numbers would not arouse the attention of the people. They feared Iaman's following.

Leading them was Bertrand. He knew about Cinnaminson Garden as he had been there in the past with Iaman and the Team. With him were soldiers, the elite of those who guarded the LampLighter headquarters and a rabble of others. They walked briskly, were armed, and carried torches and lanterns.

"I'll walk in amongst them and go up to the leader and kiss him," Bertrand reminded them. "Arrest the one I kiss!"

The Team turned to face the oncoming crowd. Steve quickly noted that they were outnumbered about ten to one. Bertrand stepped out from among them and walked up to Iaman. "Peace be with you," he said in a too loud voice and then kissed him.

Iaman knew what was happening. He allowed Bertrand to approach him and kiss him. It would be the last kiss he would ever receive.

"Is it with a kiss that you are betraying me?" Iaman looked at Bertrand. Bertrand immediately began to feel that what he was doing was wrong, but he put his feelings aside and continued with his plan. He did not respond, hardening his resolve.

Iaman then raised his voice for the entire group to hear. "Who are you looking for?" he asked.

Several of the group shouted out in a disjointed chorus, "Iaman from Barstow!"

"I am he!" Iaman responded.

At his words, the entire mob moved backwards and fell to the ground. It was as if they lost their footing from an earthquake or a stiff wind. The Team looked on amazed. Gradually they got to their feet again.

"Who are you looking for?" Iaman once again addressed them.

In disarray, again they responded, "Iaman from Barstow!"

"If you are after me, then let these others go!"

Steve could see what was developing, but he was ready. He lunged forward to the member of the gang closest to him with his knife. He jabbed right at the man's face, but the man saw Steve come at him and moved quickly to the side. The knife came down, slicing off the man's ear. Steve lost his balance and lay on his side on the ground while the other man writhed and held the side of his head. Three of the mob pounced on Steve and grabbed his knife away from him. Simultaneously, several of the team moved forward, "Shall we attack them?" Clarence shouted.

Michael looked at the crowd. "Bertrand?" he breathed.

Several of the gang who came for Iaman drew their daggers. They clinked in the darkness.

Iaman's voice boomed above the tussle. "Stop this!" Turning to the team he shouted, "Put your weapons away. Do you think I will run from the suffering the Light has put before me? If I chose, I could call on the Light and he would surround me with the warriors immortal! But then, the Old Stories wouldn't come true. This is the way it must happen." He kneeled down by the injured man. The man held his severed ear against the side of his head. Iaman leaned down, touched the side of his face restoring his ear and rose to his feet again.

"Why did you come with weapons to take me like a criminal? Haven't I been teaching in the LampLighter meeting hall regularly? You didn't arrest me there. Yet, this is what was predicted in he Old Stories, and it must come true."

With that, the rabble moved forward and grabbed him. They took him off to meet with the LampLighter leaders. The team scattered like dirrats whose nest had been discovered.

The crowd, with Iaman in tow, surged through the streets of the city. Their destination was Dermod's home, the current director of the LampLighters. After Bertrand had informed the LampLighters when he would "turn Iaman in," the leaders decided to meet at Dermod's house and wait. The crowd arrived at the back of the dwelling and stood on a large covered patio. Iaman stood in the midst of them, a bit jostled, but no worse for the arrest.

Inside the LampLighter leaders reveled in their unfolding plan. Dermod raised his hands to silence them quickly. Self-righteously he addressed his fellow leaders. "Let us remember why we are doing what we are doing. This man has discredited himself with his claims. He claims to be an offspring of the Light! He claims to have the power to defeat LiarLight! He claims to have the authority to reverse Lightday traditions. He is confusing the people with his teaching. They are leaving us—we who control the truth, or should I say *regulate* the truth—to follow his teachings!" The anger welled up in him. He raised his finger and shook it in the air. "He is the lowest form of liar; he lies about the Light!" Dermod went on like this for some time. He hoped to stir up the LampLighter Leaders, so that those outside would begin to get impatient and take justice into their own hands. Dermod achieved his goals—soon any one of those in the room would have killed Iaman with their bare hands. By the time they left the house, Iaman had been the victim of severe abuse.

As events developed inside the house, the crowd outside murmured amongst themselves. Some had started a fire in a fire pit at the back of the yard.

After first fleeing, Steve circled around and followed the crowd to Dermod's house. He was ready to die for Iaman, evidenced by his attack on the man in the garden. But Iaman was giving himself into their hands. Steve was angry and confused. He unobtrusively worked his way up to the blazing bonfire. Hay bales had been positioned around the fire for people to sit on. At that moment, several guards were sitting warming themselves by the fire.

The discussion around the campfire centered on Iaman and then moved to the recent trial of Elie and his followers. Apparently Elie pleaded guilty to the murder of the seven government workers. In graphic detail he described how he personally slit each of their throats while calling out the name of one of the LampLighters killed in the "Sopa Seven" incident. He showed no remorse, said he would kill again, and challenged the court to apply the Justice laws to him. He wanted to be a martyr, the most recent to die for his cause. He claimed he would then become immortal.

The crowd had mixed feelings about Elie's actions. They wanted to see justice done in the case of the Sopa Seven, but at the same time, the memories of the 21 years of war were fresh in their minds. Surely their lives were better than they had been even 10 years ago. They had no desire to return to days past. The consensus was, "Elie's a walking dead man."

The overseer of Dermod's household had sent several of the servants out to monitor the mob. A young woman came up to the fire to investigate what was happening there. The guards were there, and the people seemed in control, so she settled down by the fire for a moment. Surveying the faces of the men around the fire, she recognized several of the guards and exchanged a smile. Her eyes moved to Steve whose sidelong glances betrayed his efforts

155

to remain unrecognized. Picking up on this fact, she studied him all the more. Finally she leapt to her feet.

"Hey! Aren't you one of the followers of that guy they arrested?"

Those around the fire looked over at him, hardly paying any attention.

Steve looked down and shook his head. Nervously he laughed out, "Hey, I don't even know the man."

The guards turned away, but another man picked up on the girl's observation. "Yes, you are one of them. You're one of his close followers." The guards turned and looked at Steve, this time more interested.

"You're crazy!" Steve answered quickly. "I'm not *one of them*," he said disdainfully.

As they sat, the morning began to arrive. Shards of sunlight shot from behind the eastern mountains. Burn was about to light up the day.

Steve had made been making a bit of nervous small talk with a man who sat by him at the fire. Another man who had been by the fire the entire evening overheard their conversation and both the woman's and the man's questioning of Steve. He knew that Iaman and his Team were from Redlands. Having grown up there himself, he also knew some of the local ways of speaking, the idiom and expressions they would use there. Finally he couldn't hold back any longer. He rose to his feet and turned to those who were standing around the fire.

"There is no doubt that you are a follower of his. You're from Redlands. I can tell by the way you talk!"

Steve had been blindsided. He was shocked out of the conversation he had been having. He jumped to his feet and threw his hands into the air. He shouted, "What are you talking about!" he screamed. He put his hand over his heart and pleaded with them. "Light damn me dead if I know him." They continued to stare at him. "Damn it, I don't know what you are talking about!"

At that moment Burn the White peaked over the hill, beginning another day. A lone paloma stood in his cage and crowed a single time.

The entire crowd had turned to see what the shouting was about. Iaman turned as well, and his eyes met Steve's. It was a simple look but only Iaman knew the real commotion that was occurring. Hearing the cock crow and seeing Iaman, switched on a spotlight in Steve's brain. *Hadn't Iaman predicted this. Didn't I say it would never happen? What now?* he thought. He stood there stymied for a moment, and felt like he would fall over. He started to fall and put out a step to stop himself, then another, then another. Before he knew it, he was running for all he was worth. The sobs welled up in his chest. His voice cried out in agony. He put his hands to his face and wept bitterly as he ran. Suddenly his foot hit a rock and he was thrown to the ground. He thudded and ground to a stop. Finally, his breath returned to him and sobs wracked his body. He had done the worst thing he could imagine. He denied he even knew the one he loved more than any other.

Chapter 37
A VICTORY FOR THE LAMPLIGHTERS

To the crowd, the shouting around the fire had proved an interesting diversion, but nothing happened as a result. No one followed Steve. He was alone. Most of the people had not really been able to hear what Steve had said, so they just turned back to what they were doing.

After a while, the crowd began to get restless. Some of those nearest to Iaman started egging on the guards. They too were bored and began to taunt Iaman. He sat on the ground with his arms around his knees, and his head down. The taunting gradually escalated from comments to accusations, from accusations to jostling, from jostling to beating. At this point Iaman was on his feet. The guards had tied a scarf around his head to cover his eyes. Three of them would then circle around him. Suddenly one would jump forward and punch him in the face. The crowd around cheered. The guard who hit him would then feign respect saying, "Did you know it was gonna be me, oh great Leader of the Light?" The crowd laughed. This went on for several minutes. One after another, Iaman took the blows. By this time blood streamed from his nose and mouth. His left ear was swollen and red. After a while one guard got bored with this sport. He acted as if he was going to walk away, then he reeled, having grabbed a pole and cracked Iaman on the head. This blow sent him to his hands and knees. He stayed there in that position clinging to consciousness. The guard was about to hit him again when one of the other guards walked casually over and stopped him.

"Better save him for the Leaders."

"Yeah, I guess you're right." A disappointed "Ohhh" came up from the crowd.

Iaman felt terrible, but at least they were going to leave him alone for a little while. He blinked his eyes until the dizziness stopped. When he was able to see straight again, he resumed his sitting position. His head throbbed. He whispered a few words to the Light for strength. By the time the Lamp-Lighters emerged from Dermod's house, he was in pain, but he had his senses about him.

It was midmorning and the two suns shone brightly as the LampLighters walked down the steps to the patio. Iaman rose to his feet. Chairs had been set up for the leaders. After they took their places, Dermod then disinterestedly began to question Iaman about his teaching and his followers. After he

157

had reeled off about seven questions he paused. "I'm not going too fast for you, am I?" The other leaders chuckled. Dermod turned to them, appreciating their laughter. "Are you getting all this?" He looked briefly at Iaman as if to say he had permission to answer.

"Why are you questioning me? I have always spoken publicly, at times in your own meeting place. I have never said anything secretly. Why question me? Why not ask those who have been listening to me—they will tell you what I have said."

Out of nowhere, Iaman felt a smack across the back of his head. It knocked him down. A guard who had been standing behind him stood over him threateningly, "How dare you address our leader like this!"

Iaman slowly rose to his feet, rubbing his head. "If I have said something untrue, say what it is for all to hear. But if what I said was right, they why did you hit me?" The guard said nothing, as Dermod had raised his hand signaling restraint.

Calmly, Dermod addressed Iaman. "We have witnesses who are prepared to testify about you." He turned to the guards, "Bring the first one in."

A young man about 25 years old entered. "What would you like to say?" asked Dermod.

The young man pointed to Iaman, "He said that we couldn't be Light followers unless we eat his body, eat his flesh."

"Are you sure he said this?"

"I heard him, we have to eat his body!"

"Thank you," said Dermod. "Next."

Another man, about 40 years old, entered. "What would you like to say?"

The man pointed accusingly at Iaman. "He said that Paso-Lomon was a son of LiarLight!"

"Thank you," said Dermod. "Next."

An older woman was brought in. Iaman knew her immediately. It was encouraging to see a friendly face. "That man cured me of a terrible problem I had all my life."

"Did he tell you how he did it?" Dermod replied.

"Well, no, but what does that matter." She became confused. "He comes from the Light."

"It matters a great deal! Thank you," said Dermod. He gave a sidelong glance at some of the other LampLighters as if to ask, "How did she get in here?"

The testimony continued for over an hour. One person would claim that Iaman was an agent of LiarLight, then the next would claim he did something wonderful. There were others who at the prompting of the LampLighters came in and made wild claims, so outrageous that even the accusers shook their heads. In all, they were able to find only two witnesses who agreed.

They both said that Iaman claimed that he could tear down the LampLighter meeting hall and rebuild it in three days. To their dismay it was hardly a reason to put a man to death. Dermod decided to take matters into his own hands. He addressed Iaman.

"Can you refute these accusations against you?" He knew he had nothing concrete against Iaman, but decided to try that approach. Iaman was reportedly a simple man. Maybe he would think his situation was much worse than it really was. Dermod knew, however, that he had nothing against Iaman, nothing that would hold up under investigation.

But Iaman remained silent. He looked respectfully at Dermod while he questioned, but would not answer. Dermod decided to try a different approach. "Are you the Messenger of the Light, Son of the Light, Leader of the Light Team?"

"I am," replied Iaman, "and you will see me sitting at the Light's right side."

For a moment there was silence. The LampLighters realized that they had won. Iaman had given them exactly what they were after. With that, a barbarous celebration broke out. The leaders tore their garments to signify their shock at his blasphemy of the Light. One of them shouted, "You heard what he said! We don't need any more witnesses!"

Dermod was enthused. He rose to his feet and raised his hands to calm them for a moment. "What is your verdict?"

As one they shouted, "Guilty!"

"And what is the punishment?"

Again as one they shouted, "Death!"

With that, pandemonium broke out. They spit on Iaman and kicked him and slapped and beat him. He fell to the ground dazed and bloodied, but they wouldn't relent. The beating, spitting, and kicking continued as he writhed on the ground. After a while, their maniacal state slowly subsided. Iaman lay in a fetal position on the floor. The men surrounding him were breathing hard with spittle dripping down their beards. Some had blood on their shirts from where they were spattered or had wiped their hands. Iaman lay on the floor unmoving.

Dermod looked at the group, his chest still heaving. "We can't . . . We can't put him to death." He motioned with his hand, a finger extended, "Take him to the magistrate." With that, the guards picked Iaman up and dragged him out of the yard.

Bertrand watched in horror! He felt the lump of money in his pocket and realized that he had set the LampLighters' heinous plan in motion. The realization dizzied him. *What have I done?* As they dragged Iaman off to the magistrate, he sank down on one of the hay bales by the fire. His body shook with remorse. *This is wrong! This is all wrong!* He made up his mind to approach the LampLighter leaders. With his appeal perhaps they would release Iaman. Surely the punishment he had received thus far would be sufficient.

He charged up to the back door as the leaders exuberantly made their way into the house. "Wait!" he shouted. The leaders stopped on the steps and turned to face him. They smiled at their accomplice, but upon seeing his demeanor became skeptical of his motives.

"What do you want?" Dermod responded.

"I have made a mistake—it's a mistake!" Bertrand stammered with what to say. Finally he shouted, "He's an innocent man!"

Dermod pushed through the leaders and down the steps. He stared coldly into Bertrand's face. Matter-of-factly he replied, "We don't care. That's *your* problem."

Bertrand stared back aghast. Angrily, he tore the money from his pocket and threw it at their feet. "He's an innocent man!" He shouted as the tears streamed down his face. The leaders turned their backs and walked calmly into the house. Bertrand continued shouting, but it was too late. The LampLighter guards blocked his way; he was reduced to a pitiful form lying on the steps. The guards did their best to ignore him as he slumped amongst the money he had received for his betrayal. After a while, he withdrew.

One of the guards collected the money that lay on the steps and the ground and knocked on the door. "Here's the money." One of the leaders took it and went back inside.

Iaman was carried off to the Camden magistrate's office. LampLighter guards held him as they waited for their leaders to arrive. The government guards told the servants of the magistrate that the LampLighter leaders waited to meet with him. However, they refused to come into his estate, because according to their religious practices, they would be ceremonially unclean and would not be able to continue in their celebration of the Deliverance. Reluctantly, the magistrate went out to them. They stood on a portico area outside of his front door. He had been briefed that the LampLighter leaders had a man in tow against whom they had serious charges.

"Thank you for meeting with us," began Dermod. Behind him stood two guards holding Iaman and a large crowd which had followed them.

"What are your charges against this man?" asked the magistrate indifferently.

"Would we have brought him to you if he hadn't committed a crime?" challenged Dermod.

The magistrate was exasperated. "Then take him and deal with him according to your religious laws," he said and began to walk back into his house.

"The state does not allow us to put a man to death," Dermod pleaded.

160

The magistrate looked back at Dermod disinterested. "But isn't he a Sopa and a LampLighter? He's one of you!"

Dermod ignored the comment. "Honorable magistrate, you have recently won a decision against us, the LampLighters, over the killing of the police by Elie and his followers. Apparently, this crime against the state was carried out in revenge for the seven LampLighters who were killed by the lawmen." Dermod paused. "It seems we have gotten back into the game of ethnic violence."

The magistrate bristled. "Go on," he said, although he could already see where Dermod was going.

Dermod moved closer to the the magistrate. "As the leader of the Lamp-Lighters, I can be very influential in keeping the people from such tit for tat violence. But I need your assistance. How can I work to keep the people under control when insurrectionists are free to roam the landscape?" He perceived the magistrates' attention had increased. "Therefore, you might reconsider how you would apply the Justice laws. Perhaps there is one whose death would bring more healing than that of a common criminal such as the one you hold captive?" Dermod paused for a moment to allow the gravity of his words to sink in. "Examine the man we have brought to you. Consider your political future. The ramifications of his death would most certainly have a broader impact."

The magistrate went back into his house. He was no fool. He was a politician, and what was the death of one man or another as long as the Justice laws were fulfilled? He also saw the benefit in taking the life of a LampLighter the LampLighters themselves wanted dead. Through this man's death, he could both satisfy the Justice laws and win political points with the LampLighters.

He instructed that Iaman be brought to him. The wing of his estate bordering on the portico was used exclusively for government business. He sat on an elevated seat used for discourse with the public. The Magistrate looked over a sheet of charges prepared by the LampLighters as Iaman was brought in. One in particular jumped out at him.

Without looking up, he asked "Are you the 'King of the LampLighters?'"

"Is this your question?" Iaman replied.

The magistrate became irritated. "Do you think I am a LampLighter?" he shot back. "It is your own people who have turned you over to me. They claim your death will satisfy the need for justice." He studied Iaman. "So, what have you done?"

Iaman exuded moral strength. "My country is not of this world. My countrymen would have fought if my country were of this world."

"Then you are a king?"

"Yes, I am. My entire reason for being was to come to speak the truth. All who are owned by the truth listen to me."

As he was speaking, a messenger approached the magistrate and handed him a note. As he took it, he asked disgustedly, "What is truth?" The magistrate then opened the message; it was from his wife. The words made his body go cold. "Don't have anything to do with that man. I dreamed about him last night, and we suffered much because of him."

The magistrate left Iaman and went back out to the LampLighters. On his way, an idea came to him. Looking past Dermod who stood at the foot of the steps, he addressed the crowd, "I see no justification for sentencing this man to death. It was Elie who carried out the killings of the police. Shall I release this Iaman?"

A few small voices in the crowd shouted, "Yes! Release him!" But their appeal was short-lived. The majority of the crowd looked at Dermod. Dermod had anticipated this turn of events. "Give us Elie!" he shouted. When the crowd heard Dermod they screamed and shouted, "GIVE US ELIE! ELIE! WE WANT ELIE!" The shrill voices screamed for the release of Elie.

So the magistrate took Iaman away and had him whipped. The guards also took the opportunity to mock him, calling him the "King of the Lamp-Lighters!" They took a royal purple robe and put it on him and fashioned a crown from thorny red branches. As they forced the crown upon his head, large thorns dug into his forehead and scalp.

While Iaman was away, the magistrate once again looked at the note he had received from his wife. How strange to get such a message from her. The novelty of it in itself caused him to pause. He called for the guards to bring Iaman back to him. They presented Iaman to the crowds further beaten and bloodied.

"I bring him out to you. I see no reason to put him to death." The magistrate hoped the brutality done to him thus far would be sufficient. Appealingly, he said, "Look on the man."

He had barely gotten the words out of his throat when the crowd began screaming again, "Kill him! Kill him!" Their zeal for his death caused them to lose control. The guards corralled and jostled them into submission.

The magistrate increasingly became filled with fear. He went back to his examination room and had Iaman brought to him. "Where did you come from?"

Iaman looked at him respectfully but would not respond. Fear filled the magistrate. In anger he shouted at Iaman. "You will not speak to me? Don't you recognize I have the power to set you free or to have you killed?"

Iaman's physical strength was waning. He garnered what strength he had and responded, "Your power over me was given you by the Light. He who handed me over to you is guilty of the greater offense."

This response only inflamed the magistrates' fears. He sent Iaman out and struggled with how he might release him. Once again he stood Iaman before his accusers. Before he could even speak, Dermod shouted at him, "If you release him, you are not the governor's agent! The Sopas will riot!" Again the magistrate retreated, sending Iaman back to the guards. He could see no way out of his predicament. One last time he presented Iaman to the crowd.

"Here is your king!" he announced, half pleadingly.

Once again the crowd became crazed with screaming and shouting. Cries of "Kill him!" echoed in the portico.

With that, the magistrate signaled to one of his servants. He brought out a tray with a pitcher of water, a bowl, soap, and a towel draped over his arm. The magistrate poured some water into the bowl, wet his hands, took the soap and washed and rinsed his hands. As he dried them he looked at Dermod. "I wash my hands of this case. I am not responsible for this man's death."

Steely eyed, Dermod gestured to the crowd, "Let any punishment for his death be brought down on us and our descendants!"

The magistrate reconciled himself to Iaman's fate. He turned to one of his assistants, and ordered Iaman's execution.

Executions were carried out in an unusual manner at that time. A huge 'X' was constructed and the guilty party was spiked to it. The wood used for the X was heavy and rough cut.

The crowd followed Iaman as the guards took him to the place where they prepared prisoners for execution on the southern edge of town. In his condition, it was obvious that he wouldn't be able to walk the distance, so he was put onto a horse driven cart and taken to the place.

Slowly Iaman climbed down from the cart. The crowds were much greater than before and were held back by a line of guards. The guards had X's prepared and brought one outside. Two guards brought it out, but even in their good physical condition, they struggled with it. In Iaman's beaten condition, it was unlikely that he would be able to carry the X to the place, about a half mile from there, where he would be executed. Randomly, the guards grabbed someone from the crowd and instructed him to help carry the X. The man wrestled the mass across his shoulders with the two of the upper arms of the X coming out on either side of his head and the rest of the structure dragged behind him. He began lugging the thing down the road.

Iaman struggled just to carry himself to his destination. His face was hardly recognizable, a rounded mass of cuts, blood streaks, and bruises. On his head was the crown from which rivulets of blood flowed. He staggered alongside the X, occasionally reaching out a hand to steady himself on the shoulder of his benefactor.

The ignominy of the situation was exacerbated by the crowds along the way. Many cried at their leader's disgrace, but many more hurled insults and tried to spit at him from the side of the road. Occasionally, someone would throw a stone or some other object at him, accompanied by cheers with a hit.

Several times, the X bearer would fall. Impatient with his slowness, the guards grabbed someone else from the crowd who continued with the load, finally dropping it at the place for the execution. The place was known as "skull hill" because of its uncanny resemblance to a skull. The government consistently used the hill for local Justice law executions, as it proved an ongoing reminder to the citizenry of the alternative: ethnic war.

Iaman was laid down on the X. In spite of the roughness of the wood, for a second it felt good to lay down. His back rested on the intersection of boards as his head lay on the ground. That feeling quickly left him as the guards approached him with the spikes. People surrounded the spectacle at the top of the hill. One guard held his right arm in place. A second grabbed the spike and centered it on his wrist. Quickly, the third came down with the hammer. Iaman cried out with intense pain, as the guards holding arm and spike flinched back at the spray of his blood. They looked at each other disgustedly, resuming their positions. Several more strokes of the hammer and the head of the nail pressed Iaman's wrist firmly against the splintered wood. Next, the left hand, then the feet. Iaman lay with his blood dripping down the board onto the ground.

The guards then hoisted the top of the X up into the air and the bottom legs slipped into two prepared holes. As the bases of the X slipped into the holes, Iaman's body was jolted downward. He grunted in pain as the spikes ripped at him. His toes pointed down several feet above the ground. There he hung. The executioners packed up their things and left. The remaining guards brought out a ladder and nailed a sign above Iaman's right hand. It said, "King of the LampLighters." The ladder was then taken away, leaving Iaman surrounded by two guards. A short while later, two other men were brought to the place and executed in the same manner. These men struggled with their executioners, but then they had not undergone the brutality that Iaman had. After an hour, two guards remained on the hill with the three condemned men.

All day, a continuing stream of people came up the hill. Largely they came to continue their denigration of Iaman.

"So you were going to destroy the LampLighters headquarters. Uhhh, I don't think so!" This was followed by laughter and merriment.

Even the LampLighter leaders joined in. "Hey son of the Light! Come down from your "X" and we'll follow you!"

"He isn't going anywhere!"

One of the others who was being executed even derided Iaman. "So it was all just words? If you really are the Leader of Light Team, save yourself. And save us, too!"

The other criminal became incensed. "Shut up, you fool! We are getting what we deserved. But he is innocent." He then changed his tone of voice and spoke to Iaman. "Please remember me when you rule in the Country of the Light!" Iaman turned to him. "Today the Light will welcome you into His presence."

The jeering went on while Iaman clung feebly to his life.

"Weren't you going to save us from LiarLight? You'll get to meet him shortly."

"Yeah, and I don't think he'll be too happy to see you!"

"Not only could he not defeat LiarLight, but he is defeated by common thugs."

"So, you were going to save us from LiarLight? You can't even save yourself!"

Suddenly at about noon, the sky went black. The carpet wall that separated the LampLighter meetinghall was torn in two. Iaman cried out in a loud voice, "O Light, I entrust myself to you!" With that, he died.

Those around him stopped their ridicule. Someone voiced. "He was a good man."

A guard responded, "Maybe he was the offspring of the Light?"

* * * * * * * * *

Later that day, the LampLighters received permission from the magistrate to have the bodies taken down. It would be offensive to them to have the bodies remain on the hill during their ongoing Deliverance celebration. It was the custom that if those executed were not dead, the executioners would break the legs of the criminals, in that way facilitating a quicker death. As the Lamp-Lighters arrived on the scene, the guards broke the legs of the two criminals. When they came to Iaman, they found he was already dead. Therefore, rather than breaking his legs, they took a knife and stabbed him in the side, just below his rib cage. Blood and body fluids streamed from the wound, indicating he was indeed dead. Later when they reflected on the events as they transpired, the Light Team remembered the prediction in the Old Stories about Iaman which stated that none of his bones would be broken.

The LampLighters assumed that some of Iaman's followers would come to take the body away, so they also received permission from the magistrate to place guards on the body. Before the followers would be permitted to take the body, they were required to indicate where and when it would be buried.

* * * * * * * * *

Iaman did not die alone. His mother came and was there with him, as well as Kelly and Amy. Other followers also braved the angry crowds to be with him at his death.

165

Chapter 38
LIARLIGHT IS VICTORIOUS

An entirely different spectacle was occurring in the world of the unseen. Once again LiarLight's myriad of followers gathered around him as he prepared for a dance. The hilltop stage was reminiscent of a skull. In the midst of the stage, a man was suspended in agony. He hung there, clinging to life. The dance began. Fluidly, effortlessly, LiarLight moved around the grotesque figure who hung there. At times, his movements feigned admiration and love, then quickly turned to mockery and disdain. He moved around and through the X as it stood there. In anguish, the figure looked on him as he danced. The sufferer seemed to go in and out of consciousness during the macabre dance. At one point, the alarmed figure whispered to himself, "Light, why have you left me?" But there was no response. Finally, the figure shouted out some words, and the spirit of the man fell to the ground. The shell remained on the X like that of a locust after metamorphosis. LiarLight was pleasantly shocked. He stopped dancing. *Hadn't this man been a follower of the Light? Why was his spirit not transported to the Light?* His dance was in celebration of Iaman's death, but never did LiarLight think the Light would allow him access to this man's spirit.

The spirit of the man rose to his feet before LiarLight. LiarLight's face smiled deviantly. Suddenly he began again to dance. His dance became euphoric, reflecting his mood. Never was a dance performed more perfectly which expressed such complete joy as was LiarLight's dance. He leapt and twirled with perfect balance and symmetry. Finally, his movements brought him face to face with the man. He paused for a second, staring at him eye to eye. All at once, he screamed, "I've won! I've won! I've won! I've won!" The sound of it echoed for several minutes. LiarLight danced to the rhythm of the echoes. Never had he enjoyed gaining a captive as he did at this moment. As the echoes died, the dance slowly came to a stop. The man, Iaman, stood as a ghostly form before LiarLight but said nothing.

LiarLight mocked him with his stares. He studied him as a sergeant studies a recruit. "Where is the Light now?" He said condescendingly. "The Light you clung to was a creation of your imagination. Look at yourself now. Your protector has given you over to me." He paused, relishing the moment. Once again he screamed at Iaman. "Something is wrong!" His voice became that of thousands, as the crowd surrounding them spoke as one. "You have been abandoned!" they bellowed menacingly. LiarLight reiterated their words quietly in Iaman's ear. "It seems you have been abandoned." He chuckled, "Call on the Light to save you."

Iaman gave no response. He stood erect but resigned to what was about to happen to him.

After a moment, LiarLight began again. "That's correct. There is no Light in this place. Only the Light which I generate. And it is a far different light." LiarLight was enjoying his good fortune. thgiL looked on from the crowd, in her choice-induced confusion, agreeing in her mind that LiarLight's victory over this man was probably a good thing. LiarLight continued in his fear tactics, but he got no satisfaction from Iaman. There was no begging for mercy, no trembling in fear, no dashing eyes—only an erect stance and a resigned look.

At last, LiarLight said, "Be gone." thgiL knew where Iaman had been sent.

Chapter 39
DEATH

Some of his followers spent the day with him and saw him breathe his last. He was dead! The thought oppressed them, but there was nothing more to be said. His body was stiff, cold, and lifeless. As with anyone experiencing a death, in the midst of their grief, they shifted into a busy mode of trying to determine what to do with the body.

Iaman was not someone with a lot of wealth. He hadn't made plans for a burial plot. He was still a young man, with much of his life ahead of him. Additionally, he was going to bring in the Country of the Light. Surely there would be plenty of time to plan for one's burial at a ripe old age, some time in the distant future. Now that future would never come. His beaten body signified the death of the team's future.

How can the death of one who offered so much, who had so much promise, be described? Iaman's followers felt as if they had risked everything and lost. What they wouldn't give for this to be over. Childlike, they had played joyfully amongst their dreams, only to have them taken and locked away behind impassible doors. As a result, they were drifting aimlessly.

They sat together and tried to figure out what to do with his body. He had only died yesterday, but the body would very soon begin to give off the aroma of decay. The group adamantly agreed that no enemy would have the pleasure of seeing his decomposing body. Additionally, if they didn't do something soon, the government would take matters into their own hands and discard the body into a convicts grave with the others who had been executed that day. They talked among themselves and discovered that one of them, a follower named Malcolm, owned a burial cave that he would be willing to donate. The caves were near a garden on the east side of town.

The government officials gave permission for them to take the body and give it a proper burial. The team members stood by their dead leader as he hung lifelessly on the huge X. They took the body down and started back to Anthony's house, where it could be prepared for burial. They laid it on a two-wheeled cart covered with a large tarp. Steve took up the poles and pulled the cart down the hill on which Iaman had been executed and back toward Anthony's house. There was a depressing haze over the city.

Discussion on the street was mostly muted. As Steve pulled the cart through the city, most people became quiet. Most knew about the events which had just transpired. Some recognized the followers as they walked beside the cart. Occasionally, someone would laugh or point disdainfully as the cart went by. At one point someone shouted out, "Hey, there's the Light Team, or maybe we should now say the 'Cart Team!'" Those around the man laughed, somewhat embarrassed. But the Team didn't even hear his words; they were functioning as if they were in a dream. They saw their own bodies move from a distance. The cart carrying their leader was absurd. Had they the strength for words, their refrain would be, "I don't understand" or "This can't be happening" or a simple "Why?"

At one point, Steve paused. He gently set the poles in his hands down on the ground. He wiped his brow and turned to look at those who followed him. Looking back, their faces were like a dull void. By their vacant stares, some did not appear to recognize that he was looking at them. Amy's indomitable spirit offered a suffering smile surrounded by tear-filled eyes as if to say, "We've almost made it; we're almost there." Her smile was like a word of hope for Steve. He arched back to stretch, then reached down and gently picked up the poles to the cart. With a sigh he sluggishly started off again. Finally they reached Anthony's house.

Steve took the cart around to the back of the house. His desire now was to protect the dignity of his fallen leader by prohibiting anyone from viewing the body. Michael scurried to open the door, while Josh, Seth, and Steve picked up the body and moved toward the door. Hearing the door open, Anthony hurried out to assist with the body. A bare table, the one which had been used for their Deliverance meal, had been cleared for the preparation of the body.

The preparation of the body was not something typically done by grievers. People who even touched a dead body were considered unclean by the LampLighters. There was an elaborate period of waiting and procedures for cleansing which were prescribed for those who willfully or accidentally came into contact with a dead body. But the men didn't care. It was the furthest thing from their minds. They only wanted this last opportunity to show their complete love and devotion to their fallen leader.

Seven of them were in the room when Iaman's body was uncovered. Anthony was available to assist with anything that might be needed from the house. Steve, Seth, and Josh stood by ready to help in any way. Kelly and Amy were also there. Amy was the most level-headed of the entire group other than Gerald, the follower whose profession it was to prepare bodies for burial. Although he was also visibly shaken, Gerald was used to seeing dead bodies and was able to function in his professionalism. He knew they all looked to him to do what was needed.

Clarence waited outside with Edward and Michael. Edward couldn't stop crying; he blubbered like a child. Clarence and Lupe grieved in their own ways—neither wanted to see Iaman in his current condition. Michael reasoned that he brought no expertise to the procedures which would have to be done, so why enter, besides he didn't think he would be able to handle it. Clarence was dazed. Entering or not entering had not even occurred to him. He sat by the cart like a dog tethered to a pole.

Gerald stepped forward, and unhesitatingly pulled back the cloth. There lay Iaman before them. Some of them resumed the tears which had only just subsided. The stiff, lifeless form lay before them. They looked on his body and remembered who he was and what he had done. They remembered how he had moved them and made their hearts burn. They thought back to the times he had made them laugh and now here he was, dead, empty, and broken.

The eyes they had gazed into on so many occasions were closed and uninviting. His hair was matted to his head. It was caked with blood, sweat and the remnants of the perfume which Kelly had poured on his head just a short time before. The remaining evidences of the perfume on his head now seemed so out of place. Steve looked up at Kelly who stood with her hands together over her face. Her body shook as she wept. "He said you anointed him for burial." She hadn't realized until that moment that that was what she had done. Her shaking stopped suddenly as she paused and looked at Steve with a stare indicating that she understood. For some reason that realization gave her strength. Her tears continued to flow but she gained a measure of control. In the stillness of the room, the muted perfume began to fill the air. It competed with the fragrance of death. As Gerald moved to clean his head, Steve looked at Kelly and said, "Wipe only his brow and face." Gerald looked up at Steve, hesitated, and then did as he was instructed.

Gerald dipped a cloth into water and began to wipe Iaman's face. His face was difficult for his followers to recognize. The repeated blows had caused his teeth to cut through his lips, covering his chin with streams of dried blood. His cheeks and eyes were bruised and swollen. In his forehead were four large gashes from the crown he had worn of red fruit branches.

Steve remembered the words of Michael's chant. It was just like Lupe had said. Iaman was "beaten beyond recognition." His appearance was like one from whom people "would hide their faces." He lay there "cut off from the living."

Lovingly, Gerald wiped the dried blood and sweat from his face, temples, and the side of his nose. As he worked, they all stared in fascination, studying the lines of Iaman's face.

Gerald then moved to Iaman's hands. They were contorted gruesomely, partly because when the spike was driven into his wrist it had cut or tensed the tendons, and partly as an evidence of Iaman's efforts to position his hand in a way that would diminish the pain.

As Gerald worked, their eyes were drawn to the rest of his body. His feet

170

and toes, like his hands, were positioned unnaturally. Daylight was evident through the spike-shaped hole in one of them. His right side bore the hand's width open wound where the executioners had stabbed him with the knife. Once again, dried blood and body fluids were in evidence. Their trail led down his leg where they mingled with his bloody feet.

Prior to this time, they had never paid much attention to Iaman's body. He was thin, but not slight. The knot of a muscle was evident in his arms. His ribs could be seen, but he was not emaciated. The rest of him was no different than any other man. It seemed strange to them to look on his body now. They had no recollection of it in the past. His eyes and his words and, yes, his healing hands were all they had noticed of him. But now, his body would always be a specter in their memories.

For the rest of the day and through the night, Gerald worked on the body. He strived to pay attention to every detail. By morning, it laid before them wrapped in burial cloths and scented with spices. Josh opened the door to see if the cart was nearby. Michael and Edward looked up startled. Clarence hadn't moved from his position by the cart. Josh grabbed the cart and moved it toward the door. Inside, Steve, Seth, Gerald, and Anthony picked up the body and placed it onto the cart; a clean cloth was draped over it. They set off for the burial cave, only about a mile or so away.

Michael went to round up any others of the team he could find, and they met at the cave. Two guards were present when they arrived. To their credit, the guards remained in the background; they cared little about this dead man. They were instructed to be sure that the body arrived at the grave, and that was what they did.

Steve, Seth, and Gerald moved to take the body and place it into the cave. Josh stepped forward and gave Seth a glance. Understanding, Seth gave Josh his position. Michael did the same with Gerald. The three men gingerly picked up the body and placed it on a shelf in the cave. They looked on the body one last time and walked out of the cave.

For a moment they stood there waiting for someone to say something. Some looked at Michael, but he averted their gaze, looking down at his feet. Finally, Steve spoke up. He was composed, but his voice was muted.

He struggled with what to say. He thought back to his time with Iaman and remembered how he had predicted he would be killed. "Iaman knew this was going to happen to him. He knew he was going to die." He thought about all he had learned from him about the Light. "He was a great teacher. Clarence and Scott said he had a quality like the stars!" They were all familiar with that story by now. "He taught us so much about the Light!" He then remembered Iaman's repeated battle cry that he would defeat LiarLight. *What could he say about that? Hadn't LiarLight won?* "And he gave us hope that one day the Light will release us from LiarLight's tyranny." He stood there for a moment wondering what else to say. Once again he remembered Lupe's chant. "And I owe everything to him." In reality, he was crushed. He had no hope. None of them had hope. Finally, he turned to the guards and signaled that they could roll the stone in front of the opening of the cave. The guards struggled with the stone for several minutes. Clarence, having regained his senses, tugged Josh's shirt sleeve and motioned for them to help the guards to seal the tomb.

There was nothing more to do, so they went back to Anthony's house to spend the remainder of the day.

Chapter 40
THGIL IS RELEASED

LiarLight relished his victory over Iaman. He still couldn't believe that Iaman had been delivered into his hands. He puzzled over how much Iaman reminded him of the Light. *Strange, that at his death he wasn't instantly transported to the Light. Maybe he was one of the high-ranking original Light Team members who had defected.* LiarLight reminded himself that he knew all of that team. *Was not he, himself, the greatest of them? But Iaman had had such great power, greater even than his own back in the desert. Hadn't Iaman sent him away against his will?* He also had power over the wraiths. thgiL commanded them, but only LiarLight had the same power as Iaman had demonstrated over them.

To LiarLight, the real question, however, was how Iaman was able to mimic the Light so well. At one point, LiarLight actually thought he was the Light. Perhaps he'd offer him a bit of gentler treatment if Iaman would reveal his secrets.

LiarLight called thgiL, who came immediately.

"What do you think of our captive?"

"You've won!" She paused. "Haven't you?" thgiL's confused mind cringed. LiarLight's "gift" of free choice had increasingly put her in a quandary.

thgiL had played a crucial part in Iaman's demise, but she was not nearly as effective as she had been in the past. LiarLight recognized this fact. He had learned a great deal about free will from his experiment with thgiL. LiarLight assumed that the Light enjoyed his relationships with His creatures. Why else would there be the gift of choice? LiarLight, however, had no desire for relationships, so why give free will? It only made followers inept. He recognized now that he had actually impaired his greatest creation to the point of ineffectiveness. But rather than simply change thgiL back to the way she was, he decided to play out his experiment to its completion.

"Of course, I have won. And because I have won, I may grant you a wish. How would you choose between free will and no free will?"

thgiL's mind raced. Her thoughts were in disarray. *Free will?* she thought, *I have no free will. Only disobedience and punishment or obedience alone.* "I have no real choice," she replied.

LiarLight followed her thoughts. "Of course you can choose."

"My creator, to have a choice I must be able to choose a desirable thing. Not simply to avoid punishment. I must have the ability to choose you. However, you in your wisdom have not chosen me. My creator could never lower himself to relate to me. My only option, therefore, is to avoid punishment."

"Then, knowing what you know, what is your choice?"

"My creator, without free will I would lose the fear of punishment. With this free will, I live in fear of every decision. With the ability to choose, I can now do wrong. Because of my creator's high standards, I have no hope to escape punishment, as I am bound to fail. There is also no one to save me from your perfect justice." thgiL became sad. Haltingly she said, "I therefore choose to relinquish my choice."

"So be it," replied LiarLight.

The brief sadness that had fallen over thgiL was replaced with the confidence of a servant sure of her master's will. She fell on her face before LiarLight, relieved.

Chapter 41
WHY?

The Team continued to stay together at Anthony's house. They were too depressed and afraid to do anything else. The rumors were being circulated that the LampLighters were looking for the rest of the team. They planned to discredit team members in order to strike fear into the minds of Iaman's less prominent followers. In reality, the LampLighters had thought little about the rest of the team. They continued to exult in their victory over Iaman. There had been no Iaman-style teaching about the Light for several days. Many of the followers had already come back to the LampLighters after seeing Iaman die. Why should they follow a dead leader who made promises he didn't fulfill? Even the team members themselves were in conflict about their leader. It was as Steve had said at the grave site—Iaman hadn't defeated LiarLight. He had been a great teacher, but he died like any other man. The problem was, however, he made claims about being the offspring of the Light. Well if he was the offspring of the Light, how could he be killed?

Michael wrestled desperately to reconcile Iaman's words and his own experience. If Iaman's assertions about his relationship with the Light couldn't be trusted, what about his other statements? Was he really who he claimed to be, or was he a lunatic? Michael cringed to think he might have been taken in by a charlatan. In his grief he became angry with Iaman. *Why did he have to die? Didn't he realize that his death negated everything? There would be no Country of the Light. There would be no defeat of LiarLight.* Michael wondered if Iaman might not even be with LiarLight right now, getting his comeuppance for his claims. These thoughts would then be dashed by Michael's other experiences with Iaman. The way he explained the Light to them so clearly, and all the miracles he had performed. His mind seemed stretched to the breaking. He would escape by trying to sleep, but the relief was only short-lived.

The day after Iaman's burial, Kelly and Amy went to the tomb "just to look." They found the setting the same as they had left it. The guards stood by, bored, but nonetheless on duty. They indicated that a few people came by, but, "No, nothing in particular happened." Kelly and Amy stayed there for a while, just to be near Iaman's body, and then went back to Anthony's house.

The day passed by slowly. None of them could eat, and few had anything to say other than to report the latest rumors. The doors were locked tight in fear of the LampLighters.

That evening, Steve, Scott, Clarence, and Albert sat together on the ground by the back step. "It's amazing how your life can change in such a short time," said Steve. "Two days ago, we were on the top of the world. We had a future. And now?"

"Yeah, and now?" replied Albert.

Scott wagged his head from side to side. "The hardest thing is that he knew this was coming. Remember when he got angry with you, Steve?" They all shook their heads affirmatively. "Somehow, this all has to make sense. I mean he taught us the way he did and at the same time predicted he would be killed."

Michael overheard the conversation as he walked up. "That's the part I can't figure out. Somehow this all makes sense, or at least it did to Iaman. He was always very logical in his thinking, in his arguments. Somehow this all must fit together."

"You know, toward the end though, he started saying some strange things." A queer look came over Clarence's face. "Remember he talked about eating his flesh and drinking his blood? And then he said that if the LampLighters tore down the meetinghall, he would rebuild it in three days." Clarence shook his head. "What did that have to do with anything? Like somebody, especially a LampLighter, was going to knock down the meetinghall?"

"And all his talking about dying," Steve inserted. "He had an unnatural fixation on it."

Albert agreed, "I saw him both times he was interrogated—the time before Dermod and his cronies, and when the magistrate addressed the crowd. He only spoke up once. And what he said was what finally gave the Lamp-Lighters what they needed to go after him."

"You know all those people Dermod interviewed had nothing. I mean Dermod had nothing on the basis of those interviews." Clarence pointed his finger at them, "And he knew it! So what's he do? He sets Iaman up with a question that trips him up."

"I don't think he tripped him up," Michael replied. "Iaman had handled a lot harder questions than that one."

"Yeah, but he was so beat up," Clarence insisted, "and that guard had just hit him with that stick. I was amazed Iaman stayed with it. I'd have been out cold."

Scott spoke up. "Still, the way he acted. He wasn't surprised by any of it." Scott livened up as if a revelation had come to him. "And remember how upset he was in the garden? When he asked us to speak to the Light?"

"I'd never seen him so fearful," said Steve.

Michael stuttered to get his words out. "Yeah, but I get what Scott's after.

176

It, it was like, well it was like a different kind of fear. There's a fear of the unknown, like when you are startled, but there's also a fear of the known. When you know something is about to happen and you can't do anything about it. You're nervous about it, but when you realize that it can't be avoided, you do your best to face it squarely. That was the kind of fear I think we saw that night."

The others agreed and, with that, the discussion died down. They sat there in thought for a few minutes, and then the five of them went inside the house and bolted the doors.

Chapter 42
LIARLIGHT'S AMBUSH

It had been several days since Iaman's death. LiarLight had banished him to pain land, where he had been the entire time. LiarLight looked forward to seeing him upon his return. Usually when he sent followers to pain land it was only for a few moments. The pain of the punishment was such that they felt as if they had been there for an eternity. Their brokenness upon return delighted LiarLight. Although his followers' ongoing existence was painful, LiarLight would periodically send his followers to pain land simply for the deranged enjoyment he would get upon their return. Iaman would have been in pain land for almost three days.

LiarLight pondered how long he would allow Iaman to remain in the place of unbridled suffering. As he mused, he thought about the trouble Iaman had caused as a man on the earth. How his Light Team had disrupted the wraiths. With a vengeful smile, he uttered to himself, "No, Iaman will remain."

Then, in an instant, Iaman appeared before him. LiarLight was dumbfounded. He looked at Iaman angrily. "Be gone!" he shouted to send him back. But Iaman stood there unmoved, his same matter-of-fact presence staring back at LiarLight.

"Your time of lawlessness is coming to an end. I am the Leader of the Light Team, the Offspring of the Light. In the future, my followers will call me Iaman Iam, the name of the Light! The Old Stories did indeed predict my coming. My followers will have the power to resist you because I will live in them. Your fall is coming and it will be great."

With that, Iaman disappeared from LiarLight's presence. LiarLight's mind was wild with confusion. His mouth gaping, he stared back at where Iaman had been. Now it was LiarLight who trembled with fear.

Chapter 43
CAN IT BE?

The next morning, Kelly and Amy went again to the tomb. They didn't know what else to do. They gathered up some more of the spices which had been used in the preparation of Iaman's body for burial and made their way there thinking the guards might allow them to enter the tomb. As they walked up the road, they saw the stone rolled back and no guards around. Their hearts sunk. Someone had taken the body out. Hadn't the LampLighters done enough already? They looked inside and their worst fears were confirmed: the body was gone.

"Those worthless guards!" Amy whispered harshly.

Dropping their load, they ran back to Anthony's house. Breathless, they found Steve. "They've taken Iaman's body!"

"Who has? You mean, the body's gone?" With that, Steve and Scott charged out the door toward the tomb. Scott got there first. Looking into the tomb, he saw the cloths they had wrapped Iaman in lying on the bench and floor. When Steve arrived, they went in together. There was the bench where they had laid Iaman, now strewn with the cloths. They stood there for a moment and then walked back home.

Kelly ran back with them to look for the others. As Steve and Scott exited the tomb, Amy sat there crying. She stayed as they went home. After a while, she collected herself and walked back toward the tomb. As she looked in, she saw two men sitting at both ends of the bench. Slowly she went in and approached the men.

The man at the head spoke up first. "Why are you crying, woman?"

"They have taken his body away," said Amy. "And I don't know where he is."

The men didn't respond, so she turned to leave. There at the entrance was another man. He, too, addressed her. "Why are you crying, woman?" He hesitated for a moment. "For whom are you looking?"

Amy looked up at the man, assuming he was the gardener. "Please, sir, if you took the body that was resting here, would you tell me so that I can go and see it?"

"Amy," he replied in a friendly tone.

Suddenly her body glowed as a warmth shot up her spine and spread out to her body. "Iaman!" she voiced breathlessly and fell at his feet.

179

"Don't hold onto me as I haven't gone back to the Light yet. Go now to my followers and tell them I will meet them in Bernardino."

So Amy gave Iaman one last loving glance and ran back to the team. She cried and laughed as she ran, buoyed by her new-found joy. Tears streamed down her face as she skipped and laughed. She charged into the house. "He's alive!" she shouted. "He's alive! He's alive!"

The men were in deep dismay when she entered. They had been listening to Steve and Scott tell of the empty tomb and the probable grave robbers, the LampLighters.

"What are you talking about?" Steve barked at her. "What is this nonsense?"

"He's alive, I saw him! He spoke to me and told me he hadn't gone up to the Light yet! He's alive! He's alive! He said to meet him in Bernardino."

Steve got up and ran back to the grave again, with the others close behind. They looked everywhere inside and outside of the tomb but found nothing. It was exactly the same as they had left it earlier. They wanted to believe Amy; they really wanted to believe her. But the images of Iaman's body lying on the table, his limp body on the "X"—these images were too strong. They tried to calm Amy down, but wouldn't believe her. She continued in her euphoria, saying only, "You'll see! You'll see in Bernardino! We've got to go back there. We've got to leave today. Iaman said he would meet us there!" Again they attempted to settle her down, to give her a dose of reality. Some even became angry with her, but she remained undaunted. Her joy overflowed. "You'll see!" was all she would say.

Steve went off by himself to think. *What if what she said was true? Amy had always been reliable in the past. She would rarely get emotional and was well grounded. There was no reason for them to stay in Camden now anyway.* Steve sat for a while by himself. *There really was no reason for them to stay.* With little effort, he convinced the rest of they group of their next move. They would go back to Bernardino.

The preparation for the trip back to Bernardino was surprisingly quick, but then they hadn't really brought anything with them. In addition, there was no one really to tell about their departure. They felt frightened and humiliated and simply wanted to slip out of town. As they gathered, they counted the 11 followers who now made up their group. Steve hesitated at referring to them as the Light Team. The 10 gathered inside of Anthony's house. The women and others were left outside. It was the first time they had been together since the night in Cinnaminson Garden.

"Anyone know where Edward is?" No one responded. "Well then, I guess this is all of us." Steve started. They all knew what he was thinking: Bertrand was missing from the group.

Michael slowly moved forward; he was in deep depression. His political aspirations were dead; his future in a shambles. He was just a part of another small local uprising which had been squashed. "I've been looking for Bertrand. I didn't expect he would join us again, but I just had to confront him. To find out why he betrayed Iaman." He paused. "But Bertrand won't be joining us. After he saw what happened to Iaman at Dermod's house, he killed himself." Although the group was filled with anger at Bertrand, they were still saddened. "I guess they found him lying in a field with his guts spilled all over the place." Some of them looked away in horror. "It was obvious as well, that he took his own life." Michael looked around the room at the men. Some looked back and shook their heads. Others wiped the tears from their eyes. Their emotions were shredded. This was the final blow. In silence, they walked together out of the door and were on their way.

Amy glowed like a candle in the darkness, but she kept her joy to herself as well as she could. Her only words were encouragement to move along quickly, which increasingly they did. Anthony had some ayugas which he loaned to them, as well as a couple of carts. The small following collected in these and made their way home. Well into the evening, they arrived at the S & A Dry Goods warehouse and went into one of the large storage rooms.

Looking around, Steve noticed Edward was still missing. Finally he asked, "Where's Edward?"

"Who knows?" answered Albert. "He'll get here eventually." Carefully, Albert closed, locked, and bolted the doors; exhausted they fell to the floor.

* * * * * * * * *

The word got around to many of the other followers that the Light Team had left Camden for Bernardino. Throughout the day and evening, other followers also left the city and headed for home. Two men, Walter and Brad, had accompanied the team and those who traveled with them as far as Bernardino. Their homes were further ahead in Yucaipa, so after a heartfelt goodbye accompanied by words of encouragement, they left their borrowed ayugas and went on the rest of their way by foot. They hadn't had much of an opportunity to talk about the events of the preceding week in their hurry to get back home, so they started to talk as they walked. As they spoke, another figure gradually began to catch up with them. Warily they turned and waited as he approached.

"Good evening, friend," Walter started.

"Good evening," the stranger responded.

Walter sighed. "We have been traveling home from Camden."

"I have also been in Camden," the stranger replied and resumed walking with the other two. "What have you been discussing?"

Brad shook his head. "You must be kidding! You must be the only person in Camden who doesn't know about the events of the past few days!" He was clearly agitated.

"Don't be such a baola, Brad!" Walter responded sharply. "Perhaps they haven't heard about everything that happened out here yet."

The stranger questioned him again. "What has been happening?"

Brad was still exasperated but calmed down slightly, "You mean you really haven't heard about Iaman? He was the Leader of the Light Team. He was going to defeat LiarLight. Everyone who knew him was impressed with his words and his deeds. He would do miracles!"

Walter spoke up. "We had hoped he would be the One, but the Lamp-Lighters and the magistrate conspired together, and now he's dead."

"But one of the women in our group said she saw him alive!" Brad smiled and shook his head. "Can you believe it? I mean, I saw his body and there was no doubt he was dead. Believe me, there was no doubt."

"She's the only one who claims to have seen him," Walter added.

The stranger listened and then spoke up. "Don't you understand?"

The two were taken aback, but continued to listen.

"The Old Stories said all of that would happen. The Leader of the Light Team would have to suffer before LiarLight would be defeated. The Leader would die before he would go to be with the Light."

Walter thought, *Could this be?* No one in their group had made this connection before. A trickle of hope began in them. This stranger saw the whole picture. Maybe things were going according to plan. Maybe everything had not become derailed.

The stranger went on to describe in detail everything in the Old Stories which pointed to the events that they had just witnessed, had even participated in. The stranger's knowledge amazed them as they walked along the road for the hour it took to get to Yucaipa. It was as if their hearts burned within them over the connections the stranger made.

The two travelers walked slowly straight ahead while the stranger appeared to want to go further east toward Redlands. It seemed he had a different destination. The men recognized that he was about to leave them and begged him to stay with them as it was late. Apparently their home was just a short way ahead. The stranger finally capitulated, so they made their way through the last patch of red trees to their house.

Brad lit a fire in the fireplace while Walter began to assemble a simple meal. The stranger sat down by the fire and watched the meal being prepared. After a few minutes, they moved up to the table to eat.

"Thanks so much for all you've explained to us. I can't wait till tomorrow when we can go back and tell the others all you've told us." Walter chuckled. "Who knows, maybe the woman was right."

Brad spoke up. "Well, let's eat! Stranger, we would be honored if you would thank the Light for the food."

With that, the Stranger picked up the loaf of bread and broke it. Suddenly their eyes were opened. It was him! It was Iaman! He was there with them!

He is alive! As the realization entered their minds, he suddenly disappeared from them. Vanished before their eyes.

They screamed with delight and hugged each other. "He was here!" Walter shouted.

"It all makes sense now. I get it—the whole picture!" cried Brad.

With that, they pulled their boots back on and ran most of the way back to Bernardino. They pounded on the S & A Dry Goods door shouting to be let in. At first, several of those inside were shocked from their sleep. They all thought the same thing: *"It's the LampLighters!"* The pounding continued but the voices sounded familiar. Finally Clarence got up and opened the door. The two travelers burst in. Not hearing their words, Clarence tried to shush them, and locked and bolted the door again.

"He's alive! He's alive!" Walter shouted.

"We both saw him on our way home tonight!" echoed Brad.

"Yeah, he started telling us about the Old Stories, and then he came to our house. . ."

". . . And then he broke the bread and disappeared!"

No sooner had they said this when Iaman was there, standing among them. Amy and the two travelers were filled with excitement. Smiling broadly, they moved forward and fell down at his feet. The others were terrified, as if they had seen a ghost.

Iaman spoke up. "Peace to you!" But they were far from peaceful. He looked the same in some ways, but was different in other ways. His face was no longer bruised and swollen, his hair appeared clean. Marks remained on his hands and feet at the points where the nails had entered, but they appeared as if the wounds had healed. "Don't be afraid. Don't you believe it is me? Come here and look at me. See my hands and feet." Some began to look up. "It's me! Touch me and see that I have flesh and bones as you do." They were still unconvinced. "Do you have any food here?" Scott had dug out some dried fish when they arrived. He nervously brought it over to Iaman, who took a piece and ate it.

Like cowering animals ready to dart off at any quick movement, they began to gather around him, partially encouraged by the travelers and Amy who sat happily at his feet.

"Do you remember that I told you all these things would happen? Everything written in the Old Stories had to come true." At last he revealed the truth to their minds, and they understood. Only then did they begin to approach him in a manner reminiscent of their previous relationship with him.

"There is another reason that I have come to you." They were now gathered closely around him. "As the Light sent me to you, so I send you to others. Receive the Spirit of the Light!" With that he breathed on them. The breeze from his breath filled the room and their minds opened.

Their understanding was now much more complete. They saw that the events of the past week were indeed a part of his plan and were not inconsistent with his claims. Then the realization hit them: LiarLight had indeed been defeated. Their minds were awash in their new understanding. So full were their thoughts they didn't know what to say to him. After a few moments, they were then alone again.

At his departure, Lupe shouted out, "He is alive!" The statement seemed to clear their minds and they danced and shouted and hugged one another. Each of them made a special point to find Amy and apologize.

Steve approached her first, "How honored you are to have Iaman show himself to you first! Please forgive my lack of trust in Iaman, but also my lack of trust in you." Amy could only smile. She cared little for apologies at this point. Her mind and emotions and body and all that she was were flooded with joy. Her tears flowed freely as she danced with hands raised to celebrate.

* * * * * * * * *

Edward had made arrangements with another traveler to spend the night. About mid-morning he got up and made his way to the warehouse where the team was staying. The door was locked shut, so he knocked. In a moment someone was there. It was Clarence. Edward was still in the funk of death, but Clarence greeted him with the vigor of life.

"Edward, he's alive! Iaman is alive!"

"Please, I've already heard Amy's claims. I saw him; I helped bury his body."

The others heard the discussion and got up and came to him. "No really, he's alive!" Michael supported him.

Steve said, "He appeared to us last night. We touched him and he even ate a piece of fish. He is alive!"

Edward had had his hopes dashed one too many times. He became angry, "Look! I don't . . . I won't believe you! You were dreaming." He pointed to the palm of his hand, "Not until I actually touch the holes in his hands. Not until I stick my fingers in the holes in his feet. Not until I put my hand in his side will I believe you." His eyes filled with tears. "I will not believe!" With that, he left them.

The others remembered their own response to Amy when she told them she had seen Iaman alive. They thought of their own refusal to believe. For the moment, they left him alone.

The appearance of Iaman buoyed their spirits. Their hope was rekindled, alive and growing, and their trust was at a high, but they still spent most of their time locked in the S & A Dry Goods warehouse. They were still afraid of the LampLighters, and didn't really know what they were to do. They stayed there, joyful but hidden.

About a week later, they were all together eating a meal. Edward was among them. Suddenly, Iaman was among them again. They all fell to their knees joyfully. Edward's eyes opened wide. A restored, healthy Iaman walked directly over to him and held out his hand. "Here is the wound. Put your finger here." He lifted his shirt to reveal the gash he had gotten from the knife in his side. "Here is my side; place your hand in here. Stop doubting and have trust in me!"

Edward looked upon him, his trembling hands too fearful to touch and fell down before him. "My Iaman, the Iam."

"You have said rightly. You now trust in me because you see my body? Fortunate are those who will trust in me without seeing my body." He then breathed upon Edward.

* * * * * * * * *

Another week had passed without any sign of Iaman Iam. The team continued to be joyful and upbeat, but they were becoming bored. They didn't know what to do with their new knowledge. Iaman Iam's return to them had thrown Lupe into total confusion. He thought he understood much of Iaman's purpose, but his own preconceived ideas kept getting in the way of the truth that had been revealed to him. Michael walked around with a smile on his face. If addressed, he would comment on the incredible beauty and simplicity of Iaman's plan. He would slowly shake his head from side to side and say, "It all makes sense now."

Of the group, seven of them had started to work in the warehouse to resurrect the dry goods business. They had been at it for several days. Clarence, Josh, and Wendell were packing a wagon when Iaman Iam arrived on the scene. Immediately Josh ran and got the rest. Iaman sat on the back of a wagon and they gathered around him.

He called Steve forward and addressed him. "Steve, do you love me more than the rest of these men?" Iaman gestured to the rest of the group.

A broad smile filled Steve's face. He beamed at the opportunity to express his love for Iaman before the others. "O Iaman Iam, you know I love you!"

"Then take care of my children."

Again Iaman addressed Steve, "Steve, do you love me?"

Steve became a bit concerned. Half-pleadingly he replied, "Yes, you know I do."

"Then take care of my people."

A third time Iaman addressed Steve, "Steve do you love me?"

Steve was heartbroken. He didn't understand what Iaman was doing. *Didn't Iaman believe him?* His eyes filled with tears, which rolled down his cheeks. With everything that was in him he replied, "O Iaman Iam. You know me, you know my heart. I do love you."

Iaman smiled at him. "Take care of my people."

Later in his life, Steve realized the great kindness Iaman had showed him by giving him the opportunity to affirm his love three times.

Iaman motioned for Steve and the others to sit as he began to address them. "I want you to go throughout all of the world and tell people about the things that have happened. Tell them that LiarLight has been defeated. Remember, too, that wherever you are, nothing can separate you from me. I will be with you!"

Michael then stepped forward. "Is it now that you will set up the Country of the Light?"

Iaman smiled at him. He knew it would take time for them to sort out all that had happened during their time with him. "That is not for you to know. It is known only to the Light. What you should do is to tell people everywhere, all over the world, what you have witnessed."

One last time, he gave each of the men a long loving look. They were his closest friends during his life as a man. With that, Iaman Iam stood up on the back of the wagon and raised his hands up to the sky. Slowly he began to rise up into the air and continued to rise until he was finally obscured by a cloud.

The men stared in silence. As they stood there, an old codger gradually limped up. Stopping, he looked up and looked at the men and then looked up again. He took off his beat-up hat and scratched his bald head. "Hey, you men, why are you standing there staring up at the clouds?"

They looked at him. Steve was about to say something when the old man's expression softened as he raised his hand as if to stop them.

"This Iaman Iam will come back some day in the same way as he left you. In the meantime, it seems to me he's given you somethin' to do."

The men smiled knowingly at one another and shook their heads as if to say, "You have no idea of what we have just been through." Each glanced briefly up to the sky. They were joyful yet sad. Their best friend had left them. Yet they realized they were just embarking on a future like none other. They turned to address the old timer, and to their surprise discovered he, too, was gone.

The S & A Dry Goods business never did regain its place in the community. The brothers remained for several weeks only. During that time, they gathered the team together and developed a plan to take Iaman Iam's message to the world. Their individual futures held great suffering in store, but they could not contain what was within them. Yes, Iaman Iam was with them in spirit, but they were his hands, his mouth, his mind. Their enemies would never be able to have them silenced. Through them and those who came after them, Iaman Iam would loose LiarLight's stranglehold on the world. But even greater than that, he gave them a hope for the future.

Epilogue
LIARLIGHT'S REFLECTIONS

LiarLight sat silently. He reflected on the events that had just occurred. He thought to himself, *I don't feel any different!* He was angry, and embarrassed. He was not accustomed to losing. In the past, he was in control. Typically, he won most of his battles. Now, he recognized a change.

As he thought through his situation, he recognized his grip on his power was slipping. He felt like an older person who finds he can't remember things as well or doesn't have the energy he used to. The fading of abilities is perhaps the first signal to oneself that one will not live forever.

Although LiarLight's existence could not be described in human terms, there was still a finiteness about him. He knew during lucid moments that he would not have control over the world forever. The Old Stories told him that. But like a youth, he had felt indestructible. However, he never expected it to happen so suddenly, or so dramatically. He didn't know how much longer he would have; it could be a thousand years. But the events surrounding Iaman signaled the fulfillment of the Old Stories. His power would begin to wind down; it was the beginning of his end.

"What should I do?" he voiced to himself. *What is important to me? What do I want in my dying days?* he thought. He reflected on his dreams. What was it that he always wanted to do? His warped mind swiftly supplied the answer to him. *I want to be the Light,* he thought. Dreams often die quickly. His dreams crashed in fragments at his feet before he even voiced the words. He knew he was through.

Gradually anger welled up in him as he realized how cruel fate had been. *I never really had a choice,* his schizophrenic mind told himself. With that statement, something clicked in him. His mind turned to ways in which he could get back at Iaman. He remembered Iaman's words when they had met in the desert, "I lament those who have bought your lies," he had said. The only plan left to LiarLight was now clearly evident. Perhaps he could not be the Light, but he could confuse some people into believing he was the Light. He would therefore intensify his efforts to frustrate the Light by increasing his own following. He smiled. *I will give Iaman many followers to lament.*

His mind then flashed back to the recent events. He became indignant when he thought of the humiliation he had received because of Iaman. Paranoia filled

187

him. *Were the multitudes less respectful at my last dance? Didn't I detect less fear in his generals? I must devise a plan of action,* he told himself.

He determined that it should be partially aimed at damage control and partially aimed at furthering his kingdom. He pondered these two arms of his attack: damage control and furthering his kingdom.

What is the damage that I need to control? he asked himself. *I need to keep people from learning that I have been defeated through Iaman's coming back to life. People must doubt the historical fact. My chief weapon now lacks it's sting.* He pondered some more. *First, I must keep people from getting at all close to the Light, and I must discredit those who are already followers of the Light, so that their testimony about the Light will be called into question.*

LiarLight's plan was ingenious. If people didn't recognize him as a liar and a loser, there would be a greater likelihood that they might choose to follow after him.

He felt like one of his victims, trying to hide immorality from public view. LiarLight would hide the fact that his demise would come soon. He recognized that he must particularly go after people who follow the Light, as they are the only group who understand his situation. He must discredit the followers of the Light. If they lose their credibility, the message they represent will be suspect as well. Even the regular followers could be tempted to minor wrongs. "I'll fill them with guilt over their wrongs. Then I'll accuse them of their wrongs through their consciences. All the while they are trying to justify themselves, I will have succeeded in getting them to look in the wrong direction." He decided to step up his temptations. If pivotal followers of the Light fell into immoral behavior, there could be significant ramifications. He would turn this aspect of his strategy over to Lightbender.

He thought some more. Many were firmly following the Light. Sure, he could get most to make minor mistakes, but it would be difficult to get them as a group to commit the types of acts which could cause disenchantment on a larger scale. He would be fighting against a large army, and with the power of the Light in them, they would be formidable. *Their unity in the Light gives them strength.* The realization then hit him. He shouted to himself, *That's it! That's it!* He cursed himself, why hadn't he seen it all along. *Disunity! That's the Achilles heel of the Light followers.* He would allow them to go on with their devotion to the Light, but he would break them up. Better yet, they would break themselves up. He smiled to himself. *The fools already divide themselves up by the tint of their skin or the shape of their noses.*

Those like the LampLighters who study the Old Stories were always engaging in discussions and debates about points of obedience or 'luzology.' I will divide them into factions. No! They will divide themselves into factions! He reflected on his scheme. *Each group will feel that they have the stranglehold on what it means to be a follower of the Light. So much so that they will question the sincerity of those with differing viewpoints.* He chuckled to himself.

They will even doubt if the other groups are really followers of the Light at all! Indeed, in nothing will my power be more clearly seen than in the disarray of those who oppose me.

Perhaps I can even factionalize the divided groups? For the moment, he was enjoying himself. *It's easy to get these people to look in the wrong direction. People are so self-centered. They equate their personal preferences with truth. I could use music, the way they dress, or money, or any other triviality unrelated to the real mission of the Light. This is going to be easier than I thought. Because single-mindedness on the part of Light followers is now my biggest threat, this plan will be my greatest idea since death!* This part of the plan he decided to manage himself.

I wonder if the Light has a timetable for history? He thought. *If He does, then my efforts will matter little in terms of prolonging my reign. However, if He is waiting for his followers to do something like tell everybody in the world about the Light, then through my efforts I can actually prolong my reign.* The thought excited him. He felt as if he had a new lease on life.

His tactics must be subtle. He laughed to himself. *Men think themselves so wise, so clever. I will appeal to their minds. I will prompt them to seek rational physical explanations for all that is around them. They will become too erudite for the Light's simplicity. Once they begin questioning in these areas, it will be a short jump to areas of morality or life or death. I will place them on a slippery slope. Their pragmatic approach will prove their downfall.*

The brightest minds will live in darkness, never darkening the door of the meeting places of Light followers. If only they knew that truth drips from the walls. But to use Iaman's own words, "they sit in the darkness with the curtains closed saying, I can see fine. I know what is going on." Little do they know of reality. He paused. *This arm of the attack I will turn over to Dislight.*

He paused for a moment. *There is a principle here I must remember. If the Light can promise His followers that because of their loyalty to Him, their families will enjoy relationships with Him to succeeding generations, then the lack of loyalty to Him could result in my control for succeeding generations. If I can own one generation of a family, the likelihood is great that I will have that family's future. This will be our mission, "One generation for the future."*

LiarLight smiled at the thought of luring followers to himself. *How it will pain Iaman to lose followers to his vanquished foe.* He smirked. *My power might be waning and my time short, but I will see the tears of the Light over his beloved ones. The Light may defeat me, but he will feel the torment I inflict through his people. He may crush my head, but I will injure His heel. His followers will see Him limp His way into His new order.*

In spite of his plans to foil the Light, his followers noted a significant change in LiarLight. The graveyard dances ceased.

Additional Information

Jeff McNair is a professor of Special Education at California State University, San Bernardino. However, not only has he worked professionally in the training of teachers of individuals with developmental disabilities, he has spent 25 years in ministry to individuals with mental retardation. The dovetailing of his ministry and professional work has led to a program of research into the role of the church in the lives of individuals with mental retardation.

"I have observed," says McNair, "that the church is neglecting a significant area of ministry. People with mental retardation, although present in the community, have not been embraced by the church. For whatever reason, they have not been a significant focus of ministry. This is in spite of the fact that the Bible is filled with examples of Jesus himself reaching out to individuals with disabilities. Additionally, the Church has significant potential for serving this population. Somewhere we have lost the Lord's heart toward individuals with disabilities.

"Ministries toward individuals with disabilities must recognize the needs of these people for support and inclusion. It is the job of the disability ministry to introduce people with disabilities to the rest of the church group, integrating them into as many situations as is possible and appropriate.

"Ministries must recognize that the developmentally disabled are a diverse group. There are those who will largely be the recipients of ministry. However, there are others who will desire to serve in a variety of capacities. In our experience, individuals with disability have served as children's workers, volunteers for various set-up and clean-up crews, as well as in a wealth of other areas. It is up to the church to find a service niche for these individuals. Interestingly, they will rarely respond with a 'no' when asked to help!

"There are significant other areas wherein the Church can help individuals with disability. They can participate in various study or small groups, and will become valued members. The church can also be instrumental in assisting a wary community to accept all of its citizens.

"Acceptance modeled by the church toward individuals with disabilities can lead to further community acceptance. Church meetings are perfect opportunities to demonstrate for the community how to interact with disabled persons. The church setting also provides perhaps the greatest opportunity for integration across a wide variety of differences. Perhaps nowhere else is there a greater diversity in ethnic, socioeconomic, educational and vocational areas as there is at a local church."

Yet, someone might respond, "But the problem is so great, and I have no experience. Where would I start?"

"If someone who is misunderstood and ostracized came to you," McNair responds, "what would you do? Probably you would try to understand him and include him. If someone who is in need of physical, emotional or social support came to you, what would you do? Hopefully you would do what you could to meet her physical, emotional or social needs. And if someone who needed the truth of the gospel came to you, you would share it with him. If a person has mental retardation, are the needs or responses any different? Jesus doesn't call us to solve the problems of all disabled individuals in society. But there is the warning '. . . to the extent that you did not do it to one the least of these, you did not do it to Me.' In his wisdom, God did not call us to solve any problem entirely on our own. Yet he did chide us to do good to at least one of our neighbors. However, waiting for someone to come to you is insufficient.

"My brother Scott, a successful businessman in St. Louis, once jokingly said to me, 'I don't think there are any retarded people in St. Louis . . . at least I have never seen one.' Scott's comment was in agreement with a statement that I had made to him that we need to seek out people in need. If people in need do do not come in our front door, the front door of a church no less, are we no longer responsible? I would argue that the church needs to seek out individuals with mental retardation in order to minister to them."

If you would like more information about ministering to individuals with developmental disabilities, or would like to have Dr. McNair come and speak to your group, contact him at this address:

Jeff McNair, Ph.D.
P.O. Box 7415
Redlands, CA 92375